LEGACY

OF

SECRETS

Also by Helen Starbuck:

The Mad Hatter's Son

No Pity In Death

The Burden of Hate

LEGACY OF SECRETS

HELEN STARBUCK

Routt Street Press

2020

Legacy of Secrets
Published by Routt Street Press
Arvada, CO

Publisher's Cataloging-in-Publication data

Names: Starbuck, Helen S., author.
Title: Legacy of secrets / Helen Starbuck.
Description: Arvada [Colorado] : Routt Street Press, 2020.
Identifiers: ISBN: 978-0-9992461-2-2
Subjects: LCSH: Romantic suspense fiction. | Murder—Investigation—Colorado—Denver—Fiction.
BISAC: FICTION / Romance / Suspense
Classification: LCC PN3448.S86 | DDC 813 STARBUCK–dc22

Cover and Interior Design by Desert Isle Design, LLC.

For information, email info@routtstreetpress.com.

Routt Street Press

It's hard asking someone with a broken heart to fall in love again.
—Eric Kripke

CHAPTER ONE

A N HOUR EARLIER he'd pulled up the carpet in his bedroom, pried up a couple of floorboards, and deposited a small, locked, metal box in the space between the joists. He returned the boards to their former places without nailing them down and tacked the carpet back into place.

He took a steadying breath as he sat at the kitchen table, hoping to ease the shaking in his hands that made his handwriting shiver across the page. Slipping the note on top of the wrapped package, he slid the package into a padded envelope, sealed it, and reinforced the closure with tape. Turning it over, he wrote the address on the front and left to take it to the post office.

Was it right handing this off to someone else? He thought as he drove to the post office, his hands cold on the steering wheel. Maybe he should have put it in the box under the floor, but the lid wouldn't close and, with it unlatched, he couldn't make it fit between the joists of the floor. The padded envelope seemed to stare at him from where it rested on the passenger seat, as if waiting for a decision.

The precautions felt paranoid, but he knew the conversation wasn't going to go well and he wanted this "evidence" to be safe. He hoped he could find a way to discover the truth without destroying everything.

Mail it, he thought, *you're almost halfway there.*

———— ♦ ————

THE PHONE call went to voice mail. Again. That made three times today and it wasn't like her father not to answer or respond to a message. Kate Earnshaw sat at her small desk in the art gallery office where she worked and worried. Maybe he was ill? Maybe he'd taken off for a few days? He rarely went out of town without letting her know. He didn't usually say where he was headed, but he always let her know. He always took his cell phone, the one he wasn't answering. She glanced at the clock on the wall again. It was four p.m., an hour and a half left to her workday.

"Doug?" She called out to the gallery owner.

"Yeah?"

"Would it be okay if I left early? I need to swing by Dad's and check on him."

Doug poked his head around her doorway. "Everything okay?"

"Probably. I just haven't been able to reach him. It's starting to worry me. Do you mind? I can stay late tomorrow to make up the time."

Doug flapped a hand at her. "Don't be ridiculous. Go. Let me know that he's okay so I won't worry too."

Half an hour later, Kate turned into the street where her father lived. The house was in an old residential neighborhood in Lakewood, a suburb west of Denver. She had grown up in the house. It hadn't changed much over the years, although the makeup of the once family-oriented neighborhood had. Many of the houses were now rentals and a few were very much the worse for wear. She let herself into the house and immediately noticed it was unnaturally quiet.

"Daddy?" There was no response.

His car sat in the driveway, but perhaps he'd gone out with one of his buddies. She walked through the living room and into the kitchen. There was a glass on the kitchen table that held remnants of bourbon, her father's favorite indulgence. Out of habit, she picked up the glass and turned to the dishwasher, the door of which hung slightly ajar—it required a special touch to get it to stay closed.

She opened it and saw a few plates and some silverware. When she pulled out the top rack, she found a glass identical to the one on the table. Kate wondered at that. She looked at the glass she held; both were part of a rarely used set belonging to her mother's "good china," and her mother had never allowed them to be put in the dishwasher. It had always seemed ridiculous to Kate. Maybe her father had decided the dishwasher was fine.

Frowning, she returned the glass to the kitchen table and closed the dishwasher door. Habits die hard, though. She'd hand-wash them both and return them to the china hutch. It was odd that her father had used them, but maybe someone special had visited. So far everything looking relatively normal, but her apprehension was growing.

She walked toward the master bedroom. Her father's bed hadn't been made, but the room itself was tidy. *Please let him be okay*, she thought. She headed toward the den where he spent much of his time, her steps speeding up. As she got closer, a strong metallic smell hit her and lodged in her throat. It made her go cold. Her father's recliner had always faced away from the door toward the TV. She couldn't see the top of his head, but she could see dried blood splattered on the wall opposite the recliner.

"Daddy?" Her voice sounded faint and tinny, and her breath came in ragged hitches as she walked toward the recliner knowing, yet refusing to acknowledge, what had happened.

"Oh, god, no! Daddy, no!" she cried.

Her father was slumped in the chair. His hand dangled over the armrest where it had fallen. A gun she never knew he owned lay on the carpet next to the chair. She laid her head on his knees, now cold and stiff, and sobbed.

CHAPTER TWO

THE POLICE DETECTIVE sat with her in the kitchen, presumably to prevent her from seeing her father's body removed in a body bag. The death investigator had come and gone after taking multiple photos to document the scene. Crime techs, now cleared to handle the scene by the investigator, had taken the glass from the table and the one in the dishwasher with them after she'd called the detective's attention to them.

He tried to answer her questions, but he talked to her as if she was three instead of a few months shy of thirty, and it was annoying. Perhaps the shock of finding a dead relative required police to handle family members carefully and this was his attempt at it.

"I've never seen that gun, ever. My dad wasn't a gun person. This just doesn't make sense."

"Miss Earnshaw, most kids are unaware of a lot of things in their parents' lives. The fact that you've never seen the gun doesn't mean he hasn't had it for a very long time." He scratched at the edge of his jaw. "The gun's old, there's no serial number on it, and because of its age, it's most likely unregistered and untraceable. It's probably an heirloom."

"But he wasn't depressed. I talked to him just the day before yesterday. He was fine. He didn't leave a suicide note, why would he do something like this?"

"It's not unusual. A lot of people don't leave notes. And family members are sometimes the last to know if a person is depressed or desperate enough to kill themselves."

"What about the glasses? Those glasses were almost never used except for special occasions when my mother was alive, and why two? My father never used them. Maybe he had a visitor. Maybe you should try to find the person and see what he or she knows."

"Ms. Earnshaw, I'm sorry for your loss, I know how hard this is, but it looks like a pretty clear case of suicide. If he had a visitor, I'm not sure how we'd find them unless the person comes forward. The forensics bunch will process the glasses and check out the gun for fingerprints, and the medical examiner will do an autopsy. That should tell us if there was any physical reason he might have chosen suicide, and it'll tell us if he has powder burns on his hand. If he does, and there are no other prints on the gun, then…" He shrugged and his voice trailed off.

———— ◆ ————

"I HATE funerals," Aunt Ellen said as they sat in Kate's living room.

Glasses and plates and other leftovers from the reception, which Kate had held at her condo, waited to be tidied up. They sat morosely and talked, not having the energy yet to begin cleaning up. Kate had always felt close to Ellen. Despite having no children, she had always been kind to Kate and fun to be with. Neither one was having any fun now.

"I do too. The last one I attended was mom's funeral." Kate sighed. "I hope when my time comes whoever is in charge cremates me and then does whatever he or she wants with the ashes and let that be it. I certainly don't want a funeral."

"Well funerals aren't for the dead, dear, they're for the living."

"I suppose. I did what Daddy did for mom. I figured that's what he'd have wanted. I need to ask you something. Hang on a sec." She got up and walked to her office and retrieved the gun the police had returned to her. She held it with distaste, but she wanted Ellen to look at it and see if she recognized it.

She returned and held out the gun so Ellen could see it. Ellen made no attempt to take it or touch it, and Kate could see the distress on her face. "Is that…is that what he used?"

Kate nodded. "Have you ever seen it?"

"It never stops, does it?" Ellen wiped at the tears that had gathered in her eyes.

"I don't understand."

"The pain that survives some people, that seems to follow a family." She closed her eyes and took a deep breath. Opening them, she said, "It was my father's gun. I didn't know John had it. Please Kate, put it away, I don't want to see it or think about it."

Kate returned it to her office and came back to the couch. "I didn't know he had it either. I don't ever recall seeing it. And the police say there was a residue of fentanyl in the glass that I found on the table, and the toxicology report said he'd ingested a rather high dose about twenty minutes before he shot himself."

She stood up and paced. "I looked it up. It's used medically for pain control and so doctors can perform procedures without general anesthesia, but apparently you can get it in powder or pill form on the street, it's an opioid, and it's very popular. They said he probably took it to relieve any anxiety about shooting himself and as a fail-safe if he didn't succeed…with the gun."

Kate felt the sting of tears. "My father wouldn't have had a clue how to buy street drugs, but the detective said he probably asked some kid to buy it for him. He said the neighborhood where Dad lived was full of kids and adults who sold drugs or could get them for you. He said the neighborhood's deteriorated a lot since I grew up. He's got an answer for everything!"

"Oh honey, stop."

"I can't! I can't believe he killed himself. Why would he do that? It makes no sense."

"Sweetheart, it rarely does. Your father struggled with depression for as long as I can remember. I think it finally overwhelmed him." Ellen pulled Kate onto the couch next to her and hugged her. "Come back to San Francisco with me for a week or so. It'll get you away from here and give you a break."

Kate sighed. "Thank you but I can't, there's just too much to do."

Her father's death didn't feel right, it didn't make sense, but she knew no way to answer the 'why?'

———— ◆ ————

SETTLING THE estate was a far more involved process than she had anticipated. The reading of the will, the legal notices, filing probate; it was endless, time-consuming minutiae.

"What ranch? What do you mean he left a ranch to me?"

"It was his family home. Apparently, his father left it to him and since you're his only child, you inherit the place," her father's attorney said.

"Where is it?"

"It's in eastern Colorado, some place called Ardwell. I'm not familiar with that part of Colorado, but I can get you directions."

"I didn't know he owned it. What the hell am I going to do with a ranch?"

The lawyer had shrugged and suggested Kate go see it before making any decisions. Anxious to be free of one more obligation, she had to decide what to do with it.

———— ◆ ————

SHE THOUGHT about her father's family as she drove the interstate toward Ardwell. Kate knew, from the little her father had told her growing up, that the house was where her father, his two sisters, and her grandparents lived. She knew her grandmother had died when he was nine and that her father and both his older sisters had eventually left and never returned. John Earnshaw rarely talked about his life growing up or his family. He was close to Ellen, but had little to do with his other sister Madelyn. Kate never remembered him even saying where the house had been located, and she had assumed that it was no longer owned by anyone in the family.

She had no memories of her grandparents other than two photos her father reluctantly showed her, when she'd asked. He never spoke about his family unless pressed. After discovering she now owned the property, she remembered her father telling her once that her grandfather was a rancher and her grandmother kept house for the family and cooked for the ranch hands who lived in a bunkhouse on the property.

It was a hard life if the two photos her father had shown her were any indication. They were thin, spare people whose faces were not particularly happy looking, but which spoke of endless work and not many rewards for it. One photo of her grandparents was their wedding picture. It showed a stern man posing uncomfortably for the camera. It was clear he was no Mr. Rogers; he stared at the camera belligerently as if challenging the photographer to take his photo.

His eighteen-year-old bride had a sweet full face and hesitant smile as she posed next to her new husband. The photo of her grandmother taken fourteen years later, just before she died, showed a face with sad eyes and a downward pull to her lips. No sweetness left, no smiles to be shared, a woman worn down to the nub by work and childbearing.

Kate's father didn't like to talk about his mother's death. Once, as a teenager, she had asked what happened. All he said was his mother had tripped, fallen down the stairs, and broken her neck.

He said his father rarely spoke of it and when his father had it was with a bitterness that made it seem as if his wife had died intentionally to spite him.

Her father denied remembering the event and all he would say about his father was that he was a mean old bastard. He made it clear that further questions were not welcome. It seemed there were issues in his family that weren't up for discussion, just like the many things she was discovering about her father since his death.

Sometimes mean old bastards are just that, and sometimes they're mean old bastards because life has made them that way. Kate often wondered which her grandfather had been. If her father knew the answer, he never said. Maybe he didn't know. If for some reason the subject of his childhood arose, he would be out of sorts for days afterward. Kate had learned not to ask.

The questions never went away, she thought as she took the turn off to Greeley. She still had at least an hour's drive to get to Ardwell. Was he upset about something relating to his family—something serious enough to drive him to suicide? Had he been given some life-altering news by the visitor that Kate was sure had used the other glass? The police had found no prints on the glass, so perhaps she was wrong about that as well as everything else.

CHAPTER THREE

THE HOT, DRY wind blew strands of dark brown hair away from Kate's face and cooled the line of perspiration at her hairline. The tall, weedy grass swayed around her bare legs. It was hot and she'd worn shorts. *Not a great idea*, she thought. The grass made her exposed legs itch. The house, or what was left of it, waited silently for her. It sat in the midst of an overgrown field on the eastern plains of Colorado near the small town of Ardwell. The parcel of land it sat on was otherwise desolate.

A month after her father's suicide she still woke up thinking for a moment all was well, until she remembered what had happened and everything came crashing down on her. It seemed as if each day brought a revelation about her father that she hadn't known about. She felt both numb and as if she were scraped raw.

Standing in the grass looking at the two-story house, Kate wondered whether it was safe to enter. Any window glass that might have once protected its occupants from the weather was missing. Nature had done its best to eradicate the house, yet there it stood—empty, falling down in places, waiting for her to decide its future. The porch sagged, the front door lay in the grass at the side of the house, and there was a gaping hole in the roof. She couldn't see any sign of a bunkhouse, so perhaps nature had had her way with that structure.

If I turned around and got in the car and drove off, I could just let the house continue to disintegrate and be done with it, she thought.

Kate sighed. Driving off and forgetting it was an option but would only settle the issue temporarily. Her father's death had weighed her down with grief and a weird sort of inertia. Decisions often were impossible. If the property had been the source of such anger and pain for her father, holding onto it and leaving it to her was as inexplicable as his suicide. Why? What was the point?

She waded several feet through the knee-high, yellowed grass batting away grasshoppers that jumped at her as she walked toward what was left of the front porch. Her shirt was stuck to her back with sweat and she could feel it collect between her breasts. It was just too damn hot. She heard an engine approaching and turned to see an older, blue pickup truck following the two tire tracks her car had made in the grass as she'd driven onto the property.

The truck came to a stop. She heard the engine shut off and the driver's door open. Shading her eyes with her hand to better see who exited the truck, she gauged the distance to her car. She wasn't worried—yet—but you never knew what people might be like. The sun reflecting off the windshield made it hard to see who was driving.

A jeans-clad leg extended down from the cab, shod in a brown, scuffed cowboy boot, and she saw a dark-haired man stand up. He reached into the cab, pulled a straw cowboy hat out, and shoved it on his head. Stepping away from the truck, he closed the door and stood silently watching her. He was more than six feet tall, slimly built, but his white T-shirt hugged the muscles in his upper arms and chest. Several days' growth of beard left his face with a rough, unsettling look. He didn't look all that friendly.

"You wanna be careful wading through that grass, ma'am."

"Why?"

"Rattlesnakes."

"*Rattlesnakes?*" She froze. "Oh God, how do I get back to my car?"

"Did you hear any rattling near where you walked?"

"No, I don't think so."

"Then you're probably safe."

"*Probably?* Jesus, now what do I do?"

"Just walk slow and careful back to your car and listen."

"Listen for what?"

"Sort of a *sst, sst, sst* noise." His brows were knit as he stared at her. He didn't look as if he was happy about her being there. "If you hear it, stop."

"And *then what?*"

"Then you hope the snake calms down and moves off. If the noise speeds up, don't run. The vibrations set them off."

With an anxious look on her face she debated what to do as he watched her. He tipped his head to the side slightly and raised his eyebrows. "Why don't I come get you?"

"Okay," she replied hesitantly. He started walking toward her, and she was both relieved and apprehensive.

"I'm just going to pick you up and carry you back to your car." He seemed to be trying to reassure her. He smiled as he closed the distance between them, and she saw he had green eyes that flirted with blue and were fringed with black lashes. The hair that peeked below the cowboy hat had an appealing loose curl to it and was damp with sweat on the sides. The smile hadn't done much to reassure her.

"I suppose you think this is funny."

"No ma'am, rattlers are not funny."

"Stop calling me ma'am, I'm not your mother."

"You certainly aren't. My mother wouldn't be out here traipsing around in shorts. At least you're wearing decent shoes," he said, scrutinizing her ankle-high hiking boots. The annoyed frown was back on his face.

She crossed her arms over her chest and frowned back at him. "Well, how was I supposed to know there were rattlesnakes out here?"

"Don't know much about the plains then, I guess." He squatted down and wrapped his arms around her thighs just below her butt. Hoisting her over his shoulder in a fireman's carry, his hat tipped askew. He slid his hands midway down her thighs to balance her weight as he stood up and began walking to toward the vehicles.

She yelped and braced her hands against his back. "Wait! Wait a minute! Can you take me to the porch of the house so I can look around a bit?" He smelled appealingly male, a scent of laundry soap and sweat. His T-shirt was slightly damp under her hands.

He stopped. "And then what? Carry you to your car?"

"Well, yeah."

"No. The house isn't safe." He began making his way back to the vehicles. He off-loaded her by the driver's door of her car, adjusted his Stetson, and stared at her. "What're you doing over here anyway? This is private property. It's posted."

"I know that. It happens to be my private property."

"No, it's John Earnshaw's."

She blinked in surprise. "You knew my dad?"

"Yeah. How'd it become yours?"

"He…he committed suicide a month ago. He left it to me." Her vision blurred as she struggled not to cry. She had no idea why she'd mentioned his suicide. Grief was like that, she'd discovered. One minute she was reserved and cautious about what she revealed and the next she blurted out things she'd had no intention of sharing.

He was quiet for a minute. "I'm real sorry to hear that." He cleared his throat abruptly and looked away blinking his eyes a few times.

An uncomfortable silence stretched between them. She took a deep breath to try to loosen the tightness in her throat. "The lawyer asked that I come take a look at it and decide what I wanted to do with it. I was just looking around."

"I suppose you're going to sell it." He stared at her. By the frown on his face Kate figured he wasn't in favor of that. He really wasn't all that friendly.

"I don't know yet. It's kind of a mess." Her eyes narrowed. "How did you know I was here?"

"I live over there," he said pointing vaguely west. "Saw you drive onto the property; figured I should come find out what you were up to."

"What business is it of yours who comes on the property?"

He didn't say anything for a moment. His gaze was a bit unsettling. "I've always kept an eye on the place for John. You know, watching for kids getting into trouble, people wandering where they shouldn't, getting hurt. People who have no business being on the property, which is what I figured you for."

She frowned. She was going to have a permanent crease between her brows if this conversation went on much longer. "Twenty-four seven? Don't you work?"

"I work."

She gave up pursuing that line of questioning. Apparently, he wasn't inclined to say more. "I would like to look inside the place and maybe around the property just to get a feel for it. Maybe it'd help me decide what to do with it."

"I wouldn't advise that, but if you're intent on doing it, I'd suggest you come better prepared next time—long pants, preferably jeans. Your boots are good. Still, I'd be careful, the house is pretty unstable. Keep your phone handy in case you get hurt."

That didn't sound good. "You never told me your name."

Again he was silent before he said, "Evan Hastings. Yours?"

"Kate Earnshaw."

"Nice to meet you," he said, tugging on the front brim of his hat. He turned and walked to his truck and opened the door.

"I…I don't suppose you'd be interested in buying the property?"

"Nah, I have enough to contend with taking care of my property. I'm just hoping you don't sell it to some commercial bunch."

"What would a commercial developer in their right mind want to build out here in the middle of nowhere?"

"Probably nothin', but a lot of properties out here are in demand for the water or mineral rights and their oil shale deposits." Again, she got the distinct impression he wasn't happy she was here or the possibility she might sell the property.

"I didn't know that."

"Guess there's a lot you don't know. You might want to read up on the area and your property before you do anything. You could get cheated out of a fair price, being so…unaware of things." He pulled on the front brim of his hat again, grasped the steering wheel, pulled himself in, closed the door, and drove off.

Kate watched the truck reach the gate and turn west. "'Being so unaware of things.' What a condescending ass," she muttered, getting into her car and closing the door.

God, it's hot out here, she thought. No trees anywhere close; none really unless you were near a stream where cottonwoods grew close to the stream banks. Why hadn't her father just gotten rid of the place? And why had he saddled her with it? The questions were piling up and the answers weren't. She started the car, hit the down button for the front windows, and turned on the AC hoping it wouldn't take too long for the car to cool down. The more revelations about her father that occurred, the more a low-level anger had built.

She'd arranged for a two-night stay at a tiny bed and breakfast that was basically a spare room and a bath in the owners' house, done up in an unsuccessful attempt at shabby chic. Staying in a bedroom in their actual home was a little cozy for her taste, but it was the only accommodation available without driving back to Greeley. Staying two nights would give her time to look around the tiny town of Ardwell and the property. She scratched at her calf; then looked down. Her lower legs were broken out and itchy from contact with the grass. Shorts had definitely not been a good choice.

Talking to Evan Hastings had been more an extraction of words than a conversation. To say he was a strong silent type might be a cliché, but not far from the truth. Underlying the conversation was her sense that he thought she was an idiot and was laughing at her, which annoyed her. She thought for a moment he wouldn't tell her his name, which was weird, and he'd seemed to be shaken by the news of her father's suicide. His reaction surprised her. He seemed to know her father well, but Kate had never heard of Evan Hastings.

CHAPTER FOUR

O N THE DRIVE back to his house, Evan thought about Kate's father. John had mentioned his daughter from time to time, but he'd never shown Evan a picture or brought her with him to visit. He guessed she was about five-foot-six, with long nicely shaped legs. Lashes that matched her dark brown hair framed her brown eyes. She'd twisted her hair up on the back of her head with one of those clip things, which wasn't all that attractive. He'd like to have seen it down, loose around her face.

He probably shouldn't have scared her mentioning the rattlesnakes, but Christ she was wading through knee-high grass on the Colorado prairie in shorts. If he were a betting man he'd have put money on her being in flip-flops. She'd worn hiking boots, so that was something.

The weight and sadness of hearing that John had committed suicide accompanied him back to his property. Clearly he was a complete stranger to John's daughter, otherwise surely she would have told him about her father's death and invited him to the funeral. Not having known about John's death left Evan with an uncomfortable, empty sadness.

Evan often wondered why John never brought his daughter with him, but John was a private man who didn't tolerate a lot of questioning. Maybe coming up here alone had been an escape he didn't want to share. Perhaps most difficult to bear was that Evan had been unaware of John's state of mind and hadn't been able to try to talk him out of committing suicide.

He thought about the package that John had sent him. John had enclosed a note in the padded envelope that held the wrapped package. He'd asked Evan to hold onto it for him. If Evan had to guess, it was a small book. It clearly wasn't a gift, and Evan assumed John didn't intend for him to open it. So he hadn't. He wondered if he should now. Knowing John as he did, it felt like an invasion of privacy. It belonged to his daughter in any case. He'd have to give it to her.

Evan shook his head, trying to rid himself of the regrets as he pulled up to his house and got out. He hoped like hell she'd think before she just unloaded the property. What he'd told her about the land value was true. A lot of ranchers allowed fracking on their property to help bring in more money. Ranching and farming were not occupations to get into if you hoped to make money. The thought of fracking going on so close to his property worried him. Wasn't much he could do about it, though, if she chose to sell.

She'd been apprehensive and wary, which was understandable, she didn't know him from Adam. Based on conversations with John, though, he knew there was a soft, funny side to her. In some ways, he felt like he knew her. He didn't, but he'd like to. And there was his usual response to a woman in distress—he wanted to rescue her. That hadn't always been a great idea. The memory of her resting over his shoulder, her hands braced on his back, and the soft skin on her legs under his hands flashed back.

He shook his head. He should walk away while he had the chance.

IT WAS nearly five when Kate returned to the B & B, hot, sweaty, and tired. They didn't provide lunch or dinner, but breakfast had been so enormous that she hadn't needed lunch. Now, however, she was starving. Hazel, the female half of the couple who owned the place, gave her directions to the only restaurant in town. A shower went a long way to relieving her itching lower legs and ridding her of the sweat that had dried and left her skin feeling rough and dirty. Next time she was out at the house—if there was a next time— she'd wear jeans to avoid contact with the grass. After her shower, she dressed in jeans, a casual shirt, and tennis shoes. She re-clipped her hair in a twist, added some makeup, and headed out the door.

Kate decided to walk. According to Hazel, the restaurant wasn't more than four or five blocks away, and the heat of the day had dissipated some. She was frustrated and the walk would help relieve that. She felt compelled to deal with the property, her father's house, and everything that came up, and at the same time wanted to run away from it all. What she really wanted was her father. And, if she couldn't have him, then she wanted to know why he'd killed himself.

There were things that puzzled her. Her father never drank during the day. The autopsy results confirmed that he'd ingested bourbon the morning of his death, but the addition of fentanyl was a surprise. Where had he gotten it? How had he even known about it? She was considerably younger and more likely to be familiar with recreational drugs, and she had never heard of fentanyl.

And there was the gun. Surely she'd have known if he possessed one? She'd never seen it or heard her father talk about it. Not knowing about it probably meant nothing as the detective had said. She hadn't known he'd kept the property either.

Walking to the restaurant would give her a closer look at the town itself, which turned out to be pretty small and quaint. A few baskets of wilted flowers hung from porches of small houses. Some of the houses had gravel driveways and others just parched grass with the occasional car sitting on the street in front. Perhaps, she thought, this was how small Colorado towns looked.

She preferred Denver with its restaurants, theaters, shopping, and entertainment. Despite growing up in Colorado, she wasn't a hiker, biker, runner, or skier. Most of the people she knew seemed to do some or all of them. A friend recommended the hiking boots. After she left Ardwell, no doubt they'd just gather dust in the back of her closet.

Pulling herself out of her mental wanderings, she turned onto the main street. The town had a mercantile store—the sign actually called it that. An overhanging porch shaded the glass front door with its open sign hanging crookedly from a suction hook attached to the inside glass. According to the window display, the store supplied clothes and other necessities.

Across the street was a building with offices belonging to a lawyer and a doctor. The town had a small grocery store with a pharmacy next to it and a liquor store. There was a police station and a ranch store that advertised animal feed and farm supplies. Farm machinery was parked in the lot next to it, and a statue of a red-brown horse with what looked like white ankle socks sat in the entrance to the main parking lot.

What did people do for entertainment around here? She wondered.

She couldn't see her father visiting Ardwell, but he knew Hastings so he must have. And must have visited fairly frequently, based on Hastings' apparent friendship with him. What was their connection?

From the outside, the restaurant looked more like a bar to her. A number of pickups and older model SUVs were parked in its lot. She debated about going in and would have retreated to the grocery store for food if it hadn't been closed and she wasn't so hungry. Opening the door, she was hit by a wall of canned country music, the smell of beer, and a faint whiff of farm animals—accompanied by the buzz of conversation from a full house of drinkers and diners.

A few people near the door turned to glance in her direction then returned to their food and conversations. The scrutiny made her uncomfortable, but she was a stranger, and it didn't look like they got many strangers in Ardwell. There was a small hostess station and a 'Please Wait To Be Seated' sign, so she waited. And waited. At last she walked up to the bar.

"Hey little lady what can I do for you?" the bartender asked.

"I'd like a table for dinner."

"Honey, just find a place and sit down."

"But the sign…"

"Yeah, I know, but the hostess didn't come in tonight so seat yourself."

"You should take down the sign then." She really needed to eat. Lack of food turned her into a petulant snot. She was tired and the heat had wiped her out. The combination of all three left her feeling like a toddler on the verge of a temper tantrum.

He laughed. "Well, it's screwed to the stand, and Kelsey'll be back tomorrow so that don't seem worth the trouble."

Kate frowned and turned looking for an empty seat. There didn't seem to be one. "Can I get food at the bar since apparently there aren't any tables?"

He looked up from a glass he was washing in the small bar sink and glanced around. "Jerry! Bill!" he shouted to two guys occupying separate tables. "Scooch together so this lady can have a table. You don't both need tables to yourself."

The men looked up from their plates, and then one got up and moved to where the other guy sat. Kate walked over and nodded at them. "Thanks," she said, trying to smile convincingly as she eased into the chair at the now empty table.

The guy who'd moved walked over to the hostess stand and returned with a menu. "Figured you might need this, ma'am."

What was with this 'ma'am' and 'little lady' nonsense? "Thank you."

Kate perused the menu and sighed. Burgers, chicken fried steak, fried chicken, a few sandwiches, and a variety of Mexican food options seemed to be the featured items. Salads were briefly mentioned at the bottom, but she didn't think that would be a good choice. As far as beverages, there didn't seem to be any options other than beer, mixed drinks, iced tea, and soft drinks. After her frustrating day, she really wanted a glass of wine.

"What can I getcha?"

Kate looked up at a middle-aged woman with a western shirt sporting a name tag that said "Irene" and a short apron worn over jeans. The bartender wore similar clothes, minus the apron or the name tag, so apparently this was the restaurant uniform. Her hair, a rather odd shade of red, was piled up on her head and held there by a big bow-covered clip. She deposited a roll of silverware encased in a paper napkin, then fished a notepad out of her apron pocket and held it at the ready with pen in hand.

"I guess a cheeseburger and fries, no onions please. I don't suppose you have any wine."

"We don't get much call for that. The beer's good and the margaritas are killer."

"Beer's fine then."

"We got…" She rattled off a long list of beers.

"Whatever you recommend is fine."

The waitress disappeared. She returned a few minutes later and plunked a beer in a bottle on the table and quickly left to check with other customers. Kate took a sip and inwardly made a face. She didn't like beer that much, but a margarita with a burger seemed weird for some reason. She'd ask for some water when the waitress returned with her meal.

The men next to her were involved in a baffling conversation about a horse that might or might not have laminitis, whatever that was. She sat back against the chair and wondered if she could make it through another day here. The chances she'd sell the property seemed to be escalating the more she discovered about Ardwell. It was like landing in a foreign country. The conversations around her were odd and incomprehensible, and the town was tiny and seemed as if it was trapped in the fifties or sixties.

Evan Hastings seemed to fit and yet he didn't, she wasn't sure why. Under the slightly western veneer, she got the sense that he was a bit more worldly than the other residents of the town that she had met. And she wondered, again, what his connection was to her father.

She was worried about exploring the house and property, because of what he'd said about it not being safe, and the threat of rattlesnakes. There was always the option of going home tonight and putting the place up for sale. The hell with investigating the potential rights that the property might have or getting cheated out of money. Whatever she got from the sale would be a windfall.

Just get rid of the place and be done with it.

She was beginning to see why her father had done nothing; it was easier than trying to figure out what to do with the place. But why continue to visit the town? It was so out of character for the father she knew. For the millionth time, she wished she knew why he'd committed suicide. There really was no explanation that made sense. And she was beginning to wonder whether she had ever known who her father really was.

CHAPTER FIVE

ITHOUT THINKING SHE took another drink of the beer and made a face, this time for all to see.

"Not a big fan of beer, I take it."

She looked up and saw Evan Hastings standing in front of her table. He cleaned up well was her first thought. He'd shaved and he looked good in clean snug jeans, a light blue western shirt with mother of pearl snap buttons, and cowboy boots. No hat, but other than baseball caps, no guy in the place was wearing a cowboy hat.

"Umm, no not really, but it seemed like the only viable option."

"The margaritas are good."

"So I hear, but that seemed like an odd choice with a burger."

He smiled, seemingly in a better mood than earlier. "Maybe so." He indicated the seat across from her. "This taken? The place is kinda full, tonight being a Saturday."

"Feel free."

He sat down, and since the area under the table was limited he stretched his legs out into the space between tables. He really was tall. Taking in his long, lanky legs, Kate guessed he had to be at least six-foot-two. The men at the next table nodded at him and went back to their conversation, which now concerned a tractor that wasn't working. Based on their ongoing conversation, it seemed like nothing worked well in this town. The waitress returned with a burger that smelled as if it had come off a charcoal grill and not an indoor griddle. The scent nearly had Kate drooling.

"The usual, Irene," Evan said. The waitress smiled and left, returning with a glass of dark beer. He indicated Kate's burger. "Don't wait for me."

Without comment, she added the pickles, lettuce, and mustard, cut the burger in half, then squirted ketchup on the plate next to the fries. Taking a bite, she all but moaned. She didn't think she'd had a burger this tasty in quite a while.

He grinned. "The food's pretty good here."

Had she moaned out loud?

His grin annoyed her. Earlier, he'd acted as if she was incredibly stupid, and now he seemed to find her amusing. He was a handsome guy, and was more appealing now than earlier, but she felt he was laughing at her underneath it all.

Irene returned with another burger and Evan dug in. They ate without conversation. While they inhaled their food, a band appeared, set up by the wooden dance floor, and began tuning up.

I guess this is what they do for entertainment, she thought, finishing her burger.

The beer was starting to taste better. Either that or she was getting used to it. She felt a bit of a buzz and looked closer at the label, surprised by the beer's percentage of alcohol. She was going to have to go easy or she'd be drunk.

Finished with his burger, Evan cleared his throat. "I…I'm sorry about your dad. I liked him a lot."

Kate closed her eyes. Sympathy like this reduced her to tears and crying was the last thing she wanted to do here or in front of him. "Thank you," she said, opening her eyes and looking at him. "I appreciate it, but it's really hard to talk about. I'd just as soon not go there."

His face flooded with color. "Sorry. I should have figured that would be a sensitive subject."

"It's okay. I just don't want to talk about it."

He nodded and remained silent while the band fiddled with their instruments then began to play a country song she didn't recognize. Well, she wouldn't recognize *any* country songs, since she didn't listen to them.

He seemed uncomfortable and made no effort to restart the conversation. After the first song he suddenly said, "When they get warmed up, would you like to dance?"

"I'm not really in the mood for dancing." She was wary of him. Attracted—he was the type who had always appealed to her—but wary. He seemed like a nice guy and was making an effort to be friendlier than earlier in the day, but she still had so many questions about him.

"Seems like it's been a rough day for both of us. Too many surprises I guess. You look like you could use some cheering up. I know I could." He finished his beer as the band ran through a couple songs. "Not sure a dance would do the trick, but why not give it a try?"

She debated for a moment, watching him for signs his invitation was the result of pity, then decided to take a chance. "Okay, one dance."

He led her onto the small dance floor and took her in his arms. "This is a two-step. Just think walk, walk, shuffle, shuffle and let me guide you around." He listened for a moment tapping his foot then took off, guiding her around other couples who were walking and shuffling to the music, some better than others. "Relax," he said, pulling her close.

It was disconcerting being held by him. She hadn't been held by anyone in a while. There had been no one to lean on or be comforted by since her father's death other than her friend Sandi. Evan's aftershave reminded her of fresh linen. Being held in his arms made her want to lean in and lay her head on his shoulder and let go of all the grief and all the questions her father's suicide had raised. She stiffened and pulled away at the thought.

"Breathe once in a while, it helps."

She looked up at him and saw that smile.

"Are you *laughing at me?*" Her eyes flashed. "You're the one who talked me into this, so you can just find someone else to dance with."

She broke away from him and pushed through the surrounding couples. Returning to the table, she fished a twenty out of her jeans pocket, threw it on the table, and headed toward the door.

"What'd you do to piss her off, Evan?" she heard someone call out with a laugh. The door to the bar slammed behind her cutting off any response he might have made.

She was halfway down the street when she heard someone jogging up behind her. She swung around to see him approaching.

"I wasn't laughing at you." He'd stopped a few feet away with a frown on his face.

"Yes, you were. You've been making me feel ridiculous since you pulled up at my father's property this afternoon. Who the hell d'you think you are? More to the point *who* the hell are you?"

"I told you. I was a friend of your dad's."

She stepped up to him and poked him in the chest. "So you say. *I've* never heard of you, never heard my father *ever* talk about you. I didn't know he kept the property or that he came up here at all. All I have is your word for it, and you could be lying to me."

"Why would I do that?"

"I don't know. I don't know anything anymore. Just…just leave me alone!"

Tears welled in her eyes and she angrily brushed them away. Without thinking, Evan grasped her shoulders and pulled her close. He bent his head and kissed her softly at first then more insistently. Abruptly he broke off, let go, turned, and walked away, leaving her wondering what had hit her.

"You know, where I come from that could be considered an assault!" She yelled at his retreating figure as more tears spilled down her cheeks.

Without turning around, he called over his shoulder, "Where I come from, that's considered a kiss, but my apologies if it offended."

CHAPTER SIX

S HE'D SMELLED LIKE lavender from the soap and lotion he knew Hazel provided at the B & B, and holding her as they moved around the dance floor made him want to spend the rest of the night dancing with her. She'd never quite relaxed in his arms, though, except for that one brief moment. The sense that he knew her from conversations with her father was complicating things for him. She'd clearly had no idea he even existed.

She'd looked so damn sad, even out at her father's place. When he'd tried to offer his condolences, he was afraid she was going to burst into tears. The only remedy he could think of, since they both needed some cheering up, was dancing. Even that had backfired. It felt like he was making all the wrong moves. He hadn't felt this baffled by a woman in years.

He shouldn't have kissed her. He'd heard the confusion and anger in her voice when she'd challenged him about knowing her father, but the tears made him want to hold her and comfort her. The kiss had been impulsive, but it had been impossible to resist. By the look on her face and her comment, it hadn't done much to endear him to her.

He'd gone to the bar for dinner in the hope that she hadn't returned to Denver. He figured she'd done just that. If she were there he could return the package her father had left him. Despite his hope she'd be there, seeing her surprised him and made him forget all about the damn package. He'd forgotten it in the truck and hadn't given it to her. He shook his head. Hazel would probably give him her address and he'd mail it to her.

She was a connection to John and seeing her made him feel better. The smile that had irritated her so much was because she'd fit up against him just right and he'd been enjoying holding her close.

It hardly mattered.

She'll take off, sell the property, and be gone, he thought.

———— • ◆ • ————

KATE HEADED back to Denver after breakfast the next morning. She wasn't in the best of moods because of a restless night thanks to the puzzle that was Evan Hastings. His kiss had been totally unexpected and had added to her confusion. She was very attracted to him but wanted to keep her distance. Kate had too many questions about him. She wasn't sure how to find out if he really did know her father. If he did, why hadn't her father ever mentioned him? Who was he to her father?

She'd settled up with the owners of the B & B, thanked them for their hospitality, and left. It was Sunday, so her father's lawyer wouldn't be available. Tomorrow, though, she'd call the lawyer and tell him to just sell the damn place for whatever he could get for it. Get rid of one more problem, then maybe it wouldn't matter who Evan Hastings was.

Once home, Kate found her latest book, fixed some iced tea, and took up residence on her condo's tiny back patio. She intended to spend Sunday enjoying the peace and quiet and putting Ardwell out of her mind.

Evan Hastings was harder to set aside. According to him, he'd had more than a passing relationship with her father. Anger reared its ugly head. Who the hell was this guy? If he was telling the truth, how important had he been to her father?

A few chapters into her book, she fell asleep. It had taken an hour to get to Greeley and another hour and a half to get home. The long drive and her restless night finally caught up to her. In her dream, she was in the Ardwell house trying to arrange her furniture in areas that looked stable, but the roof kept releasing bits of itself onto her belongings and the floor kept giving away in spots. Her father stood in the corner watching her. Then she heard a bell ringing.

"That's for you, Katie," he said to her.

In the dream, she searched for her phone. After a few more rings, she woke and realized it was her doorbell. She grumbled to herself about the intrusion and walked to the front door.

A small man in a good suit stood on the front stoop.

"Can I help you?" she asked.

He smiled. "I hope so. Are you Kate Earnshaw?"

"Yes," she replied hesitantly.

"Wonderful. I was hoping to talk to you about buying the property you recently inherited in Ardwell."

She frowned. "How do you know about that and how did you get my address?" She was going to have a very serious conversation with her father's lawyer about releasing her personal information. She didn't think lawyers were allowed to do that.

"Your father's will was filed with Jefferson County, and you were named as the beneficiary. Wills are public information. It doesn't take much to get addresses. I hope I'm not intruding."

She frowned at him. "What do you do, monitor wills that are filed and go after the heirs like an ambulance chaser?" The poor man had come at entirely the wrong time and had woken her up. Her bitch face was in full force.

It was his turn to frown. "I assure you that my inquiry is legitimate. The company I represent has an interest in properties in that area and we get flagged when one transfers ownership. I'm sorry to bother you, but it's often easier to connect with people on Sundays."

"I'm not interested in selling it." That surprised her; she'd decided to do just that on the way home.

"I see." He fished a card out of his jacket pocket and offered it to her. "Here's my card. We would be willing to offer a fair price for it. Think about it and let me know if you change your mind."

She took the card and watched as he turned and retreated down the sidewalk, got into a car, and drove off. The card wasn't very helpful. All that was on it was Wilcox Inc., and a phone number. What in God's name were they interested in? Was Evan right about the rights attached to the land?

She sighed. There were too many questions about the property, Evan Hastings, and her father to get rid of it, she thought, as she closed and locked the door.

Kate was surprised in the intervening days by the three phone messages she received regarding the property all from various people interested in buying it or her father's home in Lakewood. She took down the names and phone numbers but didn't return the calls.

"It's a real pain," her friend Sandi agreed over lunch. "If there's any property involved they keep calling, even after its been sold. I'm still getting calls about the family home, and we sold it two years ago. I just delete the voice messages and block the number. They're like piranhas."

Sandi shook her head. "I also get credit card offers addressed to the Estate of Frederick Clarkson. You'd think the morons that send these offers would think, estate, dead person, doesn't need a credit card, but they don't. Initially, I'd call their number and tell them my dad was dead and to take him off their solicitation list, but now I just shred the damn things. I figure eventually they'll stop sending them. At least I hope they do."

"I'm surprised they'd be interested in this property, though," said Kate. "It's twenty-acres northeast of Denver out in the middle of nowhere with nothing but a dilapidated house sitting on it. The guy who lives to the west of the land said to investigate the property to avoid getting cheated out of a fair price. He said buyers were often interested in mineral and water rights and oil shale deposits on the land."

Kate held her fork over her salad thinking about what lay ahead of her. "But finding out about that involves a lot of work, and I don't even know where to begin."

"You could talk to a real estate agent."

"I could, but they always assume you want to sell, then they want you to list with them, and if you decide not to sell, they're forever sending you emails and solicitations. I don't know. I think I'm just going to let it sit for a while."

"I've heard you shouldn't make any major decisions for a year after a death. You make mistakes when something that major happens."

"Yeah, part of me just wants to be rid of it, but I can't quite do it. I can't figure out why my dad kept it. Hell, I can't figure out why he'd commit suicide." Kate's appetite, which hadn't been great since her father's death, died altogether. She picked at her lunch for a bit, as she forced herself to catalogue all the things she had to do.

"I've still got to go through the house and all his personal stuff. I'm really dreading that. The lawyer says he and I have to go to the bank to open dad's safe deposit box and retrieve the contents. I told him to hold off on that for a while. I can only face so much at once."

"People think that it all ends when someone dies, but really, for the family, it's not over by a long shot. It's especially hard with your dad committing suicide. If you need some help or just moral support, let me know."

CHAPTER SEVEN

T HAD TAKEN Kate three weeks to go through the house in Lakewood. She had collected the safe deposit box items, which amounted to legal papers, the deed to his house, her parents' marriage license, and the car title, and put them in her own safe deposit box for the time being. She'd dreaded going through her father's possessions. Her mother had been gone for almost ten years so what was left primarily belonged to her father. Together she and her father had decided what to do with her mother's belongings. Now, she had to decide about her father's possessions alone in the home she'd grown up in and the home in which he'd killed himself.

She had to sort through and deal with the contents of the rooms and closets before the house could either be rented or sold. She could understand better now the depression that had engulfed her father when her mother had passed. This sorting and decision making was interminable and heartbreaking.

Kate stood in the living room and looked at an oil painting her father had acquired some time ago. It was a landscape about two feet high by three feet wide and had always been a favorite of his.

"That's worth something, Katie. The artist has gotten real popular in the last few years," he'd told her many times. "When I'm gone, don't give it away. If you sell it, get it appraised first."

The canvas depicted storm clouds rolling across distant foothills. The prairie in the foreground was alight in spots with that weird intermittent sunshine that peeks through storm clouds periodically—like God parting the clouds and shining through, she thought with a smile. Two red rock boulders sat off-center in the midst of the prairie grass, and in the distance a streak of lightning could be seen. She squinted at the lower right corner and could barely make out the signature, EJ something, but the last name was an indecipherable scrawl. She'd keep the painting, she decided.

It took some time to go through and sort the clothes. The scent of her father's Polo aftershave that clung to his clothes was distracting and called up memories that would be forever clouded by his suicide. *Why?* The question that had haunted her since she'd found him couldn't be answered, but her unease about it persisted. She supposed anyone left behind after a suicide felt much the same. Kate set aside a few items of clothing that had particular sentiment for her, packed the rest in boxes for donation, and loaded the boxes into her car. She had called a furniture recycle store about picking up the furniture, and they were due later today.

She couldn't go into the den without seeing her father's lifeless body in his recliner. The recliner was gone, but the memory wasn't. Someone would have to go through her father's books lining the shelves in the den. They had meant so much to him and having to sort them in the room he'd died in was more than she could bear. Maybe Sandi would do it for her. There were file boxes of documents from his office that she'd have to go through as well. Perhaps something might be in the boxes that would explain his state of mind.

After dealing with the kitchen, Kate took the stairs to the basement where his office was. She decided to tackle her father's

Navy footlocker first. She tossed the cushion from his desk chair onto the floor and sat down on it. Opening the footlocker, she saw it held his uniforms—a pair of the daily blue jeans with their wide legs and his white cap with his last name inked into the inside. He'd kept his more formal whites and his dress blues as well.

Moths had gotten to the wool of his dress blues, which was a shame. Kate folded the uniforms, laying them to the side as she continued to rummage through the locker. She found some sketchpads on the bottom. Leafing through them she was surprised to see sketches of men who looked like fellow enlisted men or officers and a few women that, based on their exaggerated, pin-up girl attributes and lack of clothes, must have been fantasies rather than real subjects. She found a second sketchpad that contained drawings of people she didn't recognize, several of his two sisters, and a drawing of Kate as a baby held in her mother's arms. It astonished her to find her father's signature at the bottom of each page. They were beautiful.

It felt as if she were looking through another man's possessions. She'd never seen her father draw, and he'd certainly never spoken about it. He'd had beautiful handwriting, which, these days, was an art in itself as most people's handwriting was terrible. He was a general contractor. She supposed building things was a form of art as well. He was someone who built things for other people and sent his laborers to the house if repairs were needed. As if he wanted nothing to do with the house. The drawings, like the property in Ardwell, added more surprises to what she'd not known about her father.

Maybe you didn't know he was suicidal either.

At the very bottom of the footlocker was a bound stack of letters enclosed in old-fashioned airmail envelopes with the red and blue barber pole-like edging. She gently opened one and saw it was a letter from her mother to her father while he was in the service. In addition, there were letters from her father in response that her mother had kept. Kate gently returned the letters to the locker, carefully replacing the rest of the locker's contents, and closed it. She'd keep the locker and perhaps read the letters another day.

She walked over to the bookcase, picked up a photo album, and leafed through it. There were photos of her immediate family she recognized and photos of people she had never seen. No one, except her father's sisters, Madelyn and Ellen, were alive now. They both lived out of state. No one was handy to ask where and why some of the photos had been taken or who some of the people were. Another puzzle her father couldn't answer now.

After the furniture crew had come and gone, the house looked forlorn and empty. Kate hastily loaded her car up and made a run to the charity store dropping off the clothes and other articles that she no longer wanted or needed and returned to the house to collect what she intended to keep.

CHAPTER EIGHT

I T HAD BEEN a very long day.

Kate had lugged all the boxes into her condo and stacked them in the dining room on top of and around her mother's dining table. She planned to have her mother's china hutch brought over by a moving company. She had packed boxes with the beautiful, but rarely used, "good china" from the hutch. The image of her mother's good glasses, one sitting on the table and one in the dishwasher at her father's place popped into her head.

She shook her head. No way to know if that meant anything, but it was puzzling. Her father had never used the china or the glasses after her mother died. Well, that wasn't exactly right, she'd never *seen* him use them. Maybe he had. She sighed in frustration. All those unanswered questions, but at least the house was cleared out.

After a shower, she felt better. The dust of the day was gone and her hair was clean and dried, but she had been unable to shower the sadness and confusion away. She stood in front of the open refrigerator staring vacantly at its contents until she finally admitted to herself she wasn't hungry and shut the door. Instead, she opened a bottle of wine and settled onto the couch. She turned on the TV and surfed through the channels. Finding nothing that appealed, she turned the TV off and sat silently drinking her wine and thinking.

Tackling the family house in Lakewood had left her with a sense of emptiness. Kate wasn't sure what to do with the house anymore than she knew what to do with the property in Ardwell. Despite it being paid for and not in bad shape, the family house would always remind her of her father's death. A family with kids and pets and all that went with that, however, would probably love it. She couldn't decide whether to rent it for a while or sell it outright.

If Kate sold the house in Lakewood, all that would be left was the property outside Ardwell. Despite how busy she'd been the last three weeks, her mind kept coming back to Evan Hastings. The puzzle of who he was, how he knew her father, and how important his relationship with her father was—assuming he'd actually had one—circled endlessly in her head.

There hadn't been any more contacts about the property, but there had been several more about her family home. If she decided to sell either of them, she had the names and numbers of the people who'd called and the lawyer's card. She was leaning more and more toward renting her father's house and for the time being just hanging onto the Ardwell property.

Trying to figure out how to research the Ardwell property and whether she even cared enough to do that was something she could let sit for now. Her father certainly had done nothing with the property, so no immediate decision was needed. She wondered why he'd kept it and let it deteriorate. Maybe he'd felt the same inertia about it that she did. But then why the connection with Evan? If Evan was telling the truth, why had her father continued to visit the town?

It was about nine when her cell phone rang. She didn't recognize the number or the area code, and considered sending it to voice mail, but then answered it.

"Hello?"

There was a pause and then a male voice responded. "May I speak with Kate Earnshaw?" The voice was familiar, but she couldn't place it.

"Speaking. Who is this?" *Probably another person wanting to buy the property.*

Again, the pause. "Evan Hastings."

That surprised her. "How did you get my number?"

"Hazel at the B & B gave it to me."

"*What?* Why would she give you my number?"

"I told her we were friends and she…"

"We hardly know each other. We are *not* friends."

"I kinda thought we were, after the kiss."

She could almost feel him smiling. Her temper flared. "You kissed me, I didn't kiss you, and that doesn't make us friends."

"Okay, my mistake."

"What d'you want?"

There was a pause, again, and she wondered if there was a short circuit in his brain that caused it. "I wanted to see if you'd made a decision about what to do with your dad's property."

"Why? Did you change your mind about buying it?"

"No, but I've had to run a few folks off it lately, and I wanted to make sure that was okay with you. Wasn't sure if they were people you sent or not."

"Who's been on the property?"

"Looked to me like surveyors or maybe sales agents. None of them could prove they had a right to be there. I reminded them the property was posted, private land. You want me to let them run around on the property?"

"No, I don't. What does 'posted' mean anyway?"

"Did you read the sign on the fence? It says, 'posted, no trespassing.' The signs are posted on the fencing at intervals and it means that the property is private and if you're caught on it without permission you're trespassing. That's frowned on out here."

"Oh." She paused now. "Thanks. If you wouldn't mind, I'd appreciate it if you'd continue to do that. I could pay you."

"Nope, I don't want to be paid. I did it for your dad, I'm happy to do it for you."

There it was again, the pause.

"I'd like to invite you back," he said at last. "I didn't make the best impression, and I thought if you'd come back for a weekend I could show you why you might want to hang onto the property."

"What is there to show me?"

"Well, see, that's what you'd have to come back for." Again, she could hear the barely concealed amusement in his voice.

She thought about it and decided it was a bad idea. "Thanks, but I don't think so. For now, I'm just going to let it sit. I don't really know what to do with it, so I'm not going to make any decisions."

"Coming out for a weekend could help you decide."

"I'm not sure that's necessary right now or what there would be you could show me. I pretty much saw it all and there wasn't much to see." She was being rude, and she knew it, but for some reason she was hesitant to be friendly. Offense was the best defense she remembered her father saying.

"Chicken?" he asked, and she could just imagine him grinning.

"You are the most infuriating man. This has nothing to do with being *chicken*, which makes you sound about ten by the way. It's a boring place, with a ramshackle house on a piece of property in the middle of nowhere, and a pain in the ass neighbor."

"That'd be me, I guess."

"That'd be you."

"Aren't you just a little curious about the area and why your dad held onto the property? What his connections with it were? What the area is like?"

Kate waited for Evan to go on and when he didn't she replied, "Yes. He never said anything about it or you. I didn't know he still had the property." If the Navy footlocker was any indication, there was a lot about her father she didn't know and it worried her. Apparently, Evan Hastings did. "What'd you want to show me?"

"Come and find out. I've got a guest room you can stay in that won't cost you anything. The door is lockable, so you don't need to worry about me trying to be friends again."

When she didn't reply he added, "You could call Hazel at the B & B for a character reference if you're worried about staying at my place. I haven't killed anybody in a really long time. My parole officer says I've been rehabilitated. How about it?"

His sense of humor appealed to her, but he never stopped teasing her, which was incredibly annoying. Curiosity about what his connection was with her father finally forced her hand. "When?" she asked.

"Come up on Friday, stay till Sunday. When you get to Ardwell, head out to your dad's place, and when you get to it, give me a call at this number and I'll come show you back to my place. Deal?"

"Okay," she said at last and hung up the phone wondering what the hell she'd agreed to. It seemed her curiosity about her father's secret life had overruled her common sense.

CHAPTER NINE

SHE WAS SURPRISED when Evan's place came into view as she followed his truck into the driveway. It was a low-slung contemporary ranch with rockwork on the front, nothing like the houses in town or the occasional farmhouse she'd seen on the way to her father's property. At the center of the house, presumably where the living room was, there were floor-to-ceiling windows that looked out onto the Front Range to the west. Pine trees clustered near the front of the house and a driveway ran from the entry gate at the road around to the garage at the back of the house. She followed his pickup to the garage area. He parked, got out, and motioned to where she could park her car.

"Nice place," she said, as she exited her car.

"Thanks. Your dad helped me build it."

"My dad?"

"Yep. He had some major talent for building." Evan lifted her bag out of the back seat and headed for the back door.

———◆———

EVAN WATCHED the expression on her face as she took in the house. Seemed like there was a lot she didn't know about her father, which was kind of sad now that he was gone. He hadn't mailed the package to her. He'd been trying to think of a way to invite her back so he could give it to her personally.

It wasn't just her selling the place that bothered him. If she sold it, he wouldn't see her again. It'd taken him three weeks to admit that not seeing her would bother him a lot. He'd been hesitant to call her. Their last contact hadn't been a real success, and he figured she might not want further contact. She most likely wouldn't. He'd used the folks showing up on the property as an excuse to call her. There'd only been two of them, but he'd worried she'd decided to get rid of the place without thinking things through. And he wanted very much to see her again.

He wasn't sure what the attraction was. She was beautiful, which was always a plus, but she was as emotionally volatile as they came. He wasn't sure if that was just her personality or whether it was because of her father's death. John had always talked about how bullheaded she was, but he'd never mentioned her being temperamental.

Evan had always enjoyed it when John talked about Kate, and he was curious about her. She'd responded to the kiss, surprisingly so, but otherwise she seemed wary of him. She had a right to be, he guessed. The kiss had stayed with him for some time, and he wanted a repeat performance. Wasn't sure he'd get one, but he damn well wanted one.

"What?" he asked, realizing she'd asked him something.

"This is a nice place, and it doesn't look like a working ranch, so what do you do?"

"I lease out the property to my neighbor to run cattle on and to raise crops. I'm not a farmer or rancher, but there's no point in letting the acreage go unused."

"Must pay well," she replied, looking around as they entered the house.

Without commenting on her remark, he asked, "What do you do?"

"I work for a small, contemporary art gallery on Santa Fe Drive. You know the street with all the funky galleries and restaurants, where the art walk takes place? Or maybe you don't, living up here."

"Out in the hinterlands with all the Neanderthals?" he asked with a grin.

"I didn't say that. I wish you wouldn't laugh at me."

"I wasn't laughing at you, I was just teasing you."

"I don't like to be teased."

"Fair enough. I don't like being thought of as a hick. I know about Santa Fe Drive and a lot of things about Denver. I lived there for a while after college."

He raised his eyebrows at her and waited. When Kate frowned and said nothing he picked up her bag, turned, and headed across the open living room to the hallway leading to the guest room.

He opened the door at the end of the hallway and entered the room holding the door open for her. It was a large bedroom with a king-sized bed and an adjoining bath, a small sitting area near a window that, like the living room windows, looked toward the Front Range in the distance. He dropped her bag on the floor near the bed, walked to the doorway, and stopped.

"If you need anything, just look in the cabinets and closet. If you can't find what you need let me know. The door," he said, showing her the door handle, "locks from this side, but the kind of locks they put on interior doors are pretty easily opened. You don't really know me, so I installed a sliding bolt you can use, if you're feeling terribly insecure. That way you don't need to worry about me visiting uninvited. Dinner will be in about an hour. I'll leave you to it. Come out when you want." He left, closing the door behind him.

KATE HADN'T arrived until nearly eight thirty, so Evan figured she'd be hungry. He moved around the kitchen easily, checking on the potatoes he'd put in the oven to cook about an hour before he'd driven over to guide Kate to the house. He pulled steaks out of the fridge and seasoned them. He went out back and put the steaks on the grill he'd fired up before going to meet her and returned to the kitchen.

He hoped she wasn't a fussy eater, although he remembered she didn't like beer. She'd seemed to enjoy the burger she'd had at Joe's. Hopefully steaks would be okay. Evan felt like a damn kid on a first date, and it annoyed him. She frustrated him and intrigued him. It didn't seem to matter what he did, he could piss her off faster than any woman he'd ever met and, now that she was here, he wasn't sure inviting her had been a great idea. She was probably having second thoughts as well.

You idiot. You've got the entire weekend ahead of you. What the hell are you going to do with her?

Well, other than what he'd wanted to do with her since he'd found her standing in the weeds on her dad's property. But he'd heard the bolt slide shut on the bedroom door after he'd started to walk down the hallway, so *that* most likely wasn't going to happen.

He wasn't sure what the hell he'd thought would happen. As it stood, it would be dinner with her, a night in bed alone thinking about her, and then she'd probably go home in the morning. At least dinner would be entertaining.

Or not.

———— ♦ ————

IF YOU'RE feeling terribly insecure—what an ass, Kate thought irritably walking to the door and sliding the bolt home. She didn't really know the guy. He claimed to know her father, but she had no real proof of that, and she had committed to a weekend in his home. In retrospect that might not have been a great idea, but her curiosity about who he was and whether she could learn more about his relationship with her father had pushed caution aside. She planned to use the bolt. She sighed, she could always leave in the morning or sooner if need be.

After he'd left, Kate had wandered around the suite. The bath was well stocked with towels and a variety of unopened shampoos, conditioners, lotions, and soaps that looked as if they'd been collected at various hotels at one time or another. A large white terrycloth robe hung on the back of the bathroom door. The shower was large and tiled with an intricate pattern of blue glass mosaic tiles. The heavy sliding glass door moved easily.

Again, she wondered where his money came from. Tile work like this wasn't cheap. The main floor of the house was hardwood, and the living room had been furnished with a deep overstuffed brown leather couch and chair. A huge, raw-wood coffee table looked as if someone had cut a horizontal slice out of a very large tree and mounted it on aged brass legs. The area rug looked like it was Navaho. *Leasing your property to ranchers and farmers must pay really well*, she thought.

She sat on the side of the bed, removed her shoes, and stretched out on it. It was very comfortable. The linens were white and pristine. The colorfully patterned duvet held a down comforter, and the four pillows were soft and comfortable. She got up and opened the closet. There were additional blankets, two more pillows, and plenty of wooden hangers. He, or someone, had thought of everything. She snorted, maybe he had a wife who was out of town for the weekend.

Kate opened her bag and put her clothes away. She took her makeup bag into the bath and left it on the vanity. Leaning over toward the mirror she inspected her makeup to make sure she didn't have raccoon eyes from her mascara. Removing the clip from her hair, she brushed it. It looked nice down, but after a moment, she twisted it up and re-clipped it. It had looked a bit too nice down around her face and drifting over her shoulders. *No point encouraging unwanted advances*, she thought.

Returning to the bedroom, she changed her shirt and put her shoes back on, walked over to the door and unbolted it. Time for dinner. Kate hoped it went better than things had gone so far.

Evan looked up from the kitchen counter as she entered the living room. The space was huge and open, the kitchen separated from the living room by a large island topped with granite where he stood mixing something that looked like salad dressing.

"I was just about to holler for you. Did you get settled?"

"I did, it's very nice." Before she could stop herself, she said, "Your wife did a nice job decorating." And then cringed. She couldn't believe she'd said that.

He looked up and grinned. "I'm not married if that's what you're asking."

She felt the heat flood her face. *That was an incredibly stupid thing to do,* she thought, just one more example of how off kilter she'd been since her father's death.

"How about a glass of wine? I remembered you don't like beer."

She nodded and accepted the glass of cabernet he offered her, glad that he hadn't made any further comment about her idiotic statement. There was a bottle of wine sitting on the island next to him.

"But you do like beer. Don't feel like you have to drink wine instead."

"I like a lot of things, wine included." He held up a finger. "Hang on a sec while I go check the grill."

He disappeared out the back door carrying a plate. Kate picked up her wine glass and wandered around the living room. His bookshelves held a variety of books and genres, which was encouraging. At least he read books, and they weren't all Louis L'Amour. She stopped herself. If she was going to survive the weekend, she had to stop with the condescending city girl attitude. It really wasn't fair. He was intelligent and pleasant. Living out in the middle of nowhere, didn't equate to unsophisticated. Again, she had the sense that he fit here and yet didn't fit. She hadn't seen any other houses like this in the area.

Kate walked over to the fireplace and looked at the large oil painting that hung above the huge mantel. She worked with contemporary art but could appreciate the painting's appeal and the artist's talent. It was a prairie landscape with low rolling foothills covered in dry yellow grass. Shapes that alluded to cottonwoods ran along a distant stream in the valley, the dark hulking presence of the mountains in the background. A ramshackle fence of posts and barbed wire could be seen along with a few cows huddled near the fence. The light in the living room was such that she couldn't see the artist's signature, but the painting was beautiful, and it reminded her of the one her father liked so much.

"Okay," he said, coming in through the back door and using a foot to push the door closed. There was a scuff mark on the bottom of the door, so evidently he used his foot to close the door on a regular basis. "Dinner's ready, go have a seat, and I'll bring it over."

"Can I help?"

"No, just go sit down and take a load off."

Kate sat down in the small dining nook. He'd made an effort to set the table. None of it was extravagant, but it looked nice. He was sure trying to make a good impression. He cooked, and he created a nice setting for dinner. Either his mother had raised him right or he was gay since there was no wife. The kiss would suggest otherwise, but you never knew.

He walked over with a bowl of salad and some dressing, then retrieved two plates each holding a baked potato and a steak and deposited them on the table. The steaks' aroma made her stomach growl. There was French bread and butter, salt and pepper, and sour cream for the potatoes. Where the hell had he gotten French bread around here? She doubted the tiny grocery in town carried it. She frowned. He had obviously gone to a lot of trouble. She was pretty sure he'd noticed the frown on her face, but he said nothing.

He walked back to the island, collected the wine bottle and his glass and sat down across from her.

"Will this do for dinner?"

"This'll do just fine, thank you." They ate quietly for a few moments. "You know how to cook a steak. This is really wonderful," Kate said at last.

"I'm glad you like it. Seems like steak and potatoes are always a good bet."

It looked like dinner at least was going to go well, she thought with relief.

CHAPTER TEN

KATE SAT ON one end of the couch, enjoying the wine. Evan sat on the opposite end. It was late August. The days were still hot, but evenings were beginning to cool off. Evan had turned on the gas fireplace. She was relaxed, and the fire added to the comfortable feel of the room.

After a few fits and starts to conversation Evan rose with glass in hand. "Come outside. I want to show you something."

It was pitch black outside, so she wasn't sure what there was to be seen, but she rose and followed him out the front door into the yard. The moon hung over the plains and she'd never seen so many stars in the sky. In Denver, she rarely looked up, rarely noticed anything but what was going on in her immediate vicinity.

Evan looked up for a moment then pointed. "That," he said, indicating a swipe of stars that looked like a highway arcing across the night sky, "that's the Milky Way."

"It's…beautiful. I've never seen it before." Kate was beginning to think she was the Neanderthal.

"You wouldn't see it living in the city. The lights are too bright. You can see it here because Ardwell isn't close, and it's small enough that its lights don't interfere. The stars are always beautiful out here. When the weather is nice, I sometimes sit out here and watch them. It's very peaceful."

They stood quietly within an arm's length of each other. Kate caught his scent—clean with that faint whiff of something like the ocean or clean laundry, but more complex than that. She'd never been good at identifying scents, but it might be one of those Italian designer scents. There was also an undertone of what she'd always thought of as 'male,' never being able to quite define it further. It was the scent you found if you buried your face into a man's chest or belly hair and breathed in deeply. It was the scent she'd always fantasized about when it had been too long between lovers.

She shut that train of thought down ruthlessly and concentrated on her surroundings. She heard crickets nearby and, in the distance, the howl of a coyote. At least that's what she thought it was. The darkness enveloped them like a blanket, and the air smelled of pine and grass. There was no hint of exhaust fumes, no discordant traffic noises, no noise from neighbors. She wasn't sure if that was a good thing or an unsettling one.

———◆———

EVAN WATCHED Kate out of the corner of his eye. The wind blew softly, tugging a few stray strands of hair out of the confines of her hair clip. He wished she'd let her hair down so he could see it free. She had beautiful brown eyes that seemed to lighten and darken in response to her moods. They fascinated him. She reached up and returned the wayward strands to their place, and he wished she hadn't. It reminded him of seeing her standing in the grass at her father's place with those same wisps blowing in the hot breeze of the afternoon.

The air felt charged between them and he sighed. He thought about how soft her lips had been when he kissed her and then remembered the sound of the bolt sliding into place as he'd walked away from the guest suite door. He saw her move a bit farther away from him when she heard him sigh.

"This is nice," she said. "But I worked all day and the drive up was a long one. I'm going to go to bed. Thank you for dinner. It really hit the spot."

She turned and walked back into the house, and a few minutes later he saw the light in the guest suite go on. No doubt she'd shot the bolt home.

———◆———

EVAN LOOKED out of his studio windows the following morning and watched the sun rise. The land gradually went from dark to light gray and colors became more visible as the sun made its appearance. In the distance to the west, he could see black cows milling around waiting for workers to throw hay off Fred Johnson's feed truck. He picked up a pad of drawing paper and quickly sketched the scene in charcoal. He'd save it for another day's work. It was early—a fiery red sun was now barely peaking over the horizon and the clouds were tinged with the same color. Maybe there'd be a storm later, or maybe it was just pollution from nearby Greeley distorting the atmosphere.

It had been a restless night trying to figure out what he could show Kate that would convince her not to sell the property or lease it out to an oil and gas company. He wasn't sure what he could possibly say to sway her decision. Evan didn't want the peace of his place ruined by traffic to and from her property, the presence of workers operating drilling and fracking equipment with radios blaring, or the infernal noise of it all. He hadn't needed to worry about that with John Earnshaw. John's intent with the house had been to let it rot, and watch the progress of that slow destruction when he came up to Ardwell. Evan wasn't sure what that had been about, and John hadn't said.

But now, he had no sense of what Kate might do with the place. If she leased it, some oil and gas companies were ecologically conscious and tried to mitigate their effect on the environment, surrounding towns, and ranches. And some were not. There was no telling what you'd get when someone allowed them to operate on their land. They were all intrusive, the sites often industrial blights on the land. If she sold the property, there was even less control over what would happen to it, and he would be right next door.

Peace. That's what he'd always loved about the place. He'd lived in the east during art school and in Denver for a while afterwards, and he'd never felt like he did here. He knew that not everybody liked places like this, with no fancy restaurants, no shopping centers, no movie theaters, or theaters of any kind unless you went to Greeley. It could seem just dead boring to many people, and it seemed Kate felt that way as well.

Maybe there was nothing he could do to convince her not to sell other than buy the place himself. He didn't want to strain his finances like that, though. His canvasses were selling well and he seemed to have built a loyal, well-heeled following, but buying that property would be risky for him. He wasn't altogether sure a bank would loan him the money. And the plain truth of it was he wanted her to have a reason to visit.

He'd been sitting in front of a painting of her that wasn't going well. He'd been working on it since he'd first met her, and he couldn't get her lips right. He'd guessed on her hair—another reason he'd wanted her to take off that damn clip. He wished her father were here. He'd been so good at portraits. He could have told him what was wrong. In a way, it was good that John wasn't here. He wouldn't appreciate the thoughts that ran through Evan's mind concerning Kate.

Landscapes were Evan's specialty, which didn't help. This painting showed her in the grass at her father's place with the house in the background, turning to look his way like she had when she'd heard his truck. He was pleased with that part. It was

Kate he couldn't get right. He snorted, well wasn't that the truth? He hadn't gotten her right from day one.

He'd been thrown by the news that John had committed suicide—shaken that he hadn't known or been able to talk him out of it—and a bit stunned by John's daughter turning up. Not at his best by any measure. He stood up from his stool, picked his coffee mug up off the stand he used for his palette, brushes, and tubes of paint and walked toward the door. He turned back for one last look at the painting before he exited the studio and closed the door behind him.

"There you are," Kate said, as he walked into the kitchen. "I wondered if you were a late riser, but then I saw the coffee was made. I … wasn't sure where you were."

He couldn't tell if she was curious or worried about that. "I'm like the chickens, up with first light. The coffee pot's on auto. I don't like to have to fiddle with it first thing in the morning."

Kate held out the coffee pot, he accepted a refill and took up residence on one of the island's barstools.

"You have chickens?"

He laughed. "Sort of. My neighbor Fred Johnson has about a dozen chickens. I helped him build a chicken coop that'd keep coyotes and foxes out, and in return he lets me come over and get eggs."

She nodded as she sipped her coffee. "I wasn't sure what you had planned for today." She was dressed in jeans, intact ones, not the waste of money ones that came with ready-made holes, and a long-sleeved cotton shirt. Her feet were in socks.

He stretched his arms and yawned. His T-shirt stretched across his chest and rode up slightly. He reached down and pulled it back into place. "Well, I thought I'd take you around your property and mine and let you see it close up. If you're adventurous and careful we could take a gander inside the house."

"Are we going to walk?" She asked anxiously, most likely remembering the rattlesnake warning.

"No, I've got an ATV we can use. We'll do some walking, but I'll keep an eye out for rattlers. Go put your hiking boots on—you did bring them, didn't you?" She nodded. "Good. Did you bring a hat?"

"No."

"I'll find one that'll work. The sun gets hot out here." He eased off the barstool and headed over to the fridge where he began pulling eggs and other items out. "Finish getting dressed. I'll make some breakfast, and we can get going."

CHAPTER ELEVEN

THEY SET OUT an hour later. The straw hat he'd found sat a bit loosely on her head. Kate tightened the drawstring under her chin and held onto the seat of the ATV to avoid being bounced around on the seat. A cooler with lunch in it sat bungeed onto the back of the ATV. He'd been friendly this morning but also a bit quiet. He had some dark circles under his eyes, and she wondered if he'd slept well. Maybe having her here felt as awkward to him as it did to her. She continued to feel that push pull attraction to him and wondered if he felt it too.

Kate had considered leaving the door to her room locked but unbolted last night, then reminded herself that she really didn't know Evan Hastings at all, and had slid the bolt into place. He didn't seem like a psychopath, but then she'd heard they could be very charming—until they killed you. She was letting her imagination run wild, but she wished she'd mentioned this trip to Sandi or someone.

Evan maneuvered the ATV through a ranch gate onto his back forty or whatever it was. The land was covered in tall, dry, yellow grass some with seed heads at the tips. Grasshoppers were everywhere, leaping away from the ATV and sometimes into it as Evan drove through the field. He aimed for what she assumed was a stream based on the line of trees, and then he veered west until they got to a fence where he stopped. A number of black cows congregated in the field, some smaller than others.

"Are those smaller ones babies?"

"Calves. They were born this spring. They're gettin' big." He smiled as they watched the cows milling about. Some settled in the grass with placid faces chewing their cud. A few of the calves were wandering around near their mothers, with the mothers patiently standing guard.

"So, these are your neighbor's cows?"

Evan nodded. "Fred runs about a hundred head of cattle here until they're ready for sale. I find it peaceful to watch them. I know nothing about raising or keeping them, but it's nice they're nearby. I can watch and pretend they're mine. You could do that with your property."

He put the ATV in gear and turned away from the fence, heading back toward her father's property. Kate had a hard time thinking about it as anything other than her father's property. She could see the house gradually appear on the horizon. Evan headed out toward the road that fronted his property and her father's. It was getting warm and she was glad for the hat, the long sleeves, and the sunblock she'd slathered on her face and the backs of her hands. The sun beat down relentlessly.

Evan turned into the gate entrance and drove the ATV up toward the house and then right up to what was left of the front porch. They sat there for a few moments taking it in.

"You said it wasn't safe, how unsafe is it?"

"Depends on where you go. There's no way I'd go upstairs, it's too unstable, but the main floor will hold as long as you avoid the middle of the floor in the main room. The wood's kinda rotted out. The roof's been leaking for a very long time and last winter a fairly big hole appeared in the roof and the upstairs floor." He turned off the ATV, stepped out of it, and walked around to her side.

"Shall we?" He held out his hand for her.

Kate took it and stepped down from the ATV on alert for the sound of a rattler. He helped her step up onto the porch that creaked ominously but held their weight. She hesitated.

"Want me to go first?"

"Would you mind?"

Evan grinned at her. "Always happy to help a chicken." He hoped she took it as the joke he'd intended.

She raised her eyebrows. "I'm not a chicken, you're a sacrificial lamb."

He laughed out loud at that and stepped cautiously through the doorway as she followed closely behind him. It was in pretty bad shape, Kate thought. Sections of the ceiling had fallen down where the rain leaked and the weight of snow had broken through the damaged roof. There was a huge stained area in the middle of the main floor where water had collected for some time.

"Wow, it is in bad shape. I wonder why my dad just let it go? Surely he could have rented it out or something."

"I'm not sure why. I wondered about that at times, but your father never said. I think it had some bad memories for him. His dad, Jake Earnshaw, spent his last days here until the visiting nurse agency moved him to a nursing home in Greeley. He died there a few months later. Jake never took care of the place as far as I could tell. When he died, it wasn't in great shape, so it really wasn't rentable."

Jealousy and anger that this stranger knew more about her father *and* grandfather than she did flared. It was hard to keep the bite out of her voice. "I never knew my grandparents. Daddy refused to talk about them other than to admit they existed. Even so, it's sad to think that my grandfather was in a nursing home and I didn't know. I'd have visited him at least once to see if there was a chance of a relationship."

She was lost in thought for a few minutes. "I wonder if Daddy knew and just didn't tell me?"

"I don't know. I didn't know him then. He showed up on the property about ten years ago, which is when I first met him. I was living in a trailer on my property, and I did pretty much what I did with you, came over to find out why he was there. He'd just found out that the property had been left to him."

"My mother died right about that time and he was pretty devastated by it. If his father died then as well, that may explain why he said nothing. He was so caught up in caring for mom, and her death hit him hard, I doubt he spared any time for his father. From what I gathered, he hated him."

Kate walked carefully around the periphery of the room. There were remnants of very old yellowed wallpaper on the walls, some of it hanging off in strips. A river rock fireplace at one end had a bird's nest in the firebox that had fallen down the chimney. There were two shattered eggshells lying next to it. They seemed to Kate to echo the damaged family that had lived here.

"Still, that doesn't explain why he just let it sit and rot."

"Sometimes, that's all a person can do, just let things lie."

"It sounds like you had an ongoing friendship with my father, so he wasn't really letting things lie. Every time he came out here he'd see the house, see it deteriorate further. Why not bulldoze it and be done with it?"

"I wish I could tell you, Kate. He never wanted to talk about the house or his life there. He came and we got to be friends. He helped me build my house. He stayed in town when he was here. There wasn't any room in the trailer. You didn't wonder where he was going all that time?"

"I was in college. What college student pays much attention to a parent?" She replied, her brows drawing together in a frown. "He went through a depression after mom died. I had just graduated from high school. After a while he seemed to snap out of it. After graduation, I was up at CSU in Fort Collins. I had no idea what he did with his time, and he never told me." She turned away from him, staring at the fireplace and silence reigned.

———— ♦ ————

SHE WAS right, Evan thought as he watched her. Kids rarely paid much attention to parents unless there was something wrong. Once again, though, he felt as if he'd overstepped. She both wanted information about her dad and then seemed to resent the answers he gave her. He could tell she was both grieving and increasingly angry with her father for the way he'd excluded her. And somehow or another, he had become a target for her anger. Evan was floundering.

She turned back to him and said, "I suppose you think that's pretty self-involved, that I was a bad daughter."

"No, do you think that?"

She glared at him. He saw the glitter of tears in her eyes before she abruptly walked back toward him and pushed past. "I'm fin-ished here. Please take me back to the house."

Well, you've done it again, Evan thought. *You managed to really piss her off and the day had started out so well.*

Evan had no idea what to do, one minute she was friendly and the next withdrawn and defensive. Maybe the aftermath of suicide did that to a person.

He followed her out to the ATV, got in, and turned to her. "I'm sorry, that was…well I don't know what it was other than I shouldn't have asked. I don't think you were a bad daughter and based on how your dad talked about you, he didn't either."

He watched helplessly as she burst into tears. *Now what the fuck am I supposed to do?*

He leaned over and carefully took her in his arms, not at all sure she'd welcome it or that it'd make anything better, but she relented and leaned into him. He clumsily patted her on the back like he'd seen women do to crying kids when they held them, and it seemed to help. After a few minutes, she pushed away and used the heels of her hands to wipe tears off her face, sniffing loudly.

Evan pulled a bandana out of his back pocket and offered it. She looked askance at it. "It's clean, hasn't been used yet today," he said.

Kate took it and wiped at her face, blew her nose noisily, and then balled the bandana up in her hand. She blushed. "I don't want to hand it back with snot all over it."

"Keep it. With my track record, you'll probably need it a few more times before the day is out."

That got a smile out of her.

CHAPTER TWELVE

SHE'D LET EVAN talk her out of going back to the house. He'd used lunch as an excuse.

"Let's just go relax in the shade for a while and eat lunch, then we can go back to the house. You can go home if that's what you want, although I'd like you to stay as planned."

He drove until he came to the bank above the stream, parked, and unloaded the cooler and a blanket from the ATV. He carried them down near the stream bank and spread the rough blanket on the ground.

He'd left his Stetson on the ATV, running his hands through his dark hair to remove its imprint. He really had beautiful hair—glossy, dark, and slightly curled—the kind of hair that made you want to run your fingers through it. Trying to deal with Evan was frustrating. She was attracted to him physically, and, if she were honest, his sense of humor and easy-going way appealed to her. In other circumstances, she'd have acted on it, but that underlying anger and jealously over his relationship with her father, and all the questions that it raised, kept getting in the way. If her father had ever *bothered* to introduce them, Evan could have been someone with whom she might have pursued a relationship.

It was peaceful by the river and cool. She removed the hat he'd given her and used a clean part of the bandana to wipe the sweat off her face and neck before replacing it in her pocket. He handed her a cold bottle of water, and she drank half of it quickly before lowering herself onto the blanket.

He set out sandwiches, potato salad, and some peaches. "You think of everything," she said.

"Trying to impress I guess."

"Why?"

He frowned. "I'd really like you to see the places around here as something other than frustrating, backward, isolated, and worthless. I'm being selfish. I don't want you to sell your property to anyone or lease it to commercial interests. I don't want things around me changing for the worse."

"You could buy it and then you'd control what happened to it."

Evan sighed. "I suppose I could and that'd solve the problem. But I don't want to do that, for a lot of reasons. I want you to keep it."

"Why?" He puzzled her. She couldn't figure out what his agenda was.

"Because I think it meant something to your father, regardless of what he said, or didn't say, to either of us." He paused. "And if I bought it, then you'd have no reason to come back."

Business like, he handed her a paper plate with a sandwich and potato salad on it. He seemed embarrassed, maybe he hadn't meant to say the part about her not coming back. She took the plate and watched him as he began fixing a plate for himself.

She picked up one of the forks that lay on the blanket. "I feel like you know my dad far better than I ever did, and it makes me sad and angry at the same time. And as hard as it is to admit, I'm jealous of you. Why would he tell you things he wouldn't tell me? Why would he spend time with you and not me? Why wouldn't he tell me about you for God's sake?"

Evan looked at her for a moment. "I don't know. If it makes you feel better, I'm not sure I knew him any better than you did. Maybe I just know parts of him that you don't. My guess is you know parts of him that I don't. It might help to compare stories."

She looked over at the nearby river, listening to the water rushing over the rocks and fallen logs. "I don't know. Since the lawyer told me about this property, it feels like my father has become a stranger. It's almost like discovering your father had another family somewhere."

Suddenly she stared at him. "You're not his illegitimate son, are you?"

That startled him. He blinked a couple of times and then laughed. "No, I'm not."

She shrugged as if apologizing for asking. She took a bite of the sandwich and a drink of water. "I went through his stuff at the house and it was like I was going through a stranger's belongings. Did you know he drew?" Evan nodded. "I didn't. I never saw him draw anything. How do you not know that about someone?"

Evan sat for a while without answering. Finally, he said, "People keep all sorts of secrets from all sorts of people, even those they love. Sometimes especially from those they love. I don't think we ever know everything there is to know about anyone."

"Maybe not," she said. "I can't accept that he committed suicide. He wasn't depressed. I spoke to him the day before and he was fine. He had something on his mind, but he was in a good mood. People seem to say that about suicides though—'He was happy.' 'She was looking forward to X, she wasn't depressed.' Everyone, including the police, thinks he killed himself. I don't think so, but there's so much I clearly didn't know about him. Maybe I'm wrong."

Evan didn't answer, and that ended the conversation. She sat with her legs crossed campfire style, plate resting in the hollow her legs made. Kate ate slowly, her mind drifting and catching on things, but she didn't speak. She barely noticed when Evan stretched out on the blanket after eating and closed his eyes.

———————•♦•———————

HE'D SAID nothing after he'd stretched out on the blanket and, looking over, Kate saw that he had fallen asleep, ankles crossed, and hands folded on his chest. His face was relaxed. He was a handsome man, not startlingly so, but he had a quiet confidence that eluded many men. His hair had curled slightly around the edges where the sweat had dampened it. He was funny and kind, too. She watched him sleep, mouth slightly parted, eyes moving rapidly beneath his lids, and she wondered what he was dreaming about.

She wasn't sure what it was about him that intrigued her. Physically he was the type of man who attracted her—tall, well-built, dark haired, and green eyed. She hadn't fully relaxed with him. She didn't know whether to believe his story about her father or what it meant if he were telling the truth. She wished her frame of mind was different or she had met him under different circumstances, so she could simply enjoy him.

What she wanted to do at the moment was lie down and take a nap as well. The heat was exhausting, and the food had made her sleepy. Instead she rose and tidied up the food and plates and walked down to the riverbank. She sat on a boulder that rested against the bank.

"I'm kinda pissed at you, Daddy," Kate said quietly. "You could have told me about Evan and your connection with him. When I was in college, when I was struggling with the studio art classes, you could have helped, given me some tips if I had known about your talent. Maybe I wouldn't have been so awful at it. Why keep it a secret? Why shut me out? Why leave me? Why couldn't you have called me and asked for help?"

There was no answer, and she hadn't expected one. The fact that she knew so little about her father was disorienting. She was so sad and frustrated she didn't know what to do, and she had nowhere to go with it. For some inexplicable reason, she wanted to take it out on Evan, wanted to punish him for knowing things about her father she didn't. He had been nothing but nice so far and yet she wanted to punch him.

She heard his boots behind her and turned. He was yawning as he walked toward her. "Sorry," he said, trying to talk and yawn at the same time. He was carrying two peaches one in each hand. His hands were large and long-fingered, neither roughened with work, nor soft and unused. They looked strong and capable.

"I didn't mean to flake out on you."

"I've managed to entertain myself. You looked like you needed a nap."

"Yeah," he said, easing down on the bank near her. "Didn't sleep too well last night." He handed her a peach. "We should eat these here. They're Palisade peaches so they're nice and ripe, which makes 'em kinda messy, but they're the best peaches any-where. We can rinse off in the river."

They were messy, warm and sweet and juicy. When she finished her peach, Kate leaned over and rinsed the bandana thoroughly in the water and wrung it out using it to wash her face and hands. Evan gathered the peach pits, stood up, then scuffed a hole in the riverbank dropping the two pits into it and covering them up with his boot.

"Hoping for peach trees?"

"Well you never know, stranger things have probably happened." He knelt by the river's edge and ran his hands in the water, wiping them dry on his jeans as he stood up.

She stood up and moved next to him with the wet bandana in hand. "Here, you've got peach juice on your chin." She wiped the cloth over his chin and he reached up and grasped her wrist. It surprised her, his grip was strong and his look intense, and for a moment she was just a bit wary of him.

"Don't worry, it's clean…" she started to say.

Evan pulled her to him, took her head in his hands, and brought his lips to hers. His lips were soft, his tongue tentative, and she could taste peaches as she opened and welcomed him and her arms came around his waist. He began the kiss somewhat hesitantly but rapidly it became more insistent and hungry. He stopped abruptly, pulled away, and stepped back.

"Sorry about that," Evan mumbled as he pushed past her.

THE LAST thing she needed to convince her to go home was him trying to seduce her, Evan thought as he moved back up the bank away from her.

He wanted more than kisses, God so much more. He had nearly let his hand slide down and find her breast when he broke off from the kiss. He was painfully aroused and was glad, as he walked up the bank to the picnic blanket, that she couldn't see that. He began putting stuff away, folding the blanket, busying himself so he wouldn't look at her, wouldn't change his mind, and push things further than was wise.

Mixed in with his physical need for her was the grief over her father. Between the two, he had no idea what to do. The sensation of her lips was still strong, and the thought occurred to him that she hadn't acted as if she wanted him to stop, but she hadn't stopped him from leaving either.

Fuck me, he thought.

CHAPTER THIRTEEN

"I THOUGHT WE MIGHT go into town for dinner," Evan said when they returned to the house. It had been a bit awkward between them—he seemed embarrassed and Kate felt flustered by the kiss and the nearly instantaneous arousal it had triggered in her.

"Okay, sure."

It was probably best that they get out of the house and not be alone, Kate thought as she showered the sweat and dust of the day off. She couldn't get the kiss out of her mind or the feel of his arousal as he'd held her close. And he was clearly embarrassed by it, his neck bright red as he'd made his way up the riverbank to the ATV.

Yeah, she thought, *going into town is a good idea.*

When they arrived and found a table, a few people had stopped by to say hello to Evan. He'd explained that she was John Earnshaw's daughter. That seemed to be the magic key. People smiled and reminisced about her father and, when they found out about his death, said how much they would miss him. She noted that Evan didn't tell them he'd committed suicide, just that he'd passed, and was grateful for that.

When the last of the people walked away from the table, she said, "It's nice to know that people thought so well of my father. Thank you for not mentioning the suicide."

"No point in making it any harder than necessary for you," he said.

Their dinner arrived and neither had much to say while they ate. Evan didn't ask her to dance. He was subdued and seemed intent on keeping his distance. There was no teasing or playfulness, and she realized she'd become so used to it that she missed it.

Word had evidently spread while they were eating, and a few more people came over to say hello and talk to her about her dad. Eventually, Kate had pled exhaustion and they had headed back to the house around ten. She promptly excused herself and went to bed. He had wished her a good night and walked toward what she assumed was his bedroom as she walked down the hall to the guest suite.

———◆———

EVAN STOOD at his bedroom window looking out toward the Front Range, which was bathed in moonlight. In the distance, he could see the faint lights of Ardwell.

It had been hard to talk about John with the people at Joe's. John had been like a second father to him and had helped make his most cherished dream, this house, a reality. Without John, he'd probably still be living on the property in his folk's trailer. And he'd seen it was difficult for Kate as well, but in some way perhaps it helped to know how many people cared about her father.

Again, the regret and sadness that he hadn't known and hadn't been able to intervene and prevent John's death washed over him. Evan couldn't imagine what had gone wrong to push him in that direction. He'd wracked his brain and still didn't believe John had been depressed enough to consider suicide when they'd last spoken. He'd read somewhere, though, once people decide to commit suicide it gives them some resolution, some peace, and they often don't share their intentions.

That was the problem with suicide, it left the survivors always wondering what they'd missed, what they might have done to prevent it. And there were no answers and no chance to do anything about it.

Sighing he undressed and pulled on the drawstring pajama bottoms he rarely wore. It was a concession to having Kate in the house. He couldn't run around nude, as he'd have done if she weren't here. His bed was welcoming and he was tired, but after tossing and turning for nearly half an hour he resigned himself to another sleepless night and got up. He walked into the living room and stretched out on the couch. Maybe he'd grab a book and take it back to bed in a while. At the moment, all he wanted was to lie on the couch in the dark and think.

----------◦ ◆ ◦----------

AN HOUR after changing into her nightgown and going to bed, Kate was restless and unable to sleep. Talking with the people at Joe's who knew her father had been both comforting and sad. And like much of what she was discovering about her father there was a world of friends and acquaintances she'd had no idea existed. The discoveries made her feel as if she was the one who hadn't existed, at the very least it felt as if she hadn't been important enough for her father to share this world with her. Finally, she turned the light on and decided to find something to read. She wished she had thought to bring a book with her.

She unlocked the door and realized she hadn't used the bolt. Progress perhaps. She was far more comfortable with Evan now, but apparently not enough to leave the door completely unlocked. The hard wood floor was cool under her bare feet as she walked into the dark living room and moved toward the bookshelf. The only light was moonlight from the windows, but it was bright enough to allow her to search the bookcase without turning on a lamp.

"What type of books do you like?"

She jumped and whirled around to find Evan stretched out on the couch. "God, you scared me to death. I thought you went to bed." She switched the light near the bookcase on, not wanting to remain in the dark.

"Couldn't sleep. Looks like you couldn't either. What's keeping you awake?" He lay in drawstring pajama bottoms and no top, one arm crooked behind his head. His stare made her acutely aware that she was barefoot and in her nightgown.

"I'm not sure why I can't sleep. What's keeping you awake?" It was hard to take her eyes off his chest with its dusting of dark hair that grew in a V down his abdomen and disappeared into his pajama bottoms. In the light from the lamp, she noticed a small, blue half-moon tattoo hiding in the chest hair over his left breast.

Evan watched her with a frown on his face. "You didn't answer me. What kind of books do you like?" His green eyes were locked on her face. He had a very intense stare, as if he were memorizing her face. She felt vulnerable and wished she'd stayed in her room.

"I guess it depends on my mood. I like mysteries, historical fiction, and the classics, although an autobiography occasionally catches my attention. How about you?" She wondered why he'd refused to answer her question. He could be so open and friendly one minute and the next quiet and closed off, when he wasn't kissing her. Then he seemed to be another Evan entirely. Maybe that was what was keeping him awake.

"Kinda like you, depends on my mood. The books on the shelves are favorites. If I don't like a book, I donate it or give it to someone I think might like it. No point in keeping something you don't like." He sat up and scrubbed his hands over his face. "I could use a drink, how about you?"

"Okay. Alcohol doesn't usually help people sleep, though." Kate watched as he got up and walked to a cabinet in the kitchen and retrieved a bottle of scotch. He poured a couple fingers in two short glasses.

Walking back to the couch he said, "I'm not planning on getting much sleep tonight anyway, so might as well make myself happy." He handed her a drink.

Kate sipped at it and felt it warm her all the way to her stomach. It was peaty and smooth, but she didn't often drink hard liquor, so she planned to nurse the one drink along for a while and then go back to bed. The hell with finding a book to read.

"So, you said you work at an art gallery." She nodded.

Evan had once again stretched out on the couch, resting his glass on his chest, holding it loosely. Apparently, he didn't want her on the couch with him, so she took up residence in the overstuffed chair, pulling her bare legs up under her to give him less to stare at. She wished he had a T-shirt on. His bare chest was very distracting.

"You're what, twenty-eight or so, yeah?"

She raised her eyebrows. "It's not polite to ask a woman her age."

"If she's my mother's age it's not, but you're just a baby so that makes it okay."

"Really." It wasn't a question.

"Really."

"Thirty actually. And you?"

"Thirty-six."

Kate decided to be intrusive. "What's the significance of the half-moon tatt?"

Evan fingered it absently. "The moon waxes and wanes but never disappears. Life does the same thing. It's there to remind me that nothing is gone forever, it just takes different shapes."

She frowned. He'd reminded her of her father. She sighed, he'd changed forms too but he was gone forever except in her memories.

"What attracted you to working at an art gallery?" Evan asked interrupting her thoughts.

"I was a fine arts major at CSU. I was a complete failure at creating actual works of art, but very good at art history and restoration work. Then I graduated and couldn't get a job teaching or at a restoration facility, so I settled for selling art at galleries. Kind of a waste of a degree, but…" she let the sentence die. She had no idea what else to say.

"Are you any good at it?"

She stared at him for a moment then replied, "As it happens, I am."

"I'm sure the artists appreciate that. Are you happy doing it?"

She shrugged. "Yeah, I guess. It's a job. I meet a lot of interesting people." She was lost in thought for a moment. "If my father was good at drawing, I wish he'd helped me, given me some pointers or some feedback. But I never knew he drew until I went through his footlocker."

"That's hard to do, especially with someone close to you. You can't teach talent. You can teach techniques, if the talent is there. If it's not, then it frustrates everyone. Maybe he wanted you to find your strengths instead of trying to do something you weren't really good at."

"I still haven't found those strengths." She took another sip and watched him. "So, while other people are running cattle and growing crops on your land, what exactly do you do with all your free time?"

"I live a very boring life."

"Doing what?"

He slugged down the last of his scotch and sat up. "Either boring the hell out of people, or pissing them off, or making them uneasy—like I've done with you." He stood up and stretched. Muscles rippled. The dark hair on his chest, and the faint line of it that ran down to the waist of his pajama bottoms as they rested precariously on his hips, drew her eye. He noticed and she blushed.

"I'm going to bed. See you in the morning. Help yourself to a book."

She watched him walk across the living room and disappear down the hallway to his bedroom without a backward glance. Heard him close the door.

Why wouldn't he talk about what he did?

CHAPTER FOURTEEN

THEY SAT AT the island eating breakfast, or at least trying to. Evan ate quietly without engaging in much conversation. Kate fidgeted, uncomfortable with the awkwardness, as she picked at the omelet on her plate. It was good, he was a surprisingly good cook, but she was distracted. She was anxious to get home but wanted, strangely enough, to stay. She couldn't do both, so it was time to go.

I guess I should address the elephant in the room, Kate thought. At least, she hoped it was the right elephant, there seemed to be a number of them in the room.

"Thank you for inviting me to come. It's been a nice weekend. I see a little better why you like it up here."

"Good, I'm glad." He gave her a brief smile as he stood up, taking his plate to the sink and refilling his coffee cup. He held the pot up and looked inquiringly at her. She nodded. He refilled her cup and returned to his barstool.

"I...Evan..." She reached out and put her hand on his arm. She felt his muscles tense and removed her hand. What the hell had changed between them? "I want to reassure you that I don't plan to sell the place. I want to wait on that decision for a while. There's just too much confusion for me right now."

"That's good." He was really taciturn this morning. Evidently, she wasn't going to get much more than short replies from him. She sighed.

"If I decide to sell, I'll let you know before I list it and give you plenty of time to buy it if that's what you want to do."

He nodded. "Thanks, I appreciate that."

"Well," she said standing up and taking her plate to the sink. "I guess I should be on my way. I'll get my bag."

He made no move to get up, so she retrieved her bag and carried it to the back door. He followed her and took the bag from her. When they reached her car, he put the bag into the trunk and stood back as if waiting for her to leave.

Not knowing what else to do, she hugged him awkwardly. "Thanks again, it was a nice weekend."

She let go and started to step away when his arms came around her, pulling her into a hug that he seemed reluctant to end. "Come visit. Anytime," he said, releasing her and stepping back.

There didn't seem to be anything else to say, so Kate opened the driver's door and got in. She started the car, turned it around and drove off down the driveway. She saw him wave in the rear-view mirror and she lowered the window and waved back. She was surprised to realize she wasn't sure she wanted to leave.

———— ◆ ————

THE HOUSE was quiet when Evan walked back in. He wandered down to the guest suite and stood in the doorway. *I should just get this over with,* he thought as he walked over and began stripping the sheets to throw in the wash.

He'd been a total pig as a kid and teenager, but his mother's habits had gradually crept in once he moved out and realized no one was going to pick up after him and he didn't like living in a garbage dump. Kinda like the cooking. He'd realized quickly he didn't have the stomach to eat frozen pizza and fast food forever. Of necessity, he learned how to cook.

Her scent enveloped and overwhelmed him as he gathered the sheets into his arms. He dropped down onto the edge of the bed and held the sheets up to his face, inhaling her citrusy earthy scent. Maybe he'd just stay here for however long it took for her scent to dissipate. He shook his head, wishing in some ways he hadn't met her.

He thought about how he'd met John Earnshaw. Evan had debated long and hard about telling Kate the story, which was partly why he hadn't slept much this weekend. Watching her, he'd seen how overwhelmed she was with all she was finding out about her father, and how it upset her, so he'd decided not to. He'd also felt her anger toward him each time she heard a new revelation about him and her father. He realized, as he sat on the bed, he'd totally forgotten to give her the package John had left with him. Further disclosures could wait, would have to wait since she wasn't here.

His memory played as he hugged the sheets.

———— ◆ ————

PULLING UP behind the car that sat on old man Earnshaw's property, Evan got out and walked up to the house. The man who'd driven the car stood in the entryway and held a cardboard box in his arms.

"Can I help you, sir?"

The man turned abruptly, almost losing his grip on the box. "Who're you?"

"I could ask you the same. This is private property."

"I know it is, it belonged to my father."

"Jake Earnshaw's your father?"

"Was, he's dead. Who're you?"

"Evan Hastings, I live next door. I've been keeping an eye on the place since they took Jake off to Greeley. I'm sorry to hear he died."

"I'm not," the man said with a belligerent look on his face. "If you knew him very well, you wouldn't be sorry either."

"Okay," Evan said, slowly holding his hands up in a surrender gesture. "I've got no bone to pick with you, and since you say you're Jake's son I'll just leave you to whatever you're here for."

Evan turned to head back to his truck. "Wait," the guy said. "I should apologize, I'm John Earnshaw. I'm sorry, it's not you I'm angry with."

"No problem. What'd you plan on doing with the box?"

The man stared at the box in his arms. "I'm going to dump his ashes in the root cellar and then let the fucking place fall down around him and disappear."

Evan reached up and scratched under the brim of his Stetson. It was a surprisingly warm day for the first of May and sweat was running down the sides of his face. "Okay, I'll leave you to it. It's hot out here. If you want to stop by for a drink and to cool off, my property is just the next place over. You can't miss it. It's vacant land with a trailer on it. Close things up before you leave. Kids get into mischief when they have access to a place like this."

Evan didn't know what to make of Jake's son. Obviously he was pissed at his father. Evan couldn't remember ever seeing the guy, but he'd only lived on his property about eighteen months. Still he'd never seen visitors. He used to come over once a week just to make sure the old man was okay. Occasionally he'd bring some food his mother had fixed and leave it with Jake. Jake would invite him in and give him awful coffee—he never used enough grounds to make it drinkable—and they would talk.

The talk was pretty generic, about the weather, how the plans for Evan's house were coming along, that kind of stuff. The old man never mentioned kids. Once in a while he'd talk about the ranch, but it seemed like what he talked about happened a long time ago. Evan felt sorry for him.

About a year before, Jake had gone into a decline, and the last six months before he was taken to Greeley his confusion had gotten worse. He'd ask Evan where his wife was, and periodically he'd mistake Evan for someone named Cody and tell him to get the hell off his property. Evan had no idea who Cody was, but on those days, he'd just leave.

Finally, Evan had stopped by the doc's office in town and talked to him about the old man. The doctor came out to Earnshaw's property, took a look at Jake, and had visiting nurses come by for a month or so, before they moved him to Greeley. And now here was the son who'd never visited, who Jake had never talked about, and who was clearly angry with his dead father.

The son showed up at the trailer about an hour later. Evan invited him to sit on the patio he'd created at the front of the trailer. It gave him a cooler place to sit when it got unbearably hot out and the trailer turned into an oven. He'd enclosed it in screen so that he could sleep there without being eaten alive by bugs.

He offered the man a beer, and they sat in silence for a while enjoying the shade and the beer. "This is a nice piece of property. It's pretty country out here," John said at last.

"Yeah, my grandfather left it to me. I just need a house. This trailer is temporary, but I may have to live in it longer than I'd hoped."

"Why's that?"

"Expenses, not knowing where to start."

"Are you a builder?"

"No, well not professionally anyway. I worked construction through college, so I have the basics." Evan took a long drink of his beer. "I'd like the house to be more than basic though. I want it to be special, sort of a forever after kinda place."

"I like that idea." John sipped his beer and looked out at the property. "So, if you're not a builder, what do you do?"

"I'm an artist."

"What kind?"

"Painter." Evan stretched his legs out in front of his lawn chair. "Most of my stuff is at my folks right now, there's not a lot of room for it in the trailer. Makes me kinda nuts, not having a studio and having to go to their house to paint."

"I can imagine it does. Have you got any ideas for the house?"

Evan's face flushed with heat. "Yeah, I've drawn what I want. They aren't blueprints, just drawings. I'm not sure how to get them made into blueprints. I keep hoping I can get started on the house in a year or two. Wishful thinking I guess."

"I'm a builder. Can I see them?"

Evan fidgeted for a bit, then stood up and went into the trailer, returning with a pad of drawing paper, which he handed to John. It made him uncomfortable to show this to anyone. He wasn't a builder. These drawings were his dreams.

John looked through the pad, nodding as he turned the pages. "You've got some talent, young man. I could probably turn these into blueprints that'd pass to get you a building permit."

"I'd have to get the money to build it first. The property is free and clear, and the trailer belongs to my folks, so living out here cuts expenses a lot. I'm saving up for it."

"It could be built in phases, the foundations, the septic and water lines first, then go from there. Little steps, you know?"

"I never thought about that. What would you charge me to do the blueprints?"

"Nothing."

"Nothing? Why?"

"I don't know. I need something to do I guess. I'm sorta retired. My wife passed about six months ago, and my daughter is up at Fort Collins now so I have a lot of time on my hands."

"I'm sorry about your wife." John nodded at him. "Okay, if you're sure."

"I am. What I'd like to see you do first though is build yourself a studio." He'd continued to page through the sketchpad. "Someone with your talent shouldn't be without a place to work."

John helped him build a small studio behind the trailer and that sealed it. They began a collaboration that lasted until about a month before Kate showed up. Evan hadn't heard from John during that month and wondered how he was, but John had been a unique guy. He didn't spend time calling Evan, he'd just show up.

Evan's sales through the galleries in Denver and Los Angeles had picked up, and the studio was a godsend. Each sale brought money in that allowed him to live and build just a tiny bit more of the house. John had produced a beautiful set of blueprints and had come up a couple times a month, spending the weekend, sometimes longer, helping to build the house. It had taken them two years. Evan forced a painting on him in partial payment, and John said he'd take it only because he liked it, not in payment for anything.

Over time he'd discovered that John was an artist as well, not just with a hammer and saw, but with portraits. He'd done one of Evan in pastels and had given it to him. It hung in Evan's studio. Once the house had been built, John would stay with Evan when he came up, and they shared many easy evenings in front of the fire sipping their drinks and talking.

Evan had asked once, and only once, why John was letting the house on his property deteriorate. John had looked at him for several moments then said, "Son, my reasons are my reasons. Let's just say I want to watch that place fall down around that old bastard's ashes. Why, is my business."

So, Evan had let it drop. Once in a great while he'd see John over at the house before he showed up at Evan's. John would circle the house and then walk out into the field behind it and stand there for quite a while, then suddenly walk off and show up at Evan's. Out of curiosity he walked over one day out to where he'd seen John standing. There was a small fenced off area that was barely visible in the grass, with three small grave markers in the ground. No names, just initials and dates, of an age that might correspond to a wife and children. It had made Evan uncomfortable, and he'd walked home vowing to not go back.

———— ◆ ————

THE MISERY and grief over John's death and that low-level ache in his chest welled up as he sat on the bed. The word heartache was pretty accurate. *I should have called or made a trip to Denver. Maybe I could have prevented his death.* But he hadn't, he'd been caught up in his work and several shows. It shamed him.

Evan stood up, sheets in hand and walked out of the bedroom. John had been a complicated man with a puzzling family history, tiny bits of which he only rarely shared. And now his daughter had arrived, as hungry for information as Evan had been and just as unlikely to get answers.

CHAPTER FIFTEEN

"WHAT D'YOU MEAN you don't know what he does?"

"I don't know what he does, other than lease his land out to a neighbor to farm or run cattle on," Kate replied as she and Sandi sat on her living room floor and went through a box of papers that so far had turned out to be old bills that needed to be shredded. Sandi had been a godsend and had taken on the task of clearing out her father's den so Kate wouldn't have to. They were down to the boxes of bills. There were four boxes and Kate so far had been unable to figure out why her father had kept any of them.

"He's very…evasive, I guess would be the word. When I've asked, he told me about the lease and then just says he does 'things' or he says he pisses people off like he's done with me."

"That's kinda creepy. And you spent the weekend there?"

"He's not creepy, just private. I guess maybe that's a better word." Kate tossed another old bill into the basket for shredding. At this rate, she would have to call one of those shredding companies to come get the stuff. Her small office shredder would have a nervous breakdown if asked to handle the stack the boxes had so far produced.

"Still, spending the weekend up there alone, in his house, that's risky Kate. You don't know this guy or whether he's telling you the truth about your father."

"I realize I don't know him well, but I'm sure he's telling the truth. The people I met at the bar knew dad and had good things to say about him and they know Evan. He was a gentleman while I was there."

The memory of his kisses replayed in her head, but even then, he'd never pushed for more. "And his guest suite had a lock on the door, and a sliding bolt as well. As he said, the locks were so I wouldn't have to worry about him making any unexpected visits."

"I'm sorry, that's just creepy. Who has locks and sliding bolts on their guest room doors?"

"They were on the inside Sandi, not on the outside—they were for me to lock *him* out. Although I don't think he'd have intruded unless I asked him to. He said the bolt was a new addition before I arrived. He knew I didn't know him really and I guess he wanted me to feel safe. He was very considerate."

"Are you going up again?"

"I don't know. He knows things about my dad that I don't. It's been very unsettling knowing that my dad was so different than the dad I knew. Supposedly, my dad helped him build the house he lives in while I was away at college. I knew nothing about that. It sounds like they were good friends, I didn't know that either."

Kate sat back from the box of bills. "My dad had this whole other life that I knew nothing about and now he's gone, and I have no way to ask him about it." To her surprise, she began to cry. "I keep thinking I'm done with this," she said swiping at the tears.

"I'm not sure we're ever done mourning someone we love. It eases as we go on, but it's always there. And this is especially hard for you because of his suicide and all the surprises you've had lately."

Kate sighed and stretched her neck and shoulders. "Let's finish this box and stop, I think I've had enough for one day. I probably should just call a shredding company and hand the boxes over, but I keep thinking I should go through the contents just in case."

"I think that's best. People stash things in the weirdest places. I found most of my mother's jewelry in the pockets of her coats, and I was just going to take them to Goodwill and donate them. Listening to that little voice has kept me from making a lot of mistakes."

The little voice that Kate kept hearing was the one that said there was a reason for her father's suicide and it wasn't depression. The voice however, never said what the reason was.

———•◆•———

OVER THE next week, Kate found a number of old bills that she would need for the accountant to file her father's final tax returns, so she collected them in a folder to provide when needed. She had finally sorted the boxes and sent the contents for shredding.

She was putting the house up for rent soon. She had decided not to sell anything for now. A professional cleaning company was going to clean the house on Monday. She would then replace the carpets, which were old and very worn. The crime scene cleaning company had removed the carpet and cleaned the den. The police had recommended the company after the coroner's staff had taken her father away. It wasn't a crime scene, but they said the company would clean up "the mess" left behind.

She felt adrift.

Working at the gallery, she'd look at the paintings and wonder if her father had ever sold anything, or whether it was just a hobby for him. She wondered what he'd painted or drawn or whether the sketchbook was the entirety of it. Evan had said he was talented, but at what, just building?

She'd have to go back and talk to Evan—she had to know whatever he knew about her father—but it was awkward. Maybe Sandi was right, she didn't really know him, and maybe the bedroom door locks were a little weird, but he'd done nothing out of line. Even his kisses hadn't been aggressive or pushy. The last one had made her wish he had been, but it was probably best he hadn't. Every time she felt herself beginning to warm to him he'd say something that reminded her of what he'd shared with her father and she'd raise the wall between them.

It was Friday and Kate had run out to a nearby *taqueria* to get a quick lunch. She was sitting on the patio eating when her phone rang. This time she recognized the area code. Maybe Evan had solved the problem of getting together.

"Hello?"

"Hey, it's Evan."

"I thought the area code looked familiar. How have you been?"

"Good, and you?"

"Busy going through stuff of Dad's and working. How're the cows?"

"The what? Oh, the cows." He laughed. "They're fine."

The conversation came to a standstill and then he said, "So, I have to come to Denver to take care of some business. I wondered if you'd like to get dinner…or something."

"When?"

"I'm on my way now. I'm sorry for the late notice, the business came up unexpectedly, but I thought I'd take a chance and ask. If you're busy, that's fine."

"I'm not."

"I could pick you up around seven, if you give me your address. Or we could meet somewhere if you'd rather. You probably should pick the restaurant."

Kate hesitated for a moment recalling Sandi's cautions, then gave him her address. "What kind of food would you like?"

"I'm kinda sick of burritos and burgers and cooking for myself. How about fish?"

"Okay, I'll think of a place."

"Umm, nothing too dressy okay? I'm wearing jeans."

"It's Denver, jeans are allowed. See you at seven." Kate realized she was looking forward to seeing him.

———◆———

DESPITE THE comment about his clothes, he looked nice. His jeans were just snug enough to appeal, and his shirt was a deep burgundy that set his eyes off nicely. He'd left his Stetson at home she guessed, as it hadn't been in the truck. His hair had grown a bit since she'd last seen him—it now crested over his collar—all in all he was a handsome man. She directed him to the restaurant and, when they arrived, she noticed several women follow their progress to a table. Once they were seated and had ordered, they both seemed at a loss, and the conversation died.

Finally, Kate spoke up. "This is kind of awkward, isn't it?" He nodded. "Are you planning on going back tonight?"

"I was, but when you agreed to go to dinner, I just figured I'd get a room somewhere and go back in the morning. I didn't think this through very well." He fiddled with his glass of wine.

"There's a second bedroom at my place you could use rather than trying to get a room tonight. There's a lock on the door, no bolt though." She smiled.

"Sure you'd be okay with that?"

"Yes, are you?"

He nodded and the silence descended again until he said, "I wondered after you left how things were for you. It looked like you were pretty overwhelmed with everything."

"I was. I still am in some ways. I've gone through boxes of bills and papers and his belongings over the last few weeks, and it's difficult. Maybe it's survivor guilt, but I can't stop thinking that something unexpected happened that led to his death.

"He wasn't depressed. I'd have sworn he wasn't. I grew up with his depression—it came and went—and it was always pretty obvious. The fact that he had a history of depression has everyone convinced that's why he killed himself. I just don't believe it."

Evan didn't respond.

The waiter appeared with their appetizer, and Kate changed the subject. "I was thinking about calling you. I'd like to talk to you about Dad, what you knew about him."

"Okay."

She changed course again, not knowing what else to say. "What were you in town for, you said business…but cows…never mind." Kate shook her head. "None of my business."

The silence continued for a few moments until he said, "I'm an artist."

"A what?"

"An artist. I paint. Landscapes mostly. I was here to deliver some canvases to the gallery I work with."

Kate sat back and looked at him. "Why wouldn't you just tell me that? Why make it such a mystery?"

He shrugged. "People often don't see it as working or they hound you to do a painting of one of their kids or something. I don't like to explain or justify what I do, or have people ask me for things I don't want to give, so I just don't say. Are you pissed at me now?"

"I don't know. A little."

"I must be improving if you're just a little pissed instead of a lot." He smiled at her, and she laughed.

"You must be."

———— ◆ ————

KATE HANDED him a glass of wine and sat down on the end of the couch across from where Evan sat in the overstuffed chair by the fireplace. She'd seen the look of surprise when he'd noticed the painting from her father's house. Now that she knew he was an artist she wondered if he'd painted it. She'd ask another time; he looked tired. She was sure it had been a long day for him.

"The guest bedroom has a bath, so you should have what you need. There's a new toothbrush in the vanity, but I don't think there's a razor."

He glanced around the room, taking it in, and then suddenly said, "I should probably go home."

"No, don't be silly. It's a long drive."

He finished his wine and set his glass down on the coffee table. He stood up suddenly, surprising Kate, and said, "I should go, call me when you want to talk."

She stood up and blocked him. "Evan? Please tell me what's wrong." She reached out and touched his arm and without warning he grabbed her wrist and pulled her hand away.

"Don't," he said in a low, urgent voice.

"Why?"

"Don't. Just let me leave before we do something both of us may regret." He pulled away from her abruptly and headed toward the front door.

"Evan!" she called after him.

He opened the door and, without looking back, left closing it behind him.

Kate picked up the glasses from the coffee table and took them into the kitchen, setting them in the sink. She had offered the room out of courtesy, but the idea had obviously made him uncomfortable. She knew he liked her. His kisses made that perfectly clear. Since she had first met him, there had been a thinly disguised tension between them, an attraction and wariness that neither of them knew what to do with. And there were all the conflicting feelings she had about his relationship with her father.

She walked down to her room and undressed getting into bed and lying in the dark. She replayed the memory of his grip on her wrist as he'd pulled her hand from his arm and his low, husky voice saying, *"Just let me leave before we do something we'll both regret."*

Men, she thought irritably, including her father in the group, as she turned on her side and pulled the covers up around her shoulder. *They complicate everything.*

CHAPTER SIXTEEN

CALLING HER HAD been impulsive, Evan thought, as he drove away from her condo. He should have turned down her offer to stay the minute she had mentioned it. Her scent had filled the truck on the way to the restaurant and made it hard for him to concentrate. He could smell it still. He had yet to figure out what it was, exactly, but the scent made him want to nuzzle her neck and other things.

Over dinner it was fascinating to watch her eyes sparkle or cloud over at a moment's notice. He found himself mesmerized by her lips and was pleased to see he'd finally gotten her mouth right in the painting.

He should have left it at dinner, dropped her off, and never followed her into the condo. If she knew what he was thinking, she surely wouldn't have invited him to stay. And he'd realized, sitting on her couch drinking her wine, that staying across the hall from her would have been torture. He'd had no indication from her that she'd welcome further involvement. Her kisses seemed welcoming, passionate even, especially the last one, but he wasn't sure. So he left, but not until he'd made a complete fool of himself.

Evan was tired in body and mind. He knew he was too tired to keep driving and found a room at a motel off I-25 near the exit that would take him eventually to Ardwell and home. The room was clean, the bed was relatively comfortable, and the traffic noise from the interstate wasn't bad, yet he couldn't sleep.

He'd wanted to stay, hell he'd wanted to make love to her. But it was just too complicated. It wasn't as if this was some girl he'd picked up at a bar and gone home with. It shouldn't have made a difference who she was, but it did. Sometimes sex was just that—a way for both people to meet the urgent physical needs of the moment and then move on. His intentions with Kate were different. One night or a brief affair wasn't what he had in mind. The only solution was to leave before things got out of hand and everything went to hell.

Toward morning he dreamed of Kate's father. He stood in Evan's studio and watched Evan with a forlorn look on his face.

"You take care of her, Evan. No matter what happens, you take care of her."

"I will, John, I swear I will."

He nodded. "I'm counting on you, boy," John said and walked past him out of the studio.

Evan opened his eyes, shifted slightly, and sighed. What the hell was that supposed to mean? The little he knew about John or his family was nothing alarming, but then he didn't know much more than Kate did, just different bits. Over dinner Kate had talked about the difficult job of going through her father's belongings and had again mentioned that John had suffered from depression. John had never seemed down or depressed when they had been together. And Kate insisted that, before his death, her father hadn't been depressed. She clearly believed that something other than depression had been at the root of his death.

The last time John visited Evan he *had* been upset about something. He never said what, but asked Evan what he'd do if he'd come across something difficult, something he wanted to avoid, that needed tending to. Evan had no idea what he was talking about, and John wouldn't elaborate, but Evan told him that if it needed tending to then he'd tend to it. John had nodded and left.

A few days later a package had arrived in the mail from John. Inside the padded envelope, he'd found a book-shaped object wrapped in brown paper. The note from John, taped to the wrapping paper, asked Evan to keep it for him until he returned to get it. He'd put the package away without opening it, and hadn't had any further contact or news from John until Kate showed up.

The closed off aspects of Kate's family puzzled Evan. How does a family survive when the people involved don't talk to one another? Keeping so much of themselves hidden was baffling. There just didn't seem to be a good reason for all the concealment.

He turned onto his back, remembering the small stack of sketchpads and loose drawings John had given him when he last visited. Looking back Evan now wondered if the gifts had been some subtle clue that John had made up his mind to kill himself. He wondered whether he should give them to Kate. He didn't want to, they were all he had of John other than memories. He looked at his phone. It was four in the morning.

"Christ!" He rolled to his side and punched the pillow trying to settle down and possibly get some more sleep. Half an hour later, he admitted it was pointless. He should just get up and head home. He could be there in a couple of hours. By then maybe he'd be tired enough to go to bed and sleep, or awake enough to just get on with the day.

He showered, dressed, and headed down to the front desk where he checked out and left. Next time he had to come to Denver he was not calling her, he decided. He'd leave it up to her to get in touch.

———◆———

AS SHE was having her morning coffee, Kate's phone rang.

"Ms. Earnshaw?" It was the manager of the company she'd hired to tear out and replace the carpeting.

"Yes?" He was probably calling to tell her it had taken them longer to install the carpet or taken more carpeting than he'd estimated. That would probably cost her another couple hundred dollars.

"I called to find out what you want me to do with a small box we found. We were pulling up the carpet in the master bedroom yesterday, and there were two loose floorboards. We normally re-nail those before we replace the carpeting, but they wouldn't lie flush with the floor, so my guy pulled them up to see what the issue was and found a small metal box."

"What was in it?"

"No idea, it's locked. I didn't want to pry it open. We have to be careful about handling things we find, especially when it's a job in a vacant house and it's an estate. I can't have clients accusing us of stealing things."

"Okay, thanks. Can I come get it today?"

"We're open 'til six on Saturdays. It'll be at the front desk. My secretary has it, and she'll ask for identification, just so you know."

"Okay, no problem. I'll be over this afternoon."

———◆———

KATE RETRIEVED the box from the carpet store and headed home. *No point in waiting to tackle this,* she thought walking into the house with the box and putting it on the kitchen table.

After fixing some iced tea, she retrieved a screwdriver and hammer from the garage and sat at her kitchen table. She tried to pry the box open with the screwdriver, which didn't work. So she took the hammer and beat at the locked hasp. The hasp began to give way and she was able to insert the screwdriver between the weakened hasp and the box and pry it off. It looked far worse than when she'd picked it up at the carpet store, but it was at last open.

The box contained three photos, one of which had been torn in half, and a stack of letters. The first was a photo of three children standing by a corral—two girls and one boy. This had to be her father and his two sisters, she could see the resemblance to the adults she knew. They were dressed in clothes that looked like those worn by kids in the late fifties and early sixties. The girls' sleeveless blouses had Peter Pan collars, the eldest girl wore jeans rolled up to mid-calf, and the younger girl wore long shorts. The boy wore a T-shirt and shorts. The boy and the younger girl were barefoot. The older girl wore dark, flat-heeled slippers.

She turned the photo over and saw that someone had written in pencil in what looked like a man's handwriting, *Madelyn, Ellen, and John*. So, these were of her father and her aunts. In all probability, the handwriting belonged to her grandfather who'd most likely taken the photos.

All three kids were smiling and the two younger ones looked a little shy, as if neither was used to having their photo taken. Madelyn's smile was different, as if she was smiling at someone she wanted to attract. She had cocked her hip and held her right hand on its crest. It was a worldly expression and pose. Kate didn't think the girl could be more than thirteen or fourteen. Kate wondered who had taken the photo; who was the recipient of that look—surely not her grandfather.

The second photo was of a thirty-something woman in a dress—not a fancy one—one of those everyday dresses women wore in the fifties and sixties. It had short sleeves and Kate could see her well-defined arms. She wore slipper-like shoes. She looked tired and careworn but she had a soft smile on her face and dreamy eyes. Again, Kate had the impression the look was aimed at whomever had taken the photo and was pretty sure the woman in the photo was her grandmother. It appeared as if the photo had been taken in the summer at the same time as the children's photos. On the back in the same handwriting someone had written, *Franny.* Her grandmother's name was Frances, Franny must have been her nickname—so the woman *was* her grandmother.

The third photo had been taken later in the year and someone had torn it in half. Piecing it back together, she saw her grandmother on one half and a man on the other. Her grandmother wore a heavy sweater and the photo showed her standing with the man against a corral fence. He was good looking in that rough ranch hand way—tanned skin with squint lines at the corners of his eyes and an engaging smile. He wore a long-sleeved shirt, well-worn jeans, and cowboy boots. They were both smiling and the man had an arm around the woman's waist. The photo had been taken from a much lower focal point. Perhaps by a child?

The man was not someone Kate recognized, but he was most certainly not her grandfather based on the photo of him she'd seen. She turned the photo over and re-aligned the torn pieces. Someone had written the name *Cody Westerholt* on the man's half. The handwriting was not the same as that on the other two photos.

Who the hell was Cody Westerholt, and where was my grandfather? Kate thought.

She doubted seriously he had taken the photo. Most men wouldn't condone a photo of their wife held by another man or with that look on the wife's face, and a husband certainly wouldn't take the photo.

Kate looked at the innocuous box that sat on her kitchen table and its contents, and wanted to put it all back, re-lock the box somehow, and get rid of it. It felt like Pandora's Box. One more mystery, one more thing she didn't know.

She pulled the bound stack of letters toward her and undid the string holding the stack together. There was a letter on much different stationary attached to the top of the stack that read:

May 1, 2018
John,

I'm trying to weed out extraneous things that I have kept for unknown reasons, and I discovered this stack of letters in a box of keepsakes. They are the ones you began sending me right after Janet died. They hold no sentimental value for me, and I am tired of hauling this stuff from one place to the next, so I am sending them to you along with a diary I came across in the box of Pa's stuff you gave me when he passed. With the move, I haven't had time to read it; I don't really want to. I think it belonged to Mama, but I don't know for sure.

Ellen

There was no diary in the box and Kate wondered what had happened to it. She laid the letter aside and took the next letter in the stack, reading it and passing on to the next. The letters were from her father to her Aunt Ellen and her replies. They began in 2009 and ran through 2012, in which her father asked his sister about their mother's death and what Ellen remembered about what had happened. Her father had interspersed the letters he'd received from Ellen with the other letters.

The letters to Ellen were sporadic after 2011. Her father mentioned Evan and the house they were building, how he was feeling better, and not much else. Her father announced to Ellen in late 2012 that the house was finally finished, and he'd helped Evan move in. Then the correspondence with Ellen appeared to stop until May 2018, when Ellen had sent the letters and the diary she'd found to Kate's father.

Kate opened the last letter. It was dated ten days before his death.

May 12, 2018

Ellen

I think I know why the dreams have been so hard to remember. Some things are best left buried, but once dug up they have to be faced. I think I know what happened, but I have to know for sure. Keep me in your thoughts.

John

Kate's brow creased into a frown as she read the note again. What had been worrying him so much? What did he mean about the dreams? What dreams? There was one final sheet of paper left. It was a series of scrawled questions in her father's handwriting. The writing was hard to read as if he'd been very upset when writing it.

Is what I remember in the dreams accurate? What should I do? Is he still alive?

What had so unnerved him about the dreams? Had what he'd found led to his death?

"Oh God, Daddy, what did you find?" She whispered.

CHAPTER SEVENTEEN

A T HER KITCHEN table, she opened her laptop and Googled the name Cody Westerholt. Perhaps he was the person her father had been thinking of when he'd written, "Is he still alive?" If Cody Westerholt were alive, he'd have to be in his late nineties. Her grandfather had been ninety-five when he passed. Her grandmother had been seven years younger, so perhaps this Cody was closer to her age.

She worked her way through the men listed, ignoring the younger men with that name, until she found one who'd been featured in a local Greeley newspaper for celebrating his ninety-eighth birthday the previous year. According to the article he was the oldest Greeley resident and he would be ninety-nine come January. *Assuming he was still alive*, Kate thought as she did the math.

If her grandfather had died at ninety-five, this man would have been eighty-eight at the time, ten years later he would be this man's age. He could be the Cody she was looking for. Greeley wasn't too far from Ardwell. It looked like he was a resident of a nursing home called Happy Acres. Why, Kate wondered, did they choose such horrible names for places like that? It didn't fool anyone.

She sat back and massaged her neck. She wasn't sure she wanted to tackle this alone. Evan knew her father and also knew her. Maybe he would help her. Maybe he could go with her to see if this Cody she'd found was the one in the photo.

The phone rang several times, and she was about to hang up when Evan answered. "H'lo?" He sounded distracted, busy, and for a moment she was sorry she'd called.

"Um, hi. It's Kate." She paused—maybe his pauses were contagious. "I was wondering…wondering whether I could come up."

"Sure, when?"

"Thursday? For the weekend, if that's okay." She couldn't leave before Thursday because of a big gallery party on Wednesday.

"What's wrong?"

"I just…I just need someone to help me sort through some things I found today. I'm sorry to intrude, but I don't want to do this alone."

"You could come now if you want."

"I can't. I have to help Doug with a gallery party on Wednesday. I'll come up on Thursday, if that's okay."

"It's fine. You want to talk about whatever this is?"

"Not now. I need some time to think about what to do. You're sure you don't mind if I come up?"

"I told you to come anytime. I meant it."

"I just thought…I don't know why you left the other night. Well, I do or at least I think I do. I don't want to…"

"For God's sake woman, just come up. I'll see you when you get here."

Kate disconnected and called her boss at home to let him know she needed to deal with something related to her father and might need to be off on Thursday and Friday. Doug had been great since her father's suicide and had been encouraging her to take some time off anyway. He told her to keep in touch and if she needed more time to let him know.

SHE HAD put off leaving home until afternoon, hesitant to go for some reason she couldn't identify, so she arrived around six in the evening. She pulled into the parking area behind Evan's house and shut the car off. She gathered her small suitcase and the paper carrier from The Tattered Cover bookstore that she had put the box and its contents into. She walked to the door just as Evan opened it. He took the bags from her and held the door open.

"Glad you made it. Come on, let's get you settled. Have you had dinner?"

Kate shook her head. It felt so good to be welcomed and treated like she belonged, she thought, as she followed him to the guest suite. He put the bags down by the chair near the window and turned to her.

"You look beat. You can put your things away after dinner, after you tell me what's going on." Evan was completely taken aback when she stepped into him and wrapped her arms around him and began to cry.

"Jesus, Kate, what's wrong?" He held her close and waited for her to tell him. Her hair was down and it smelled of lemon. Holding her was torture.

"I…I'm not sure. The guys installing the carpet at Dad's house found some things of my father's that really worry me. I need your help with sorting through all this, whatever it is."

"Of course." He stroked her back a few times, then took her shoulders and held her away from him so he could see her face. "Whatever it is, it can wait until you've had something to eat. It's a long drive, and you look beat."

She nodded, wiping her cheeks off with her hands. "I'm sorry for the meltdown. I guess I'm more tired than I thought."

"Don't apologize. It's fine."

She followed him out to the kitchen and sat on one of the barstools. When she'd gone through the box, and in the intervening days, she'd felt as if the weight of the world had landed on her shoulders. Now she felt it lifting.

He handed her a glass of wine and donned some oven gloves, before taking a casserole out of the oven and setting it on the kitchen island. "Come on, come sit down and let's eat. I hope you don't mind a casserole. It's a recipe of my mother's. Sort of a shepherd's pie kinda thing."

She smiled. "No, that sounds fine to me. I'm so sorry to just disrupt your life like this."

"It's no disruption. It's nice to see you again." He dished out the food onto the plates on the island and carried them to the table. He seemed unsure what to say or what to ask. Kate hoped he'd let her eat and then they could talk once dinner was over, and he seemed to pick up on that.

"So, tell me what's happened," he asked at last as they settled on the couch after dinner with the remains of the wine.

Kate took a deep breath and explained the box and its contents. "I'm worried that the letters to my aunt or the photos may have played some part in my dad's suicide. The last piece of paper… his questions…he was clearly really upset. He hid the box under floorboards. People don't do that. Maybe whatever he'd discovered led to his suicide. I don't know what to do, but you knew dad, and I thought perhaps you could help me sort through all this." She fiddled with her wine glass uncomfortably.

"Would you mind if I read the letters and looked at the photos?"

"No, I'll go get them." Kate retrieved the letters, photos, and the note from her father, and handed them to Evan. "I don't know what happened. Dad said he thought he knew what the dreams meant and that he had to ask, but I have no idea what dreams he's talking about and he didn't say who he had to ask or what he needed to know. What if something he learned contributed to his death?"

She watched him as he shuffled through the letters in their envelopes. "I found a Cody Westerholt in a nursing home in

Greeley. I have no idea if he's the one in the photo, but I wanted to visit and talk to him. I don't want to go by myself."

Evan looked at the photos. Kate bore a striking resemblance to her grandmother. "Well, my take on the photos is someone didn't want your grandmother and this Cody together. You found these in the box?" She nodded. "Don't jump to any conclusions about your dad till we have more information."

"This whole thing just makes me so crazy. I no longer know who my dad was. How does that happen? I just…I can't…" She began to cry.

He put everything she'd given him on the coffee table and pulled her to him. "Kate, you have a choice here. Nothing you do at this point will bring your dad back, and you have no idea what this relates to. You don't have to pursue this, you could put this away and not get involved."

"I could," she said, regaining her composure and wiping at her eyes. He released her and she sat back. "I know that, and maybe I should. Dad said some things should be left buried, but I can't reconcile suicide with my father. He struggled with depression when I was growing up and after mom passed, but he made it through all those years after mom died and didn't kill himself. Why now? It has to be related. I have to know what happened."

Evan nodded. "Okay, but promise me you won't do anything without me. He was a friend, one I valued. I want to be involved."

She nodded and felt a stab of yearning as she watched him. He was such a grounded, kind man. Someone who'd be there whenever you needed him, and she was such a mess that she couldn't climb over the wall of self-protection that kept her from him. It really wasn't his fault that her father had confided in him or kept that from her, but despite her growing feelings for him, she just couldn't get over feeling betrayed and angry. It seemed as if it was always that way, some fatal flaw that kept her from finding 'the one.'

THEY HAD talked of other things, topics that relieved the apprehension she felt and helped her relax. They eventually finished the wine and finally Kate rose. "It's been an upsetting few days for me, and the drive was tiring. I guess I'll go get settled and go to sleep. Thanks for letting me come up."

Evan stood up. "Sleep well. Let me know if you need anything." He watched as she walked down the hall to the guest room. He was trying to keep his distance, physically, because what he really wanted was to take her in his arms and make love to her. But he could see how vulnerable she was, and it just wasn't right; at least not now. He wondered if it ever would be.

He tidied up the kitchen and then picked up the letters and the photos and carried them, along with a shot of scotch, to the bedroom. He searched for the drawstring pajama bottoms and put them on. Seemed a bit silly, but with his luck there'd be some emergency he'd have to attend to that required leaving his bedroom and he wouldn't be able to find the pajamas. He stretched out on the bed, legs crossed at the ankles, sipping his scotch, and gradually read through the letters, John's final letter, and the note with his scribbled questions.

He remembered the odd conversation he'd had with John and was sure it had been related to this, whatever *this* was. What the hell had he found out? Did it have anything to do with his suicide? Evan laid the letters on his bedside table and finished his scotch. Was the package John had sent him related to this? Maybe it was the diary his sister had mentioned. And the big question was, did he give it to Kate?

He picked up each half of the torn photo and held them together. Kate's grandmother was a handsome woman. Tired and overworked it looked like, but that smile that was Kate's smile. He put the pieces of the photo on the nightstand and picked up the photo of Frances Earnshaw taken in the summer. He studied her face and the way she had looked at the photographer who'd taken the photo. She had to have been looking at this Cody.

Based on the torn photo, Kate's grandmother and Cody had some sort of close relationship, one that someone hadn't been happy about. He remembered the times that Jake Earnshaw had mistaken him for a man named Cody and the anger it had caused, the threats the old man had directed at him in his confusion. It made sense now. He wondered whether Jake had played some part in his wife's death.

He put the photo back on the bedside table and picked up the one of the three kids. He stared at the teenage girl. What was with the look? He knew what it would mean to him, it was a blatant come on. Was it directed at the photographer or was she just replicating a pose she'd seen in some magazine? He put it back on the nightstand and reached to turn the light off when he heard a light knock on his door.

CHAPTER EIGHTEEN

HE GOT UP, went to the door, and opened it. Kate stood outside the door in her nightgown, feet bare, hair around her shoulders, and he hoped whatever she wanted could be handled quickly, before he gave into the need to kiss her again.

"Everything okay?"

She looked embarrassed. "I…" she shook her head and began to turn away.

He reached for her arm. "What? Talk to me, please."

"I don't want to be alone." She ran a hand distractedly through her hair as she stepped into his room and the door slowly swung toward its jamb. "I can't sleep, the bed's too big, the room's too dark, I…oh never mind."

"Do you want to talk?"

"No, I want you." She stepped toward him and wrapped her arms around his neck, resting her head on his bare shoulder. Her cheek felt warm against his bare skin.

Evan held her. The wine and the scotch made him want to throw caution to the wind, but he gently pulled her away from him and forced himself to say, "Kate, I don't think this is a good idea, much as I hate to say so."

She watched him, a puzzled look on her face.

"I'm not sure you really want me or if you just think you do. All you've found out about your father—the letters and the photos—I think it's thrown you off balance. God, I want you, but I don't want to wake up tomorrow and have regrets. I don't want *you* to have regrets."

In answer, she stepped into his arms, tipped her head up, and kissed him. Her lips were soft and she tasted like toothpaste. It made him smile. He took her head in his hands. "Be sure Kate. If this goes any further, I don't know if I'll be able to stop."

"I don't want you to stop. I want to be with you tonight, please."

He noticed she'd just said '*tonight*' and shut off the voice in his head telling him to back off that this wasn't a good idea; that she was upset by everything that had happened and might not be thinking straight. But she kissed him again, deeply, and his resolve melted despite knowing he was venturing into deep, uncharted water.

He responded to the kiss by pushing her back against the door forcing it closed in his haste and pressing himself against her. He nearly rucked up her nightgown and took her there against the door, but held back. He pulled away and slipped the nightgown off over her head, letting it fall to the floor. Kissing her he dropped his pajama bottoms and kicked them away. He reached out and caressed her breasts.

"God, you're beautiful," he said as she ran her hands through his hair.

He let his hands roam over her as she dropped her hand, took hold of him, and stroked him. He closed his eyes and moaned, then walked her to the bed. He sat on the side of it, pulling her down onto it, and laid beside her. Evan planned on taking his time and enjoying this whether it was ill advised or not. His mouth roamed slowly over her, breathing in her scent. He tasted her lips as he caressed the softness of her breasts, moving down her throat, he took the hardness of her nipple into his mouth, using his tongue to play with it then sucking on it. He heard her sharp intake of breath as she took hold of his head and held him against her.

At last he let go and worked his way down her body, tasting her as she willingly opened for him, reveling in the scent of her. She stroked his hair, her breath catching in her throat. She held his head in place as he explored her with his mouth and tongue. The sounds of wanting and pleasure she made as she pressed up against him nearly undid him.

"Now please," she said huskily, pulling him up to her. "Don't make me wait any longer."

He pushed her knees up and thrust into her. He heard her cry out. Her orgasm pulsed around him, holding him, squeezing him in the hot wetness of her and he lost himself in it, in her. He thrust hard again, and again, hearing her moan and pull him closer with her legs. At last he let go, easing himself down on her when the spasms of his orgasm had passed.

She stroked his back as they lay quietly in the dark. She let her hands drift down the ridge of muscles that ran on either side of his spine, running her fingers down to the crease in his buttocks, making him tighten them as she cupped both in her hands and pulled him against her.

A few minutes later she lowered her legs, and he rolled to her side. She curled up against him, and he held her. She had just about fallen asleep when she felt him jolt.

"Oh Christ," he moaned.

"What? What's wrong?"

"I forgot…we didn't use protection. I didn't think, God I'm sorry. I don't have any…you know, STDs, but you could get pregnant."

"No, I can't. My cycle was really affected by all the trauma and stress over my father's death. I ended up going back on the pill to regulate it, so I can't get pregnant. I don't have any STDs either, but I guess we should have talked about that first."

"Yeah, it's a little late to be discussing all this." He let out a breath of relief. "You just turn my brain to mush."

She curled into him, threw her leg over him, and rested her hand on his chest. "Your heart's beating pretty fast."

He chuckled. "I just scared myself to death, so I guess it's not surprising. It was careless and stupid, I'm sorry."

"My fault, too. I didn't ask." She pressed close against him. "I've been so off kilter since I got the box, I'm not thinking straight either."

He said nothing for a bit. "I've been thinking about making love to you since I saw you standing in the weeds that day."

"Why did you leave the other night?"

"Because, I didn't want to take advantage of you. You've been through a lot lately." He stroked her hand and arm as it rested on his chest. "I worry that this is more about what you've been through than it is wanting me. I'm crazy about you, Kate. I don't want this to be a mistake."

"You worry too much." She moved onto him, her hands resting lightly on his chest, her eyes serious. She leaned over and kissed him softly on his lips, then urgently, taking his face in her hands, she kissed his chin, his cheeks, and his closed eyelids.

"Maybe I do," he replied, reaching up and running his hands up her body until he held her breasts, stroking her nipples with his thumbs.

"I do want you," she said, rising up and guiding him home, taking him in, moving slowly against the finger that he'd placed between them.

"Oh God, you feel so good." He whispered, as she moved in a steady rhythm on top of him.

She arched back, closing her eyes and beginning to move faster. Leaning forward, she placed her hands on either side of his head, moving faster and faster, eyes fixed on his until her orgasm broke. He grasped her hips and clamped her to him, pushing deeply into her and emptying himself.

Kate lay down on top of him and sighed, nuzzling and kissing his neck. "Sleep now," she whispered, stretching her legs out and rolling to his side. She slid an arm under his neck and wrapped her other arm around him as they both let sleep take them.

———◆———

HE WOKE early, as he always did, and watched her sleeping. He wanted to paint her like this, with the soft light of early morning caressing her face, lighting the curves of her shoulders and breasts, leaving the hollows in shadow. He wanted to paint her hair as it tumbled around her face, which was still relaxed in sleep. Her lips were slightly parted, a bit reddened and swollen from their lovemaking that had continued through the night, fired by the endless delight of new lovers.

He retrieved a sketchpad from his studio and returned to swiftly sketch her. He wanted that memory, just in case her coming to him last night was a need for someone—anyone—to be there for her, to comfort her. Just in case it was irrelevant in the end that it had been him.

CHAPTER NINETEEN

KATE SMELLED THE coffee first, then remembered where she was and what had happened last night. She lay on her back and stretched, staring around Evan's room. It was comfortable and masculine, with touches that said Evan, sprinkled here and there—a black felted Stetson hung off the corner of the dresser's mirror, a pair of trainers lay near the closet. A pile of what looked like running clothes lay on the floor next to them.

A sketchpad lying on the floor next to the bed caught her eye, and she leaned over the side of the bed to retrieve it. She paged through it and was impressed by his talent and then quite startled to see a pencil drawing of herself lying nude in tangled sheets that didn't leave much to the imagination, her face and body relaxed in sleep. She blushed and at the same time was struck by the tenderness that the drawing reflected.

She closed the pad and returned it to the floor feeling like a voyeur. Sitting up, she swung her legs over the side of the bed, stood up, and retrieved her nightgown that Evan had evidently draped across the foot of the bed. Her last memory of the nightgown was him removing it and dropping it on the floor by the door. She pulled it over her head then moved to his bathroom and used the toilet. She washed her face and ran her hands through her hair. She'd brush her teeth after breakfast, she thought, as she walked toward the bedroom door.

Kate knew Evan was worried that coming to him last night was a reaction to her discoveries and her distress. Perhaps it was, she wasn't sure, but she had needed him last night. And this morning? There was no undoing what had happened, and she wasn't sure she wanted to. More and more, she felt a connection with him that went well beyond his relationship to her father, but always the wall went up. She could feel it slowly rising as she paused before the bedroom door.

Time to see how awkward the morning after will be, she thought opening the door.

———◆———

EVAN STOOD at the living room window clad in his pajama bottoms, holding a mug of coffee in his hand as he stared out the window. He turned at the sound of her entering the kitchen. She was stunning, he thought, hair mussed, face still a little sleepy looking, her nightgown covering the body he'd explored and come to know last night.

"Morning," he said with a smile.

"Morning. What're you staring at out the window?" Kate moved to the coffee pot and poured a cup, doctored it, then walked toward him.

"Couple of deer on the front lawn. Come see." He held his arm out to her and saw her eyes rest on the definition of the muscles of his arm and chest and the small half-moon tattoo. He remembered telling her it stood for life waxing and waning. He wasn't sure since he'd met Kate what was waxing and what was waning. All he knew was everything was in flux including himself.

She moved into his arm, and he pulled her up against him. He pointed with the hand holding his coffee mug at two deer that stood eating the grass.

"Do they do that often?"

"Winter's coming, so they eat what they can. I don't see them every day, but often enough." He kissed her temple. "Sleep well?"

"Yeah, but this guy kept me awake for a very long time."

He chuckled. "Funny how that happens." They watched the deer for a while, drinking their coffee. At last, he said, "Do you want to go see this Cody today?" He was sorry he'd said anything when she moved away from him and walked to the kitchen island. "You don't have to do it at all."

Evan followed her and set his coffee mug on the island. He began pulling a bowl, measuring cups, and ingredients from cupboards, hoping to conceal his annoyance with himself for ruining the moment at the window.

"I do. I can't spend my life wondering what Dad found or whether it was the reason for his suicide." She paused, and watched him with a puzzled look on her face. "What are you doing?"

"Making breakfast."

"You cook a lot."

"I like to eat, and I finally figured out I couldn't live on pizza and fast food." He laughed. "Plus, there's only the one restaurant in town, so I asked my mom for some lessons. It's kinda necessary living out here." He turned the oven on then mixed butter, sugar, and cinnamon into a crumble. When he'd beaten the batter into shape, he poured it into a pan and sprinkled the crumble over it before sliding it into the oven and setting the timer. "I figure coffee cake would hit the spot."

"You're a surprise, Evan Hastings."

He smiled and loaded the used dishes and utensils in the dishwasher and was taken aback when she said, "Would you show me your studio, your work? I'd like to see it."

He hesitated. "It's not contemporary art."

"I know."

He was uncomfortable. He rarely allowed anyone into his studio. The work was often unfinished and rough, and his art was very personal. Until it was finished, he felt exposed if anyone saw it. Finally, he shrugged and took her hand, pulling her to a closed door near his bedroom. The scent of oil paints and turpentine was strong when he opened the door.

It was a large room with a wall of windows and two skylights. There were multiple easels each holding a painting in various stages of completion. On one there was a painting of her standing in the field on her father's property, the crumbling house behind her. The sensuality in the rendering of her face was arresting. She approached the easel and stood there for a moment, her head tilted first to one side, then the other.

"It kind of reminds me of that Andrew Wyeth painting 'Christine'."

"A bit I guess, although you're not crawling up a hill, and you're certainly not as wasted looking as she was."

"True." She moved closer to the painting. "I don't know what to say. Is this how you see me?"

"It's how you look."

"It's not what I see when I look in the mirror."

He smiled. "It's what I saw."

"Did the reality compare favorably last night?"

He nodded and watched her blush. "Well, um, I guess that's good."

He stepped toward her and brushed a stray strand of hair behind her ear. Leaning down, he kissed her. "Don't be embarrassed. You're beautiful and sensual and making love to you was all I'd hoped it would be. I hope it was for you as well."

She wrapped her arms around his waist and laid her head on his chest, then finally said, "It was." The note of hesitation—perhaps regret—wasn't lost on Evan.

She smelled of lemons and sex, and desire for her flared. He started to kiss her again, and the timer on the oven began chiming.

"Well hell," he said breaking away. "I guess breakfast is ready."

CHAPTER TWENTY

S HE USED HER laptop to investigate Happy Acres further after breakfast and, as she had anticipated, it didn't look like a happy place, and it wasn't near any acreage. It was the oldest nursing home in Greeley, and it was a Medicaid facility. That didn't bode well. She only hoped Cody Westerholt was still alive and capable of talking.

She called and discovered he was alive, although not in the best of shape. When they arrived, the director told them that he had taken a turn for the worse during the previous week and spent much of his time in a recliner in his room or in his bed. The room was what Kate had expected—institutional looking, small, and drably painted, its walls banged up from moving furniture. The sight of the elderly man dozing in the recliner, lap covered with blankets, shocked her. She felt Evan take her elbow as they followed the director into the room where she stopped at the man's side.

"Mr. Westerholt?" the woman said, touching his arm and then patting it. "Cody? You have visitors. Can you wake up and visit with them?" She patted his hand again and then turned to Kate and Evan. "It's getting harder to wake him up. That happens toward the end. Perhaps if you wait here for a bit, he'll wake up on his own."

Kate nodded, and the woman left. Evan pulled two chairs up to the recliner and they sat watching the sleeping man. He looked wasted—his mouth hung open as he slept, his cheeks were hollowed, and his hands twitched on the armrests periodically. His white hair was sparse over the top of his head and whoever had shaved him had missed a few spots. Kate could see his eyes moving restlessly under his eyelids. His breathing was so quiet that she had to watch the rise and fall of his chest closely to confirm it.

"Maybe this was pointless. I'd hoped to be able to talk to him." Kate leaned closer to him. "Cody? Can you wake up for a little bit?"

Evan watched as the man's eyes blinked open, casting around as if searching for where the voice had come from. His eyes found Kate, and a smile creased his face. He didn't look so wasted anymore, and there was softness in his eyes.

"Franny," he whispered. "I knew you'd come for me. It's so good to see you again. I've missed you, missed you so much."

Kate realized that he thought she was her grandmother and reached out and took his hand. "It's good to see you too, Cody."

"I shouldn't have left you there. It near killed me when I heard what happened to you. I'm so sorry."

"Why did you leave?"

"Knew about us, said…you'd get hurt. Took the pictures. They were th'only ones I had of you." His breathing hitched ominously, and a tear escaped his eye. "I planned to come back and get you… then you were gone. Didn't save you after all."

"Who Cody? Who knew?" Kate spoke softly as she stroked his arm.

"I love you Franny, always have."

Kate smiled at him. "I love you too, Cody."

"You're the most beautiful woman I ever knew. I'm sorry I let you down." His breathing had become more labored. "You came for me, though. D'you forgive me?"

"Oh Cody, there's nothing to forgive. It wasn't your fault. Can you tell me who made you leave? Who took the photos from you?"

He sighed and squeezed her hand, the smile still on his face. "I have a hard time staying awake these days, so tired, so ready to be done with all this. I can't wait to be with you again. Maybe today's the day, since you came for me. You'll stay 'til I can go with you? You'll stay?"

"I'll stay, Cody. Please tell me, who made you leave?"

"Not important anymore, Franny. We'll be together, that's all that matters. So tired." His eyes closed, his breathing deepened, and he slept.

Kate held his hand and was surprised at the tears that had welled up and spilled down her cheeks. "I'm going to stay. You don't have to," she said to Evan.

Evan passed her his handkerchief. "Kate, there's no predicting when he'll pass. It could be days."

"I know, but I can't leave him. He thinks I'm my grandmother. How can I leave him to die alone? Did you see his face when he saw me?"

Evan wrapped an arm around her shoulders and pulled her to him. "Stay then, at least for a while. Let's see how things go." He withdrew his arm and stood up. "I'm going to go talk to the woman who brought us back here. Are you okay?"

"Yes."

———— ◆ ————

EVAN HAD watched her holding Cody's hand and thought she was far from okay, but she'd made up her mind to stay, and he couldn't blame her. He'd felt her pull away slightly when he'd put his arm around her. She'd been withdrawn since they'd left the house, and the sense that something was brewing worried him.

The smile on the old man's face and the way he looked at Kate spoke volumes about how Cody felt about her grandmother and the regret he'd carried for leaving her to her fate. If Kate's presence gave him some peace, what was the harm? Evan's only concern was what it would put Kate through. And he had to admit he was worried that what had happened between them the night before had somehow derailed in the light of day.

The conversation with the old man didn't help to resolve much other than to confirm that there had been something strong between him and Frances Earnshaw. And now, it had cast some doubt as to whether Kate's grandmother's death had been an accident.

Evan waited in the foyer of the nursing home for their escort to be located, struggling with a decision he had to make. Did he give Kate the package John had sent him before his death or just burn it? He had no idea what it contained, and he feared further traumatizing or alienating Kate if he gave it to her. Giving her the package wouldn't bring John back, and John's quest to find out these family secrets may have had a hand in his suicide. He didn't want to perpetuate the secret keeping that seemed to run in her family. Unfortunately, he'd been one of those secrets, one for which Kate seemed to hold him responsible. Trying to decide made him feel as if he were walking a tightrope over the Grand Canyon.

Evan returned to the room half an hour later and sat down by Kate. "He's in hospice and has no relatives. He never married and never had children, so there's a court appointed guardian arranged by the attorney who's the executor named in his will. Mrs. Williams, the woman we spoke with, says that he's doing what they call 'actively dying.'"

Evan sighed and scrubbed his face. "The terms they come up with these days, never cease to amaze me, but from what she said that means he's near death. Like she said it could be today or it could be days, but she said not much longer."

Kate nodded. "I'll stay. I want to be here if he wakes up."

"He may not wake up according to her. I guess that's what they do. She says people who are dying sleep more and more and then lapse into a sleep they don't wake up from. She's fine with us staying."

"You don't have to, Evan."

"I'm not leaving you here."

------◆------

FORTY-EIGHT HOURS later, Cody Westerholt passed without waking up. Staff members had moved Cody to his bed a few hours after Kate and Evan had arrived, and it was where he'd stayed until his death. He died so quietly that it was Evan who finally noticed he was no longer breathing.

Kate had held the old man's hand with few interruptions since their arrival. Through the room's window, she'd been watching a bird on one of the feeders that the staff had mounted outside the windows to the rooms that faced the courtyard.

He reached out and touched her arm. "Kate," Evan said softly. "He's gone."

She turned abruptly. "When?"

"Just in the last few minutes. It took me a while to realize he wasn't breathing."

She stroked the old man's lifeless hand. "I hope he knew I was here."

"Even if he didn't, he saw you before he passed. You gave him some peace and happiness."

"It's just so sad," she said at last. "God, we screw up our lives so badly sometimes."

"I'll go let the nurse know he's passed."

CHAPTER TWENTY-ONE

VAN DROVE BACK to the house and neither of them spoke. Fatigue weighed on him; they hadn't gotten much sleep in the last two days. The staff brought another recliner into the room so, in theory, they could sleep during the night. The theory hadn't quite panned out. Kate had insisted on sitting by the old man's bedside and holding his hand. If she used the recliner to do that, then it was in the way of staff members. Evan had finally stepped in and was able to get her to agree to at least lie in one of the recliners for several hours and get some sleep.

Staff members, who were grateful that someone had wanted to stay with Cody, had brought them food, but institutional food was pretty unappealing. Evan was relieved to finally arrive home. Kate had fallen asleep during the drive, her head resting on the headrest at an awkward angle.

He parked and got out, walking around to the passenger side and opening the door. "Kate, we're back at the house, come on let me help you inside." He eased her down out of the truck and walked her into the house. "You need to sleep and so do I. Let's go get a couple hours, and then I'll figure out something for dinner."

"I want a shower and a toothbrush." She yawned and walked tiredly toward the guest suite.

Evan watched her go, wondering whether she'd want his company or not, then decided to get his own shower. Half an hour later, he walked into her room and found her curled up on the bed, hair wet, a T-shirt and panties on, and out cold. He walked over and pulled the covers up over her. She didn't move.

She'd been withdrawn the entire time they'd spent at the nursing home, and he debated now whether to leave her alone or crawl into bed with her. God, he was so tired. Finally, he walked around to the other side of the bed, lay down, pulled her to him, and dropped off to sleep.

———— ◆ ————

HE WOKE in an empty bed in the dark, disoriented for a few moments before he remembered where he was. He sat up, scrubbing his hands over his face and wondered where Kate was. He found her sitting in the dark living room with a glass of wine in her hand, staring out the windows.

"Hey," he said softly as he walked into the living room. "Did you sleep well?"

She looked exhausted. "I sat down on the bed to comb my hair and I don't remember anything till I woke up. How about you?"

"Not bad, could use a full night's sleep though. Are you hungry?"

"Not really."

Evan nodded, walked over to the kitchen island, and poured himself a glass of wine. It was awkward. He felt as if he'd done something wrong, but wasn't sure what it had been. He'd felt her hesitation in responding to him the morning after making love to her and her increasing withdrawal while they stayed with Cody. He stood at the kitchen counter watching her gaze silently out the window at the darkness. Whatever the problem was he was sure it didn't bode well for him. At last he returned and sat on the couch within touching distance but not close. He had no idea what to do or say.

Finally, she turned to him. "Tell me about my father. Who he was with you."

"Okay." Evan thought for a moment before he spoke. "He was a very private man. He never explained what had happened to him growing up or why he hated his father or why he was letting the house fall apart. He made his hatred for his father clear the very first time I met him, though. I met him much like I met you—I saw his car on the property and came to see what was going on. He was carrying his father's ashes in a box."

Evan took another sip of the wine. "All he said was he was going to spread them in the root cellar and hoped the house fell down around the old bastard. The one time I asked why he was letting the house deteriorate he told me, essentially, to mind my own business. So, I did."

"He never said anything to me about the property or the house or my grandfather. At least you got that much."

"It can be hard to talk about things like that, Kate."

"He talked about it with you!"

"Barely." Evan paused and took a drink of his wine. He wished he'd gotten some scotch instead. This didn't look like it was going to be an easy conversation. He could feel anger radiating off her, but wasn't sure if he was the target. He changed his position and thought for a few moments.

"He was funny. He was a very talented builder. He taught me some tricks to improve my carpentry skills."

"He *was* funny. I knew he was a builder, but he never showed me how to build things and he never told me he could draw. He never offered to *improve my skills*," she said, her face a mask of resentment and anger…and hurt.

Evan took a deep breath and released it. "Is this about me or your father?"

She turned on him, eyes flashing. "This is about *me!* And it's about my father who kept himself from me, who showed himself to you, but not to me."

Evan didn't know what to say. Kate got up and paced.

"Here's what I know about my dad. He has two sisters who live out of state. I'm close to my Aunt Ellen, but not Dad's oldest sister Madelyn. She's hard to deal with and doesn't encourage any closeness. He never made any attempt to get together with her and he didn't see Ellen much either, although they were close. They were both at his funeral. Madelyn left right afterwards, didn't even stay for the reception."

Kate turned and faced him. "I knew Dad was a builder, a contractor, and according to you he was good at it. I wouldn't know, he did next to nothing around our house, he had laborers come over and fix things if needed."

Evan listened without comment. It was painful to hear.

"He suffered from depression, incapacitating depression, when I was little. As I got older that changed, it was less debilitating for him. Antidepressants helped. I grew up in a house where certain topics were off limits. Why he was depressed, for example, wasn't talked about, ever."

She resumed pacing. "And I know what you're going to say, that he probably had a recurrence of one of his depressive episodes and decided to kill himself. That's what the cops said, that's what everyone assumes. But he hadn't had an incident like that in years."

Evan said nothing as she paced. "He loved my mother almost to the exclusion of anything else. He loved me, but if he'd had to choose between my mother and me I'm not sure who he'd have chosen—my mother at a guess."

She ran her hands through her hair then rubbed her neck. "He was good to me, loved me, but never showed me these other sides he showed to you. Maybe once mama was gone, I was of less interest. He never confided in me. Christ, that's minimizing it! He shut me out completely from all of this." She cried, swinging her arm around to indicate the house and Evan. "And now he can't share any of that, and I can't find out what he knew because Cody's dead and…and…oh hell, who cares!"

Time to bite the bullet he guessed. "Kate…your dad left some stuff with me, before he died. I should have given it to you the first time you stayed. I just…you seemed so…I guess it doesn't matter why, but I'll get it for you now."

She rounded on him. "*No!* I don't want any more reminders of how important you were to him. He didn't leave anything for me other than endless work to settle his estate and endless rude surprises about his life. He didn't even leave a fucking suicide note!"

Evan let his exasperation get the better of him. "How the hell is that *my fault?* What d'you want me to do about it? I can't change what your father did or didn't do any more than you can. We're both victims of his damn secret keeping, but I won't apologize for being his friend. I didn't keep secrets from you, *he did!* I wasn't your father's friend to spite you."

"I know that. It's not your fault, Evan, you're just the collateral damage he caused." She turned and walked toward the guest bedroom. "I'm going home, I can't stay here."

He shot up and closed the distance between them, taking hold of her shoulders. "Kate you're exhausted and so am I. Please, if you need some time to yourself, go to the guest room and get some sleep. You're in no condition to drive back to Denver. We'll get to the bottom of…"

She pulled away from him roughly. "Don't tell me we'll figure it out. Don't tell me everything will be all right. I *found* him Evan! I found him after he'd shot himself. It'll *never* be all right."

She stabbed a finger at him, tears running down her face. "And *you*—he gave you everything he kept from me. Keep what he gave you, I don't want something he never intended for me to have."

She turned and stalked into the guest room and slammed the door. Evan heard her shoot the bolt into place. Heard her sobbing behind the closed door. Totally baffled, he stood in the living room and wondered what the hell had just happened. He knew she was angry with her father, for the suicide, for what he'd had with John—that had been pretty clear from the beginning. But she'd never said she'd found her father, or how John had taken his life. No wonder she was so torn up about it, the violence of his death must have just added to her despair. And now it looked as if he was the lightening rod. It was understandable, he guessed, but it pissed him off. How the hell was it *his* fault?

He dumped the wine down the sink and poured himself a generous helping of scotch. He walked into his bedroom and shut the door. He ditched the pajama bottoms and got into bed, weariness engulfing him. The look on her face when she'd said she didn't know who her father would have chosen if asked to pick between her and her mother broke his heart. And there was no way he could change what her father had shared with him.

CHAPTER TWENTY-TWO

KATE WOKE. SHE checked her phone and saw it was five a.m. She hoped Evan wasn't awake, she didn't want an argument or for him to try to talk her out of going home. She'd packed the night before but he'd been right about one thing: she was exhausted. She'd gone to bed and planned to return home in the morning.

Sitting with Cody until he passed felt like a cruel joke. It had been more than she could bear. To be so close to finding out what had happened to her grandmother and then have Cody die before he could tell her was frustrating beyond belief. Nothing had been gained by talking to him other than to confirm that he'd loved her grandmother. Every dead end she hit infuriated her.

It had been a mistake asking Evan to tell her about her father. Hearing him talk just stoked her anger. This blow up with Evan had been slowly building. She just hadn't realized how consuming the anger would be. Every time she heard or stumbled on something about her father that he'd known and she hadn't, the slow burn had intensified. And then, because she was so tired of being alone and struggling with her father's death by herself and just wanted to be held and comforted, she'd slept with Evan. Jesus, what had she been thinking?

She'd realized when they'd returned to Evan's house that she wished she'd been able to sit by her father's side and be with him when he died—of old age. Instead, she'd found him dead, a bullet through his temple. And it was hard to admit how angry she was with him.

Kate shuddered and shook her head as if trying to shake the memory of finding her father from her mind, but it would always be waiting to sneak up on her and hit her when she least expected it. She was fairly successful at walling it off when she was busy, but it was never gone.

She dressed and picked up her bag, easing the door open. Evan either wasn't up or was in his studio. She hoped he was asleep. She moved soundlessly through the living room past the kitchen and out the back door, easing it shut behind her and walking to her car. She got in and started it, hoping that wherever he was he wouldn't hear the motor or the car as she drove past the house and out onto the county road.

Right now, she couldn't be with him. She'd needed someone to hold her and soothe her, but going to him had been a mistake. She should have stayed in her room, shouldn't have initiated their night together, and now she had no idea what to do other than leave. His efforts to stop her, to make sure she wanted to make love to him, not just anyone, hadn't overruled her need for comfort. She wished she'd listened or that he'd refused her and, irrationally, that added to her anger toward him.

————•◆•————

EVAN DIMLY thought he heard a car, but couldn't fight his way out of sleep enough to be sure. When he woke around eight, he pulled on a pair of jeans and went into the kitchen to get coffee. The house was quiet, he could hear the wind blowing around it, and it sounded like a storm was on its way. The door to the guest room was closed. Perhaps Kate was still asleep, but he had an uneasy feeling about it. He walked to the back door and confirmed his suspicions—her car was gone.

"*Shit!*" He pounded on the door in frustration.

He stepped outside and took a deep breath. The skies were overcast, and the temperature had dropped. Goosebumps covered his arms as the wind hit him. It was the middle of October, so snow might be coming or maybe just cold sleety rain. Whatever the clouds and wind portended it matched his mood. He walked back in the house, retrieved his phone, and dialed Kate's number. It went to voice mail.

He waited for the beep. "I wish you'd stayed. I don't know what happened, and I'm sorry it did, but I'd appreciate it if you'd let me know you got home safely."

He hung up and turned toward his study where he kept his desk and laptop. He sat in the chair by his desk and hunted for the package her father had sent him. Christ, he should have given it to her the first time she showed up. All he'd done by waiting was royally piss her off and drive her away.

He'd figured making love to Kate would be enjoyable but hadn't been prepared for just how enjoyable it'd turned out to be. She was sensual and responsive, and just thinking about it made him close his eyes and groan feeling his nearly instantaneous erection. The thought that she might consider it a mistake was infuriating. A sick, frustrated feeling washed over him when he thought that it might never happen again, and he didn't like the ache that had settled in his chest.

"Just calm down," he said under his breath. "Give her some space. Take a fucking cold shower for Christ's sake, if you have to." When the thought of a cold shower didn't work, calling to mind his grandmother standing in the doorway frowning at him, arms crossed over her chest took care of the erection at least for the time being.

He resumed looking through the drawers of his desk to no avail then remembered he'd put the package in his studio. Once in the studio he riffled through a drawer in the supply cabinet until he found the package. He didn't know what was in it and had never thought to ask John.

It didn't feel right opening it, John hadn't meant for him to read it. He would mail it to Kate. Before he did that, he wanted to do a little research. He looked at the package sitting in his hands for several moments and then put it back in his desk and picked up his phone.

"Hey, Mom."

"Evan! It's good to hear from you, how are things?"

"I'm fine, Mom. How're you and Dad?"

"Good sweetie, the usual aches and pains but otherwise just fine." Evan hesitated, not knowing where to go with the conversation. "What's wrong?" she asked.

He laughed a little. "What makes you think anything's wrong?"

"Evan Jonathan Hastings, don't try to buffalo me. What's wrong?"

Evan sighed. What was wrong? That was a long list, so he tried to redirect the conversation. "When you lived in Ardwell, did you or Dad know or did Grandma or Grandpa know the Earnshaws, the ones who lived out near Grandpa's land?"

She thought for a moment. "I sort of remember them. Not well, I was just a kid. I remember seeing the man coming into the feed store once in a while, and I would see his wife occasionally at the grocery store when I was there with your Grandma. Why?"

"I'm doing a little research into the family. The old man passed about ten years back. I'd gotten to know him casually and then got to be friends with his son. John helped me build this house. I don't think you ever met him. He died about six months ago. His daughter showed up after inheriting the property, and…and I'm just curious about the family. Jake Earnshaw basically let the farmhouse fall down and John did nothing with it either."

"I knew it had to have something to do with a girl."

"Mom, it doesn't. Maybe peripherally, but it's not what you think." He could almost see her raise her eyebrows at him and give him that 'don't bullshit me' look. She'd never say bullshit, at least to him, but he knew what she was thinking. He was glad it was a phone call.

"Well, I was only about twelve then. Your dad was sixteen, he may remember more. I do remember all the talk about the wife. You know how kids eavesdrop on grownups. Women friends of your grandma's said she'd fallen down the stairs and broken her neck, and there was a lot of gossip. Some said there was something going on between the wife and a ranch hand. Some wondered if her husband had found out about it. The ranch hand disappeared shortly before she fell. I don't think he'd been gone but a day or two when she died. There was a lot of speculation but no proof of anything."

She paused and sighed. "After that, all I know is the husband was pretty unfriendly from what I overheard my folks talking about. All of the kids ran off eventually. The oldest daughter left first I think. I'll ask your dad what he remembers and let you know. He's off fishing with Tom Casey for the week."

"Okay, thanks."

He was about to hang up when she said, "Now tell me what's wrong. And don't tell me 'nothing.'"

There was a long silence. "He was a friend, a good friend, and I didn't know that he'd committed suicide until his daughter showed up. She's pretty messed up about it, and I haven't helped. She didn't know about me, didn't know a lot of things about him or his family."

"You like her, I take it."

He laughed quietly. "Yeah I like her. Not sure she likes me much."

She made a sort of 'psh' noise. "You're both in a hard place. You lost a friend, and she lost her father to suicide. That's never easy. Have you slept with her?"

He could feel the heat flush in his face. "Mother! That's none of your business."

"So, you have," she said. "That's a bridge you can't walk back across son. You know that as well as I do. Give her some time and let her make the moves next time."

She made the moves the first time, he thought, *and look where that got me.* He had no intention of making that mistake again. Too many things needed to be cleared up first, no matter how badly he wanted her. "Thanks for the advice, Mom, embarrassing as it is coming from you."

"Oh, for heaven's sake, Evan. You're a grown man. I'm fully aware you have sex."

He closed his eyes and felt the heat swamp his face again. "Mom! Just stop okay? This is embarrassing." And it made him feel about sixteen again.

She laughed heartily at that. "You're such a goose. Or gander perhaps is more correct. Come to the house for dinner soon, I miss seeing you. We're not that far from Ardwell."

His folks had moved to Fort Collins—his mother's reasoning being they weren't getting any younger, and it was better to be closer to a bigger city in case one of them needed a hospital or help. That thought had left him depressed.

"Okay, maybe when Dad gets back. Let me know if he remembers anything okay?"

"I will sweetheart." She paused then said, "You might want to talk to Ida Stueben, you know, Josie Shoemaker's grandmother? She's got to be in her nineties and if I recall she knew the Earnshaws or at least was around when the wife died."

"Thanks, I'll check into that."

"This girl? She'll come around if she has any sense, Evan, just be patient."

He rolled his eyes and again was glad it was a phone conversation. "Thanks, Mom, love you."

"Love you too. Don't be a stranger."

He smiled as he hung up. He often wondered if his mother was psychic, nothing got by her. He needed to get out of the house, it was closing in on him. Deciding to take a run and work out some of his frustration and low mood, he suited up and headed out the door. A cold wind hit him, needling his face with little icy pellets, and he almost turned back, but a few minutes into the run he heated up. As he jogged near the abandoned Earnshaw place, he saw a truck parked near the house and turned into the property, jogging up to two men who were about to enter the house.

"This property is posted, private land," he called out. "What are you doing here?'

They halted on the front steps turning toward him with frowns on their faces. "We're taking a look at the place. What's it to you?" The man on the left seemed to be the dominant one of the pair. The other stood shuffling his feet.

"You have some proof the owner knows and agrees to this?" The discomfort on their faces said they didn't.

"We're just looking around, no harm done."

"Actually, there is. One, it's private property, and you're trespassing. And, two, the house is falling down and you could get injured. You need to leave." Evan pulled his phone out of his pants pocket. "I'll have to call the sheriff if you don't."

Their frowns deepened, but they left the porch and walked to the pickup truck parked a few feet from the porch. Evan noted the energy company logo on the side of the truck as they got in, started it, and drove off. He entered the name and the phone number on his phone, then entered the number on the truck that indicated which company truck they'd been driving.

It was nearly one in the afternoon, he'd call the company when he returned to the house and let them know Kate wasn't interested in selling and to stay away. Maybe he'd put up a ranch gate and lock it so people couldn't get in so easily. He'd never offered to do that with John or John's father. There didn't seem to be that many people interested in the property then. He shook his head. It was her property. He had no right to do anything. He could call and ask if she'd mind, then remembered his mother's advice.

Fine, he thought as he began to run again. *I'll just keep an eye on the damn place.*

CHAPTER TWENTY-THREE

KATE WOKE IN the dark, a hand clamped between her thighs in the throes of an orgasm. The memory of Evan's touch played in her head and reverberated through her body. When it had subsided, she rolled over onto her side and checked the time. Four thirty. There'd be no going back to sleep now.

She hadn't called Evan back, but had texted that she'd gotten home safely. It had been cowardly to avoid calling him, but she was afraid that any contact other than a text would open the door to the conversation they'd had the night before she left. Aside from that, she had so much going on in her head that she couldn't imagine allowing him back into her life. He hadn't responded to her text in any event.

She sighed. He'd asked her if she was sure about making love with him, and she had been at the time. Then she'd taken everything he'd offered and given nothing back. No, she was pretty sure he'd had enough of her to last a lifetime. Rightfully so, and she was sorry for it. She was tired. Tired of being pulled between her attraction to him, the anger and resentment at what he'd shared with her father, and the need to find out why her father had committed suicide. She wished she could push a fast forward button on her life and get past this part of it.

She couldn't honestly say whether she was mad at Evan or whether he was just a convenient stand in for her father. Perhaps she would be able to resolve the anger if she could find out the why behind her father's suicide. She wasn't sure she'd ever know why he'd kept the property and Evan a secret.

Kate got out of bed and walked into her bathroom. She left the lights off and turned the shower on to let it heat up. Standing in the dark under the pounding spray, she leaned her head against the tiled wall and cried for herself, her father, and for Evan. Finally, feeling nearly boiled, she washed and got out. Toweling off and pulling her bathrobe on, she wrapped a towel around her hair and wandered down to the kitchen for coffee. She turned the under-counter lights on. They cast a low light over the counter and not much else. She really didn't want to deal with the day yet.

Through the sliding door that led out to the patio, she could see an inch of snow on the ground. She'd figured the snow would start on her drive home, but the skies hadn't relinquished their burden until the middle of the night. Their leaden color now mimicked her mood, which had not improved with a night's sleep.

It was too early to call Aunt Ellen in San Francisco. She'd have to wait a bit before placing the call. Kate hoped that her aunt could help her sort through some of her questions. Ellen had been the sister her father had been closest to and the one he'd corresponded with, perhaps she was the one he'd planned to talk to.

She couldn't think of a reason why he'd want to talk to Aunt Madelyn. They'd never been close, politely friendly when they happened to be together, but they never made any attempt to visit or stay in touch. If Ellen couldn't answer her questions, then she'd call Madelyn.

She didn't look forward to that. More to the point, what would she ask?

EVAN STOOD on the front porch of the small, white clapboard house just off Ardwell's main street, waiting for someone to answer his knocks. He'd called Josie Shoemaker earlier in the day and asked if he could speak with her elderly grandmother. He wasn't sure whether there was much to be gained by it, but it took his mind off the endless *'What the hell did I do wrong?'* loop running through his mind.

The front door of the house opened. "Evan! It's good to see you, come on in."

He smiled. Josie Shoemaker looked much as she always had. She'd been a few grades behind him in school and still wore her blond hair in a ponytail caught up at the back of her head with a barrette. Her jeans were well-worn, accompanied by what looked like a hand-knitted sweater. She was a mother now if the baby she was holding was hers. Josie had told Evan that she watched her grandmother a couple of days a week to give her mother a break.

"Josie, good to see you. Who's this?" The baby was flapping one hand in the air, so he reached out and caught the baby's hand between his thumb and index finger, waggling it and making the kid give him a toothless grin.

"This is my son, Ben. Don't stand there, come on in."

Evan moved past her into the living room, removing his hat, as she closed the door behind him. It was cold outside and the inch or two of snow on the ground made it feel colder. "Hope I'm not intruding."

"Heaven's no, it'll break up the day for Nana, and it'll give me a break, too." She walked into the living room. "Can I get you some coffee or something?"

"No thanks, I just wanted to talk to your grandmother for a bit, if I could."

"Sure, let me put Ben in his playpen, and I'll take you to her." She settled the baby in a plastic and net contraption sitting in the middle of the living room and tossed in a couple toys lying on the floor outside of it. Ben crawled over to them, picked one up, and sat back on his butt playing with it as Josie led Evan down a hallway.

The room where her grandmother resided was small but pleasant. A south-facing window let in what light there was to be had on an overcast cold day. The bedspread looked like the one his grandparents had used, little lines of fluffy stuff running in a pattern over the surface. He hadn't seen one of those in ages and couldn't remember what his grandmother had called it. The old woman was seated in a rocker with a crocheted afghan over her lap and one draped around her shoulders.

"Nana, this is Evan Hastings. You remember Evan? He was a couple years ahead of me in school. He's Dan and Carolyn's son."

"I remember just fine, Josie. I'm not feeble-minded yet."

Josie laughed and kissed her on the cheek. "No ma'am you're not. Evan wanted to visit with you for a bit, so I'll leave you two to talk. Holler if you need anything."

The woman had to be in her mid-nineties if she was a day. She was tiny and wizened with wispy, white hair escaping the bun that rested on top of her head. Her eyes looked huge behind her glasses.

"Mrs. Steuben, it's good to see you. How are you?" Evan fiddled with his Stetson, running the brim with his hands before he laid it down on the bed and shrugged out of his sheepskin coat, placing it next to his Stetson.

"I'm as good as a person can be who's ninety-three. You don't want to know the details, and I don't want to dwell on them. It's nice to have a handsome man visit—perks an old woman up."

That made Evan laugh.

"I appreciate the visit, but I'm not sure what prompted it. Most young ones like you got better things to do with their time than visit an old lady."

"I wondered if you remembered the Earnshaw family. I have some questions if you do."

"The Earnshaws? My, I haven't given them a thought in years." She rocked several times staring off into space then returning to fix her gaze on him. "I remember them. Troubled family, in my opinion."

"Why's that?"

"Seemed like something was wrong right from the get-go. Jake courted Frances in Yuma where she lived, he'd traipse over there every weekend he could get away. That put a few mamas' noses out of joint around here, seeing as there were plenty of marriageable girls here in town."

She laughed at that. "'Course there's always something to get upset about if you put your mind to it. He married her about six months later. I never knew how he'd met her in the first place. He brought her home with him all of a sudden, married and all, and I think his ranch was a bit of a shock to her."

Mrs. Steuben closed her eyes and fell silent for a few moments. Evan was afraid she'd drifted off to sleep like Cody had, but she opened her eyes a moment later and focused on him again.

"I gathered she'd come from a family that had a bit of money, and I don't think she was prepared for the isolation out there or the work, and my guess is he was a whole different person when he was courting her than after he married her."

She let her eyes drift up, apparently thinking. "He introduced her at the fellowship get together after church once they'd gotten settled. She was a nice little thing—pretty, well-bred—you could see why he was attracted to her." She stopped and then hollered in a surprisingly loud voice, "Josie! Bring us some tea. I need to wet my whistle."

Evan hid his amusement. She was an entertaining old woman, but he bet she wasn't easy to live with. Josie had evidently figured the request would come as she showed up shortly with a small trolley holding a teapot, two cups, sugar and cream. She had also added some cookies.

She smiled at him and fixed a cup for the old woman. "Okay Nana, here's your tea. Let me know if you need anything else."

Mrs. Steuben took a sip and sighed. "That's better. She's a good girl. Where was I?"

"You'd gotten to the part where everyone met Mrs. Earnshaw."

She nodded. "We didn't see much of her after that. He'd never been one for church. We'd see her when she'd come into town with him to get groceries and supplies for the ranch. I got the impression he didn't want her coming in by herself. He was a nasty piece of work, in my opinion. Never very friendly, rude at times. He spoke to her like she was a hired hand instead of his wife."

She rocked, and sipped her tea. Evan had taken a cup and was nursing it along. He'd have preferred coffee but didn't want to trouble Josie. "I'd have never put up with that from my husband, Robert. You got to start 'em out right if you expect to spend the rest of your life with the damn fools."

Evan laughed. "Yes, ma'am, I suppose that's true."

"You find yourself a good woman, you treat her like the prize she is. I was married to Robert for sixty years till he dropped dead of a heart attack. I still miss him." Her eyes glittered for a minute before she cleared her throat and began again.

"The Earnshaw kids were generally good kids. My son and daughter went to school with the two younger ones. The boy was a quiet thing, same with the youngest girl. The oldest girl was a piece of work, a chip off the old man's block. She was downright nasty at times if you believe what the kids said. I never had any contact with her, other than to see her in town, but she had that look about her, like she was too good to be here. I gather she gave the boys a run for their money."

"Do you know what happened to the mother? I heard it was an accident that resulted in her death."

"That was the story. Earnshaw said she fell down the stairs and broke her neck. I was never sure I believed that, but there was no proof otherwise so maybe I'm just a suspicious old biddy." She winked at Evan.

"Why did you question it?"

"There were rumors about her and one of the ranch hands. Apparently, another ranch hand had run his mouth off after a few too many beers. He said he'd seen the younger girl taking a photograph of them together when the husband was in Greeley buying cattle or horses, I forget which. He kept his mouth shut after that, told people he'd been mistaken. Not sure who did it, but somebody beat the bejeezus out of him the day after he'd run his mouth off. The ranch hand he'd implicated left not long after that, maybe a week or two, and a few days later the wife was dead. I watch *Castle* on TV, that's what Beckett calls a coincidence, and she don't believe in coincidences. So, I don't think it was an accident."

"But the sheriff thought it was?"

"Well, no one was there to see it, were they? And it was a different time. We didn't have *CSI*. There was only one sheriff and one deputy and they mostly handled drunks on the weekend or other small-town escapades or concerns. People didn't get murdered here so they figured it was an accident. She did fall down the stairs, which could have been an accident, and there was no one to say otherwise. Still, I always wondered."

The old woman returned her cup to the trolley and began rocking again. "Jake Earnshaw just got meaner after that. The two younger kids took it hard, the older one? I was never sure. She was upset at the wake and the funeral. Afterward, she was good at concealing whatever she was feeling from others, always had been."

"You said the two younger ones took it hard, what can you tell me about that?"

"The little girl was withdrawn, and you'd see her crying every now and then when she walked to school or home. The boy seemed disturbed. He got quiet, jumpy, and had that look in his eye that I remember from some of the boys who came home from

Vietnam. Troubled, you know? He eventually seemed to snap out of it. Maybe it was just his way of grieving."

She sighed and continued to rock. "All the kids ran off eventually. The older one just left. About sixteen I think she was, no idea where she went, and no one here heard anything more about her. The younger daughter married Cal Waters a couple years later, and they left right after that. The boy left for Denver I heard, when he was about seventeen. I'm not sure I can tell you much else. Jake Earnshaw kept the ranch running into his seventies and then stopped and let the place deteriorate. Guess his son did too."

"Do you think the boy saw something, maybe knew something about his mother's death? His reaction does sound like returning soldiers with PTSD rather than a nine-year-old's grief."

"I guess it's possible, but I'm not sure how you'd find out."

"I'm not either. He died a few months ago."

"I heard that. Also heard you were squiring his daughter around town a while back. You sweet on her?"

Again, he felt the heat climb up his neck and spread to his face. What was it with women? It seemed like they could read your mind. "No, I…I met her when she visited the property and was just showing her around."

The old woman cackled and grinned at him. "Boy, you don't lie very well, and if you get any redder you may pop something important. I hear she's a looker. My advice? If you like her, make a move and don't let her get away. Time'll come when you're too old to fix mistakes."

Evan nodded and stood up, leaning over to take her hand. "Thank you for talking with me. I really appreciate it."

She surprised him by pulling him to her. "Give me a hug and a kiss on the cheek, boy, so I can say a good-looking man's still willing to do that."

He did, and she laughed. "Thank you, boy. Now go find that girl you like and kiss her proper."

Driving home he thought about what she'd said. It sounded to him like Kate's father had seen something or knew something, but he had no idea how to find out. If he found something, he'd have to figure out a way to tell Kate without causing more strain between them. He sighed. Seemed like a no-win situation to Evan.

"'*Kiss her proper*' Christ I can't get close enough to even do that," he muttered pulling into his driveway and parking behind the house.

CHAPTER TWENTY-FOUR

"**H**ONEY, I DON'T know why your father was so obsessed with Mama's death. Now you're asking, why do you want to know?"

Kate could feel her frustration rising as she listened to her Aunt Ellen. "I want to know because it seems like it was important to Daddy, and I wonder if what he found out led to his suicide."

"Kate, your father struggled with depression from the time he was small. Nobody called it that then. Everyone thought he was just grieving for Mama or moody or overly sensitive, but it was more than that. As an adult, he went through periods of depression, too. You remember, don't you? I suspect one of them just overwhelmed him."

Kate didn't think so, but she pressed on. "Tell me what you remember about her death. Please."

She could hear her aunt sigh. "When he first asked about Mama's death in the letters, I didn't tell him much. I knew he was grieving over your mother's death, and I didn't think it was good for him to revisit Mama's. But he seemed so obsessed with it. We wrote back and forth for a while and I told him what I remembered. Then he seemed to let it drop.

"Before our move last year, I was going through boxes of stuff and getting rid of as much as possible. I came across a box from the house in Ardwell that John had given me. He said it was what was left after Pa died. He never went through it. He was so angry with Pa that he didn't want anything connected to him. I'm kind of a pack rat, and I kept the box."

If that was true, why had he supposedly kept his father's gun? That made no sense. Her aunt was silent for several minutes and Kate held her breath. "I glanced at the contents when he gave it to me and most of it looked like junk. There was a small book that looked like a diary. I didn't go through it. I wasn't in the mood so I just stored it. When I was weeding out stuff, I found the box and sent it to him. That was probably a mistake, but after all his questions I thought perhaps it would help for him to have it."

"So you don't know what all was in the box or the diary?"

"No. Kate, when we were growing up our lives were miserable, and I didn't want to be reminded. I didn't want the stuff, but I didn't want to throw it out, so I sent it to him."

Kate heard her sniff and blow her nose. She felt terrible about dredging all this up for her aunt, but she needed to know what Ellen remembered. "Tell me what happened the day of your mother's death, what you remember. Please."

Ellen huffed out a breath. "What I remember is Mama sending me out to feed the chickens and look for eggs. I was out of the house when it happened. Madelyn was up in our room. She'd been there for most of the morning, said she was doing homework. She told me to leave her alone when I asked if she wanted to come help me. Mama was heading upstairs to clean when I came down, we spoke briefly, and I went out to take care of the chickens."

Kate held her breath, afraid to speak for fear of derailing her aunt's memories. "I'd been gathering eggs for about twenty minutes when I saw Pa go into the house through the back door. A few minutes later I heard him…I don't know how to describe it… it was almost a howl. I dropped the egg basket I was carrying and ran into the house. I found him at the bottom of the stairs cradling Mama in his arms and crying. John was nearby cowering in a corner. I heard a door open upstairs and heard Madelyn ask what had happened. She came to the top of the stairs and then collapsed on the landing crying."

"I didn't know what to do, so I ran outside and grabbed one of the ranch hands. I told him what had happened, and he drove into town and brought the doctor back. She was dead, though, there was nothing to be done."

"You said Daddy was cowering in the corner, had he been there the whole time? Did he see something?"

"I don't know. Kate, I don't see the point of this. It just stirs up painful memories. And then with John's suicide—it's more than I can bear."

"I'm sorry to cause you pain, but something happened right before his suicide that he was very upset about. I need to try to find out what it was." Kate was near tears with frustration. She ran her hand over her mouth trying to figure out a way to chip at Ellen's resistance, to get her to open up.

"He mentioned dreams. Do you know anything about dreams he may have had related to his mother's death?"

"He never talked about her death. We were always close, but for a while he was so shut down that he wouldn't talk to anyone. He did what he was asked, answered when he was asked something point blank that required an answer, but otherwise wouldn't talk." Kate could hear her voice waver, and she felt terrible about asking Ellen to relive the memories.

"Madelyn and I shared a room, and John had a room to himself. I heard him cry out in his sleep, it often woke me up, but he denied having dreams or nightmares. Honestly, Kate, I think he was a traumatized little boy in an age when people pretty much ignored kids unless they were in trouble or the grownups needed them to do something. If Pa noticed what was going on, he never said so, and he certainly never did anything about it."

The bitterness in her voice triggered by speaking of her father echoed that of Kate's father. "He never noticed any of us unless it was to tell us what to do, or reprimand us, or punish us. He had always been intimidating, but after Mama's death he became angry and hateful—mostly, it seemed, with John and me."

She paused for several seconds then resumed. "He'd take his temper out on Madelyn, but she was very self-possessed. Unless she openly defied him, he would never challenge her. I never saw her cry after one of his beatings. It was like she wouldn't give him the satisfaction of thinking he'd gotten to her. He was why we all left. I'm sorry, Kate, but I can't talk about this anymore."

"I understand. I'm sorry to bring all this up for you. I have no one else to ask except Madelyn, and she's a little intimidating."

"Madelyn's a lot like Pa was. There's a hard core to her, but she means well. She was upset about Mama's death. She just wasn't one to talk about how she felt."

Kate said goodbye and hung up, weary and frustrated. The conversation hadn't helped much. It had fleshed out the story a bit, but raised as many questions as it had answered. Then it dawned on her that she hadn't asked Ellen if she knew Cody. She wasn't sure that it mattered. How much would an eleven-year-old have noticed about a budding attraction between her mother and a ranch hand?

The only two people left who might know anything were her aunts, and if Madelyn's memories were similar to Ellen's, then there was most likely nothing to find. Still she remembered the note her father had written. Who had her father wanted to talk to? Ellen had told her he hadn't asked her. Was it Madelyn? She realized, with a start, that she'd left the letters and the photos at Evan's. She sighed. She'd ask him to mail them to her.

Kate had never felt close to Madelyn. Her father hadn't either. Her aunt had never been a very demonstrative person.

"Katie, she's a hard person to get close to," he'd said after one of the rare family gatherings when Kate was in grade school.

Kate didn't like the reproving stares from her aunt if she got silly and loud. She complained to her father that evening as he sat on the side of her bed having finished reading her a bedtime story.

"Running away from home like she did when she wasn't quite sixteen was a mistake, I think."

"Didn't she have anybody to look after her like I have you?"

Her father smiled and ruffled her hair. "No, she didn't. She married, but her husband died a few years later, and she doesn't have any little puddings like you." Kate had giggled.

Kate had been a little more forgiving of her aunt after his explanation. She never knew if her aunt's childlessness was by choice or fate, but it seemed to have left her unable to relate to children in any comfortable way. Her father had remarked once that after his mother's death, Madelyn had been forced to take care of him and Ellen and she had resented it. Her husband had been wealthy and when he died, she'd never remarried. Still Kate felt sorry for her and had always tried to be extra nice whenever she was around. It hadn't been easy. Fortunately, they rarely saw her.

She wiped away the tears running down her face. She wished her father hadn't kept the letters or the photos. Why save them? Why not burn them and the sheet of paper instead of leaving the box under the floor? All they had accomplished was to stir up questions that no one could answer.

CHAPTER TWENTY-FIVE

H E WASN'T WORKING, and he knew he should be. The galleries Evan worked with would want more paintings eventually and the ones he'd completed before Kate had shown up had to cure so the paint was dry before transport. At this rate, he would have nothing to send them in the next few months.

But he couldn't leave the questions raised by the hidden documents Kate had found alone. He felt almost as driven to find answers as she did. Realistically, he wasn't sure that was possible, but he'd been unable to let it go. He wondered if it weren't an attempt to present Kate with answers for which she'd be so grateful she'd...she'd what? She'd sleep with him again? And for how long? Maybe she'd hang around until she got the answers and then disappear again.

She pissed him off. It was clear to him now, when she'd said she had wanted him, it had just been for comfort. There was nothing wrong with that, necessarily, but that wasn't what he'd wanted. He was pissed off at himself as well. Inviting her to the house the first time had been a mistake, but letting her stay the second time was an even bigger mistake.

The night with her had been intense. He'd had relationships along the way, some more serious than others, but none of them had stood the test of time. In between the more serious relationships, he'd had more than his fair share of brief encounters. Women seemed to like him, and there had always been wealthy women at his gallery openings who managed to find a way into his bed. He'd never resisted them. None of them expected or wanted any long-term connection. Attracting women had never been a problem; having any long-term interest in any of them had been. But Kate…Kate was different, had been from the start.

And too damn bad, he thought. *She was gone and not coming back. Pining over her was stupid.*

He kicked the couch before he flopped down on it. It had gotten so bad that it was hard to sleep in his bed because of the memories it stirred up and the physical consequences of those memories. He sure as hell couldn't sleep in the bed she'd slept in, so the couch seemed like the only option.

Lovesick teenagers do that, he thought, *not grown men.*

And he'd never done it.

He'd contacted his friend Craig Williams, the family practice doc in town, thinking perhaps he might have access to old medical records for Kate's grandmother. Unfortunately, it was Friday and Craig's schedule was full, but he'd told Evan to come by his house on Saturday over lunch and he'd feed him. Evan doubted that Craig knew anything about John Earnshaw's family or his mother's death, but maybe he could find the old records.

Evan couldn't remember much about the previous doctor who Craig had replaced. He'd rarely been sick as a kid and other than inoculations, sports physicals, and the occasional strep throat or tonsillitis, he hadn't spent much time with that doctor. Still it would be interesting if Craig were able to tell him anything. Maybe, if the old records were stored somewhere, there would be something worth finding and reading.

———◆———

"EVAN, COME on in." Craig, a friend since grade school, stood aside to let Evan enter his living room, and he closed the front door behind him.

After graduation, Evan had attended The Rhode Island School of Design on a scholarship to study fine arts. Craig had gone to the University of Colorado to study medicine helped by a scholarship as well. When he'd been accepted into medical school, the community chipped in to help pay his expenses. The caveat was that he would come back to Ardwell and provide a much-needed family doc for the community. Evan thought he might have felt a little like a hostage if it were him, but Craig seemed to enjoy the practice. He was a good doctor and had done well by the town.

"Thanks for the lunch invite," Evan said, holding out the six-pack he'd brought with him.

"Anytime," Craig said, taking the beer in hand. "You're not sick, are you?"

"No. I just wanted to talk with you."

"I always like to ask. It's a small town, some people get a little antsy about making a regular appointment."

"I don't envy you your job, man."

"Practicing in a small town can be tricky with everybody in everybody else's business. Come on in. I fixed some chili last night. It's always better the next day."

Evan followed him into the small kitchen, the aroma of the chili making his stomach growl in appreciation.

"Have a seat. The chili's ready, I just have to dish it up."

Evan sat in one of the old-fashioned chairs with tubular chrome frames and vinyl seat covers that surrounded a table with a scarred Formica top and chrome legs. It was a dated but homey kitchen. The physician before Craig had left the house to the city with the stipulation that it would be used as an enticement to whoever was recruited to take his place. It was small, but the town didn't charge Craig rent. It was furnished as it had always been with serviceable furniture. Craig seemed happy here. Evan hoped he was.

Craig dished up the chili and deposited a bowl by Evan, along with a plate of warmed tortillas. Small dishes containing shredded cheese, cilantro, diced onions, and diced jalapeños sat on the table.

"You serve a mean bowl of chili as I recall," Evan said, spooning all the condiments into his bowl. "Am I going to regret the jalapeños?"

"Nah, the chili's tame. I let people spice it up to their taste." He handed Evan a beer and set one down on the table for himself, loading his chili up with everything as well. They ate companionably for a while.

"So, how're things? Paintings're doing well I hear."

"Yeah, they are. There seem to be more and more people who like them. How about you? You still happy here?"

"I am. It's a nice town, always was. Good people. I'm content, which not everyone can say, these days."

"True."

"So, my old friend, what brings you here to talk to the doc? Hope you haven't caught yourself something nasty from the ladies."

Evan laughed. "God no. There haven't been a lot of ladies lately, but I'm always careful." *Except with Kate that night*, he thought. Nothing about Kate had been careful.

"Good to hear. What can I help you with? Doesn't seem like this is a social call."

"Did Doc Caulfield keep patient records? Or, for that matter, did the doc before him do that?"

"Why?"

"If they did, I'd like to look at the ones for Frances Earnshaw. She's the mother of a friend of mine, John Earnshaw, who recently passed. I'd like to see if the records could fill in some blanks about her that he didn't." Evan scooped up the last of his chili, wiped the bowl with a tortilla, and ate it.

"Kind of an odd request, man."

"I know, but John was a friend. He committed suicide, and some questions have come up as to whether he found out something about his mother's death that may have led to it. Any chance the medical files would still be around? Her death probably occurred around 1958, give or take a year."

Craig sat back in his chair and took a long swallow of his beer. "Lord that far back, probably not. Doc Caulfield practiced from 1980 until I got here in 2010. He took over from McClelland who'd been practicing in Ardwell since the forties. God only knows where those records are. And honestly, if they do exist, legally you don't have a right to go through them. You'd have to get a next of kin to sign off on that or a court order, I think. What're you looking for?"

"John was upset about something before his death, and his daughter showed up to look at the Earnshaw homestead a while back. She's concerned, based on some letters and other items she found recently, that he may have stumbled onto something relating to his mother's death that led to his suicide."

Craig smiled at him. "Yeah, I heard about his daughter. Nice looking lady, and you seemed a bit taken with her based on what the gossips report."

"Jesus, I hate living in a small town sometimes."

Craig laughed. "They're a hotbed of gossip, are they not?"

"They are." Evan sighed and used his napkin to wipe the sweat off his brow. The chili had been great but pretty fiery. "Okay, yeah I like her, a lot. But she doesn't like me so that's going nowhere. I did, however, have a long-standing friendship and…I guess love… for her father. He was like a second dad to me. If there's something to her concerns, then I'd like to find out what it is."

"I'm sorry, Evan. Suicide is the worst. Most people can come to terms with a loved one's death, eventually, but suicide just perpetuates the loss and the heartache." They finished their beers. Craig opened two more and handed one to Evan. "So tell me about this daughter."

"Why? So you can gossip with the rest of the town?"

"Hey! It's covered under doctor-patient privilege. It goes nowhere."

"I don't know what to tell you. It's like I said I like her a lot. She apparently doesn't like me much."

"How serious is it?"

"Christ, you sound just like my mother. I don't know how serious it is. It feels serious to me, but…oh hell, just leave her out of this."

Craig held up his hands in surrender. "Okay. What do you need from me?"

"Can you find out if there are records that still exist? I know you said I'd need her permission, but Craig, John's father and his mother are dead, and so is he. Why would it matter?"

"His daughter's not dead, and she's the next of kin. Sorry Evan, it's private information unless she gives you the go ahead, or a court says you can look at them. That assumes they even exist now. Record keeping wasn't as regulated as it is now. Hell, out here? Half the time they just got dumped in an incinerator after a while. But if they exist, I have to follow the rules."

"Then forget it." He pushed his chair away from the table and stood up. "I appreciate the lunch. I owe you one."

"I'll check it out. If any exist, then you can ask her. Who knows? It might give you a reason to contact her." Evan frowned at him.

"Evan, if you're that crazy about her, what's the problem? Take whatever opportunity presents itself."

Evan walked into the living room and picked up his coat and Stetson. He turned to Craig. "Thanks for lunch. If you find something let me know." He shrugged into his coat, settled the Stetson on his head and opened the door. The cold wind hit his face and he burrowed his chin into the collar of his coat as he walked to his truck and drove home. He'd realized the day after she left that he still had the letters and the photographs she'd brought with her. And he had the package.

The package and the rest of the stuff belong to her, he thought. You need to send it to her. Then let go of her and this curiosity, and get on with your life.

He snorted. As if that were going to happen.

CHAPTER TWENTY-SIX

KATE SAT AT the kitchen table and stared at her phone. It had been a very odd conversation with her Aunt Madelyn. Not that any conversation with her had ever been 'normal.' Madelyn didn't have a cell phone or an answering machine. At her mother's funeral, Kate had heard her father complain about it taking nearly a week to contact her about the death. She heard Madelyn tell him she didn't want to be at everyone's beck and call, nor did she want to feel obligated to return messages. It had taken Kate two days to finally connect with her via the older woman's landline.

"I've been traveling and haven't been home to answer calls, but I'm home now. What did you want?"

"Do you have some time to talk?"

"I wouldn't have answered the phone if I didn't."

No, she probably wouldn't have answered. Kate squirmed. Madelyn had always been able to make her feel like a child. "I um…I have some questions about your mother and what happened to her."

Madelyn cut her off. "Oh God, not you too. I spoke with your father about this after your mother died. What I told him seemed to satisfy him although I have no idea why he'd want to know about her death at this late date."

"I think my mom's death and your father's death being so close together set it off. I don't know. He was depressed after mom died then he gradually recovered. He was busy with other things that seemed to help him let go of his questions. I think he stumbled onto something before he died and it fired up all the questions again. I was hoping you'd tell me what you remember."

"What did he find?"

"I don't know, whatever it was is gone. At least it hasn't turned up. Do you have any idea what it might have been?"

"Haven't a clue. If he found something, he never told me about it." Kate could hear her rustling papers around. "I don't see the point of this. Why do you want to know?"

"I think it may have played a part in his suicide."

"Kate, your father struggled with depression all his life, or at least after Mama died anyway. Depression, that's what killed him. Not some theory or discovery about Mama's death."

"Would you humor me and tell me what you remember? I never knew about any of my grandparents. My mother's parents were dead by the time I was old enough to know or remember them, and Daddy never spoke about his parents. I'd like to know. Maybe it had nothing to do with his suicide, but I'd like to know." Kate hesitated a moment then said, "Please?"

Madelyn sighed loudly. When she responded, her voice was sharp and angry. "This is just so pointless, but fine, this is what I remember. I was up in my room that morning. I was studying, trying to prepare for a test that was coming on Monday. Ellen came up and wanted me to come help her with the chickens and collecting eggs."

Her voice lost some of its sharpness. "She was always terrified of the chickens. I told her they were just stupid birds and to scatter the feed as soon as she walked into the coop so they wouldn't flock around her. That's what scared her usually, but she kept whining about it until I got cross with her and told her to leave me alone."

She paused then resumed. "She left to get her chores done, and I heard Mama coming up the stairs speak to her. Probably twenty minutes later? Maybe less, maybe more, I can't remember, I heard a noise. Afterward I realized it was the sound of her falling down the stairs, but at the time it was just a bumping noise. I didn't think anything about it. John was always banging around the house, I figured it was him. Not long after, I heard Pa shout and he began wailing at the top of his voice. I wondered what had happened, so I opened the bedroom door and walked to the landing. I saw him cradling Mama in his arms, rocking her, and crying."

She stopped speaking. "Then what?" Kate asked softly.

"She was dead, that's what. She was lying at the bottom of the stairs. The laundry basket had tumbled down with her and there were clothes and towels scattered down the stairs, the basket lay next to her upside down. And Pa was sitting at the bottom holding her and crying. There's nothing else to tell you, Kate. It was an accident."

"Where were my father and Aunt Ellen?"

"Ellen ran in a minute or two later, said she'd heard Pa's wailing and John was crouched in the corner of the living room near the stairs. Ellen disappeared, and a while later, a ranch hand showed up with the doctor. There wasn't anything he could do," she barked a nasty laugh. "Except charge us for his damn visit and tell us what we already knew."

"Did my father come in? Or had he already been in the house?"

"No idea, I'd been in my room. He may have seen her fall though. I don't think he ever got over her death. I've often wondered if he played some part in it. I think it was at the heart of his depression, but he never spoke of it to any of us."

"What d'you mean he played some part in it?"

"As I said, he was always banging around the house, leaving things lying around, and he liked to play tricks on us. I wondered if perhaps he surprised her or maybe left one of his trucks on the stairs, something like that. Maybe it caused her to fall. I don't know and neither does anyone else."

"I don't think he remembered anything other than she fell and died. Aunt Ellen said he had dreams…"

"You've spoken with Ellen?"

"Yes. She said he had nightmares that woke her up. Did he talk to you about them, or what they were about?"

"No. We weren't close. I was five years older than he was, that's a huge age gap when you're young. He never confided in me, he talked to Ellen."

"She said he denied having dreams."

"He may well have done that. I didn't ask him. Ellen was always closer to him and nosier."

"Did you know anyone named Cody Westerholt?"

That stopped the conversation cold, and Kate had the sense that the question had surprised Madelyn. "No. What does this Cody Westerholt have to do with anything?"

"Probably nothing. His name was on a piece of paper in Daddy's footlocker," she lied. She didn't want Madelyn to know she had found the photos. She wasn't sure why, other than Madelyn had always put her on the defensive. It felt like the fewer details she gave out the better. "I just wondered if it meant anything to you."

"He was probably a friend of John's, or maybe one of the ranch hands. John often made friends with them. They were always around, but they came and went all the time. A few stayed for a while, most were gone within months of hiring on. Pa was hell to work for, and he was a horrible father. John probably latched onto one of the hands and got his strokes from the guy. He certainly never got any from Pa. None of us did."

"Okay, thanks." Maybe she didn't remember Cody. But he'd taken the photos. How could she not know him? Remembering the look Madelyn had directed at the camera, Kate doubted that but could think of no way to ask.

"Kate, let it go. It's ancient history, and it won't bring your father back."

"Thanks, probably good advice."

"It is. If you're smart, you'll follow it." Madelyn hung up without a goodbye.

Kate had forgotten to ask Madelyn if her father had talked to her about whatever was bothering him. She sighed, maybe there was no point to it. Surely she would have said if he had.

CHAPTER TWENTY-SEVEN

EVAN WAS RESTLESS. The visit with Craig had resulted in nothing helpful. He needed a change of scenery, so he headed for Greeley looking for a bar with food, a dance floor, and lonely single women. He intended to get shit-faced drunk and have some fun instead of wallowing in self-pity at home. He was in a reckless mood. Maybe he'd get laid. Who knew?

The place was loud and crowded. He found a spot at the bar, draped his coat over the back of the barstool, and flagged the bartender down, ordering a beer as he settled in to scope out the crowd. Eventually, he ordered some wings and ate a few, raising his index finger to signal the need for another beer. He had a buzz going and he did not want to lose it.

He'd checked in at a motel two blocks away, knowing, if he was lucky, he'd be in no condition to drive home. Worst case, he could walk to the motel. And, whether he walked or drove, the motel room might come in handy, he thought, as he indicated the need for another beer a few minutes later. At this rate, he might have to crawl back to the motel and that'd be just fine with him.

"You look lonely."

Evan turned to see a woman he'd guess was in her mid-twenties standing near his right shoulder. "Do I?"

"You do. Want some company?"

Evan shrugged and pulled out the barstool next to him "Have a seat."

She wasn't a stunner, but she was nice looking. She'd be prettier with less makeup he decided, but he liked the tight jeans she wore, the way her top clung to her breasts, and the way her nipples stood up when she brushed against his arm as she sat down. And that was just fine with him, too.

"Want some?" He asked pushing the wings in her direction. She helped herself to a couple as the bartender walked over to them.

"What can I get you?"

"Um, I'll have what he's having."

"Put it on my tab," Evan said.

She turned to him and smiled. It was a nice smile. "Why thank you, that's kind of you."

"You're welcome." The bartender returned shortly after with her beer.

"You look like you need some cheering up." She smiled at him and ran her hand up his thigh.

He blinked. Had she actually done that, or was he buzzed enough that he'd imagined it? "What kind of cheering up did you have in mind?"

"Maybe some dancing? Then who knows?"

"Sounds cheerful."

The band tuned up and began playing a couple of fast country songs, then the predictable couple of slow ones. He held her close and was taken aback when he felt her grind up against him more than once.

"I'd be careful if I were you," he mumbled into her hair. It didn't smell of lavender or lemon like Kate's did, but it smelled nice. Kinda fruity, he decided. "Keep that up and you could be in trouble."

"What kind of trouble?" She ground her pelvis against him again, and he closed his eyes as she pressed against his erection. "That kind of trouble?"

"Yeah, that kind of trouble," he said, placing his hand on the small of her back and pulling her tight against him as they swayed to the music.

"That sounds like fun, not trouble."

"It can be both." He was hot from the dancing and light-headed from the beers and suddenly wanted to fuck her brains out. The hell with Kate. He was tired of jerking off in the shower. It was getting downright embarrassing.

"Why don't we go find out?" she asked.

He nodded and steered her back to the bar. He closed out the tab and helped her into her coat then shrugged into his and they made their way out of the bar. They hadn't gotten more than a few feet into the parking lot when she wrapped her arms around his neck and kissed him, forcing her tongue into his mouth. It surprised him, and he pulled back.

"Let's go somewhere a little more private, okay?" He guided her to his truck and they climbed in. He wasn't totally drunk and could drive back to the motel, mostly because it was close by. He figured he could get there without getting into trouble. He put the key in the ignition, but before he had a chance to turn the truck on she began rubbing him through his jeans. He let his head drop back against the headrest. "Oh Jesus."

She unzipped his jeans, freed him, and began stroking him from base to tip, lingering to play with the tip of his erection. She stopped just short of making him come, pulled a condom out of her jeans pocket, tore the package open, and in a suspiciously expert way unrolled it down over him. She quickly shucked her jeans, climbed over his legs, and straddled him. He dimly registered she wore no panties and thought it odd—convenient, but odd.

He gasped, feeling her settle on him then begin to move energetically, rocking and gripping and releasing him till he thought his brain would explode. He raised his head and ran his hands up under her top and grasped her breasts. It didn't take long until he did explode. His head fell back against the headrest and his breath came in gasps. He kept his eyes closed, not really wanting to see the girl, not wanting to see she wasn't Kate or confront the fact he felt like he'd cheated on her.

Goddammit! He thought bitterly, *I can't even get laid without her interfering.*

The girl rose up off him and retrieved her jeans from the floor of the truck and slid back into them. "Thanks, baby, that was good. That'll be fifty bucks." She held out her hand.

"What?" He blinked at her several times in confusion.

"You heard me, fifty bucks. If you don't have it on you I know where there's an ATM."

"You're a prostitute?"

She frowned at him. "I don't care for that term one little bit. I'm putting myself through school. This helps."

"Jesus, whatever happened to scholarships or having a job?"

"I don't qualify for a scholarship, and this *is* a job. You gonna pay me or not?"

Evan carefully slid the condom off, tucked himself back into his jeans, and zipped up. He glanced around the cab of the truck trying to locate the paper fast-food bag from his lunch earlier.

He pointed to it. "Um…could you hand me that?"

She reached down, picked it up, and handed it to him her eyebrows raised, still waiting for the cash. He opened the bag and stuffed the condom into it. That was embarrassing, but he wasn't going to wander around, used condom in his hand, looking for a trash barrel. The sooner he got out of here the better.

Fishing in his back pocket for his wallet, he hoped to Christ he had fifty bucks on him. He really didn't want to spend any more time with her than he had to. He pulled the money out of his wallet and held it out. She took it and tucked it into the front pocket of her jeans.

"Thanks," she said, opening the passenger door and stepping down. "See you around, cowboy."

"I'm not a cowboy," he said to the empty truck cab. He watched her disappear back into the bar and realized he hadn't even asked her name. Honestly, he had to admit he didn't care.

You are totally fucked up, he thought as he started the truck and drove off. *Totally fucked up.*

CHAPTER TWENTY-EIGHT

ONE OF THE big mistakes of the evening, aside from sex with the working girl, was stopping at the liquor store next door to the motel and getting a six-pack of beer. He'd had too much to drink already, and he knew it, but the need to erase his thoughts about Kate and what had just happened was more important than the way he'd feel in the morning.

He saw a trashcan outside the liquor store when he got there, so he grabbed the fast food bag and dropped it in the can. It sat, embarrassingly, on the top of the garbage. He pushed at it trying to force it deeper but the can was too full. He gave up and entered the liquor store. The fast food bag sat accusingly on the top of the garbage when he emerged from the store. He shook his head in embarrassment and drove to the motel.

The problem with drinking too much, was you did things that weren't very well thought out. Like calling Kate at one a.m.

"Evan?"

He heard her sleepy voice. It washed over him like…well he didn't know what. He was having a hard time focusing, but her voice warmed him and made him wish he were holding her.

"Yep, s'me, Evan."

"Are you *drunk?*"

"Yep, totally shi-shit-faced. How 'bout you?"

"You're drunk, and you're calling me at one in the morning? Where are you?"

"Uh…oh yeah, Greeley…motel here all by my losnum, I mean lonesome. Wanna come keep me company?"

"No. Why are you in Greeley?"

"Came here to have some fun. Drank waaaay too much. Won't feel good in the morning."

"And did you have some fun?"

"Not really. Mos'ly just drunk." He sighed. He was suddenly very tired. "Miss you."

She didn't respond, but it felt good knowing she was on the other end of the call. He closed his eyes and dropped off to sleep.

———— ◆ ————

EVAN GROANED and covered his eyes with his arm. The early morning sunlight from the slightly parted curtains hit him square in the face. His mouth, which tasted vile, was dry, his tongue was stuck to the roof of his mouth, and his head pounded unmercifully. He sat up slowly, trying to forestall the pounding pain from escalating, but it didn't help.

He was sick to his stomach, and his pounding head made him feel like throwing up as he walked carefully to the bathroom and used the toilet. Standing in the hot shower, hands braced against the preformed plastic walls of the tub and shower enclosure, he wished he could think himself home. The drive back to the house was the most unappealing thing he could imagine at the moment.

Drying off, he walked to the tiny fridge sitting next to the dresser and pulled out a bottle of water. He downed most of it in several gulps and sat on the bed staring blankly at the dark TV screen sitting on the dresser top. After several minutes of staring, he finished the water and got dressed.

The drive home was torture. The sun was bright and in his eyes the whole way. He hadn't been that drunk in quite a while, and his body was not letting him forget it. He'd dropped a can of Coke out of the machine near the motel office when he checked out and sipped it on the way home. It helped relieve the nausea, and God knew he needed some relief.

He turned into his driveway and parked. The house was quiet and welcoming. He found a bottle of aspirin and swallowed several. In the bedroom, he shucked off his boots and fell onto the bed, dragging the comforter over himself and dropping off to sleep.

What the hell was ringing? He thought groggily. *Phone. It's the phone.*

He felt the top of the bedside table and found nothing. Realizing he was still dressed, he felt his pockets until he found it and fished it out. Squeezing his eyes closed and then trying to focus on the screen he saw it was Kate and his mood lifted. He hit the green button.

"Hello?"

"Did you get home okay?"

"What?" *Oh fuck me,* he thought, *did I call her last night?*

"Did you get home, or are you still in Greeley?"

Jesus Christ on a boat, I did.

"Uh, yeah. I…guess I must have called you."

"You did, at one in the morning."

Evan closed his eyes and sighed. "I'm…sorry. I was…"

"I know, shit-faced, you told me."

God, could it get any worse? "Look Kate, I'm sorry. It's no excuse but I was drunk, very drunk. I'm sorry I bothered you."

There was silence for a minute. She sighed heavily. "I owe you an apology. The excuse for your behavior last night is being drunk. My excuse is a head that's totally screwed up. You're sober, I'll probably always be screwed up. I'm sorry for what happened."

He tried his best to tamp down the hope that her comment had meant anything. "I can deal with screwed up if you can deal with shit-faced drunk phone calls late at night."

"I can't do this, Evan, I'm sorry. I just wanted to apologize for my behavior. I shouldn't have come to you or led you on or treated you so badly. I'm sorry," she said softly. More businesslike, she said, "I imagine you're not feeling all that well right now, so I'll say goodbye and let you recuperate. I just wanted to make sure you were all right."

He thought he'd heard a hitch in her voice. "Kate?"

"What?"

"I miss you."

"I know, you mentioned that last night," she said, her voice softening.

The phone went dead, and Evan saw she'd disconnected. He was done trying. She wasn't interested and wasn't going to be. He'd just have to get used to it.

CHAPTER TWENTY-NINE

"**YOU WANT TO** look at what?" Sheriff Taylor frowned at Evan.

"The official police record for the death of Frances Earnshaw. I think it happened around 1958, but it could have been '57 or '59."

"Why?"

"John Earnshaw was troubled before he died, and his daughter has found some notes that make both of us believe he discovered something that led to his death. I'd like to see the police report and see what it says."

"How'd he die? I heard he just passed. Was there something that makes his death unusual?"

"He committed suicide. Kate, his daughter, is trying to find out why. There was no note."

Taylor shook his head. "I'm sorry to hear that. I didn't know him well, but he seemed like a nice guy. Suicides don't always leave notes. I wouldn't take a lack of one as a sign that his death was anything other than suicide. Did the police indicate that there were reasons to think otherwise?"

"I don't think so, Kate never mentioned that. Would it be possible for me to see the record?"

Taylor watched him for a moment, then raised his eyebrows and blew out a breath. "Evan, that's quite a while ago. My deputy put the old paper records on digital files a few years back. It's a small town. There weren't a ton of them to copy. They were mostly the usual shit—vandalism, drunk and disorderly, the occasional neighborly dispute, but nothing serious, no suspicious deaths or murders. Still, I'm not sure we have records that far back."

"Would you look?"

"Yeah, I can look, but we don't make police files available to the public."

"It happened a long time ago. None of the participants live here, or they're dead. What harm would it be to let me look? I'd do it here, with you present."

"I'll see if I can find them. If I do, don't ya think the daughter ought to be present as well, since she's next of kin?"

Evan sighed. "If you find the report, let me know and I'll talk to her."

"She doesn't know you're looking into this?"

"She knows," Evan lied. "I don't want to bother her if it turns out there's nothing to look at."

"Okay, I'll let you know. I should be able to tell you in a day or two. I'm not familiar with searching those records on the computer so I'm gonna have to have my deputy help with that. And don't let it out that I let ya see the report or I'll have every Tom, Dick, and Harry in here asking for a look at reports."

"Thanks, Sheriff. I appreciate it."

———◆———

THE GALLERY was slow. There hadn't been a visitor in several hours even though it was a Saturday. Kate sat at her desk and used the computer to research Evan, while listening for the tinkle of the bell over the door alerting her to a visitor. She wasn't sure why she was checking him out other than curiosity about his art. He worked with two galleries, one in Denver and one in Los Angeles. Clicking on the links to the galleries, she found photos of his canvases and was taken aback. They were stunning.

She smiled seeing several canvases depicting cows in various situations. He really did like them apparently. But to be fair, they were beautiful renderings of life on a ranch or farm. One depicted a blizzard with cows huddled together seeking shelter from the wind and snow under winter-bare cottonwood trees. Another showed cows queuing up to a feed truck with a ranch hand dropping bales of hay off the end of the truck bed.

Kate sighed. All her life she'd wanted to be able to paint like this and couldn't. His talent could have been what attracted her father. Her strength lay in finding paintings that were destined to be great amid the general chaff of paintings for sale. Doug, her boss, relied on her for that, and she supposed it was a talent of sorts. She had a talent for restoration as well, but that wasn't creation as much as repairing what had already been created. She certainly didn't have the talent Evan had.

He was doing very well. His small canvases were selling for nearly five thousand and his larger ones ran anywhere from ten to twenty thousand based on their size and complexity.

"You're not planning to jump ship, are you?" Doug asked, surprising her. He'd come up behind her and saw what she was looking at.

"No...no of course not. I've just heard of this artist and was curious."

"He's pretty hot, if you like representational western art." Doug sat a hip on the edge of her desk. "He was interviewed in *Art Digest* recently and one of the Barkheists bought several of his canvases for their home and a couple for their hotels."

Kate's eyebrows lifted. The Barkheists were a very wealthy family in the Denver area, patrons of several charities, and they owned a four-star hotel chain. She hadn't thought of Evan as quite that successful. Once again, she'd let her disdain for Ardwell color her opinion of Evan. His "miss you" kept replaying in her mind. If she were honest with herself, she missed him too. She shook her head. He clearly was better off without her in her current frame of mind, and that was unlikely to change.

———•◆•———

"I KNOW you're going to think this call is just a ploy to get you up here and try to talk you into resuming whatever we started, but it's not. The doc and the sheriff have found the original records of your grandmother's death and you need to be here to see them—at least to see the medical stuff. I can't access those records without your consent, and the sheriff thought you might want to see the police report. It might be worthwhile to see them."

"You've been looking into this?"

Evan sighed. This was either going to go well or it was going to blow up in his face. "Yeah, I've been looking into it. It's none of my business, but I cared for your dad and I wanted to help if I could. I'm sorry if I've overstepped."

He was about to hang up when she said, "I'd like to see them."

"When?"

"I could come up on Thursday, I'll need to ask for Friday off."

"Okay, let me know."

"I'll stay at the B & B."

"Oh, for Christ's sake, I'm not going to try to seduce you. There's no reason to pay for a room when you can stay here for free. Up to you. Let me know if you change your mind. I'm not entitled to look at the medical records unless you're there, so I'll wait to hear from you. Or not." He disconnected.

"*Goddammit!*" He swore and kicked the overstuffed chair in the living room sending it skittering across the hardwood floor a few feet.

———◆———

KATE WANTED to see the records, badly. She had no idea what they'd contain or whether it would help solve the riddle of her father's death, but she wanted to see them. The conversations with her aunts had been disappointing, and after talking to them, she hadn't had any idea how to proceed. She had begun to think it would be better to just let go of the whole search for evidence or an explanation. But Evan had found the medical and police records, and the need to know had fired up all over again.

His meddling was just one more irritation. He acted like he had some right, because of his friendship with her father, to butt into this. He'd had the presence of mind to at least ask about them, though, it had never occurred to her. Their existence was the only hook she needed to be drug into this again.

She should have told him she wasn't interested and then made private arrangements to view the records. But it was a small town. If she showed up without him, the whole town would hear about it and so would he. She didn't want to hurt his feelings or embarrass him, and she had to admit he had cared for her father. Maybe he did have a right to see them.

Doug had closed the gallery at noon, heavy snow was predicted and traffic in the gallery was slow. At home, she added the last item to her overnight bag and headed to the car. She'd made reservations at the B & B and only planned to stay overnight. If nothing was gained by looking at the old records, then she was letting go of the entire puzzle. It was past time. Despite her sense that there was something seriously off about it, her father had killed himself, and in all probability, she would never know why. After she saw the records, she was going to let go and try to get on with her life.

When she got to the B & B, it was snowing steadily, and she was glad she'd arrived before it got dark. Hazel seemed glad to see her and showed her to the same small room she'd stayed in before.

"It looks like the snow's really starting to come down, it's good you got here early. I was worried the drive would be awful," Hazel said as Kate set her bag down on the bench at the foot of the double bed.

"I was relieved to get here. I don't like driving in the snow. I grew up in Colorado, but snow makes drivers here a little nuts."

Hazel chuckled. "Yes, it does. I'll leave you to settle in. There are extra blankets in the closet if you need them. It's getting pretty cold. If you don't want to go out for dinner, you're welcome to join Bill and me. Nothing fancy, just meatloaf, green beans, and mashed potatoes, but there's plenty of it."

"Thank you. Let me get settled and think about it. I'll let you know in a bit." She unpacked her bag and then debated about calling Evan. Maybe it'd be better to call him in the morning and figure out a time to meet. In which case where she stayed wouldn't be up for further debate.

———◆———

IT WAS Friday night and Joe's Bar, being pretty much the only entertainment in town, meant that anyone who wanted to be entertained was there, including Kelsey the hostess who'd been absent the first time Kate had come to the bar.

The drive up in the snow had been long and stressful. She'd declined the offer of dinner, and Hazel had given her a key to the front door before she left. The walk to the bar helped to stretch her legs and get outside her head. Kate didn't plan to stay at the bar any longer than it took to eat, then head back, get cozy, and hope to get some sleep.

No wine to be had, and she wasn't going to drink beer, so she ordered one of the much-touted margaritas and the chicken enchiladas. The drink was strong and, as advertised, delicious, as were the enchiladas. She dug in and began to relax. About half way through her meal she caught the shadow of someone who'd approached her table and looked up.

"How about some company, little lady?"

She hated the way men in this town talked to women. He was a big, beefy guy with a shaved head, one of those long, mustache-less beards that seemed to be popular for reasons that mystified her, and half sleeves of tattoos on both arms. What she could make out were skulls and dragons.

"No thanks, I'm just here for dinner."

"Dinner's a good time for company," he said, pulling out the chair on the opposite side of the table.

"Thanks, but I really don't want company."

"Not very friendly, are you."

"Not tonight, I'm not. But I'm sure there are plenty of other women here who are."

She saw Evan enter the bar and closed her eyes momentarily. He probably had guessed she'd arrived and would eat at Joe's. The big guy didn't move, so despite not being through with either her food or drink and not wanting a confrontation with this guy or Evan, Kate gathered her purse, shrugged into her coat, and stood up, signaling the waitress for the bill. She motioned for Kate to come to the bar, but as she tried to move past the guy, he reached for her arm.

"Hey now, just sit down and we can talk. No harm in that is there?"

"Take your hand off me. Now."

He laughed. "Or what?"

"Or you're going to get your fucking arm broken," she heard Evan say.

Kate glanced up sharply and saw Evan standing next to her. The look on his face left no doubt that he'd follow through with the threat, and the guy let go.

"No need to get all riled up, I didn't know she was yours."

"I don't belong to *anyone*, you ass." Kate pushed her way past him and ignoring Evan, headed to the bar to pay her tab. Handing the waitress the money and a tip she made her way out into the street and began walking toward the B & B.

"When did you get here?" Evan called out behind her.

She stopped and turned around. "A couple of hours ago."

"Were you going to call me?"

"In the morning." Kate could see the flash of anger on his face before he could suppress it.

"I'm surprised. I didn't figure you'd call at all."

"Evan…"

He held his hand up to stop her. "I'd appreciate it if you'd let me come and hear what the Sheriff and Craig have to say. Up to you though."

"That's fine."

"Thanks." He dipped his head, touched the front brim of his Stetson, and started to turn away.

"Evan…"

He stopped. "No, I get it. You don't belong to anyone, certainly not me. I get it, I'm not stupid." He turned around and began to walk away then turned back. "But I *want* you to belong to me. I get that's not what you want, so it's not going to happen. But it's a damn shame."

With that, he turned and walked away, leaving her standing in the street with snow falling around her and an ache in her heart.

CHAPTER THIRTY

AFTER ALL THE work he'd done to find the records, it made no sense to exclude Evan from the results. Kate called him the next morning to give him a chance to decline coming with her, if being with her was too awkward after his comment last night. He agreed to come and pick her up at the B & B. Conversation between them, however, had been minimal and uncomfortable on the phone and on the way to the sheriff's office.

"Complete fracture of the C3 vertebra which severed her spinal cord. You'll have to talk to the doc for a translation of the rest of the report." Sheriff Jackson said holding out the autopsy report to Kate. "The sheriff at the time interviewed Earnshaw, the kids, and the ranch hands."

He swiveled back and forth on his office chair. "The ranch hands were unwilling to talk for the most part, claimed they hadn't seen anything and wouldn't comment on the Earnshaw's relationship. My guess is they were afraid Earnshaw would fire them if they said anything about his wife or his relationship with her. There'd been rumors about her and one of the ranch hands, but the guy had left the ranch three to four days before her death. When they tried to locate him for an interview, he couldn't be found."

"Earnshaw allowed them to interview the kids. The two girls hadn't witnessed the fall, but related what they knew. The son wouldn't respond to their questions. He seemed pretty shell-shocked, and they figured he witnessed her fall. It looked like an accident and there was nothing to say otherwise, so that was that."

"Can I have copies of these reports?"

His brows drew together, and he pursed his lips. "I'm not supposed to do that, but it's an old closed case so I guess there wouldn't be any harm in it. Why do you want them?"

"Just to have them." Kate clutched the papers in her hands. "After talking to both my aunts and you, I think my father saw something. He never talked about his mother's death to his sisters, or anyone that I know of. He had nightmares after it happened but claimed he didn't."

Kate sat back in her chair and sighed. "Maybe it's as simple as he remembered what happened and he couldn't live with it. Little boys play tricks on people, they're noisy and boisterous. Maybe he surprised her or startled her, and she missed a step and fell and he felt responsible. I'll probably never know. If I could have copies, I would appreciate it."

The Sheriff nodded and took the reports from her, disappearing into a back office. Evan hadn't spoken at all, and Kate wasn't sure if he was angry with her or simply taking a back seat as an observer. She planned on returning home after they met with the doctor who had found her grandmother's medical records, so it really didn't matter, she guessed, but she was sorry it had come to this.

It had continued to snow through the night, and there was about six inches on the ground with snow continuing to fall. If she were to get home and not be stuck in Ardwell she needed to leave in the next few hours. If the weather was bad, she'd drive to Greeley and spend the night. She didn't want to stay another night in Ardwell. What Evan had said to her had rattled her and she was becoming more and more claustrophobic in the small town. She wished to God her father had gotten rid of the property and hadn't left it to her. She wished he'd burned the letters and destroyed what was in the metal box. None of this would have happened if he had. But, like his suicide, there was no undoing it.

———•◆•———

THE DOCTOR, who Evan had explained was a long-time friend, had asked that they meet him at his office.

"Craig thanks for doing this." Evan tilted his head toward Kate. "This is Kate Earnshaw, John's daughter."

Kate shook his extended hand, and he ushered them into his office. "I'm surprised I found the chart. Dr. McClelland apparently kept his records pretty well. They were stored in the basement here, so they're a bit musty."

Kate handed him the autopsy report. "Can you decipher this for me?"

Evan sat, as he had at the police station, without comment or questions as Craig read through the autopsy report. "With the fracture she sustained, there really was no chance she'd survive. C3 is a high vertebral fracture site." He pointed vaguely to a place high on the back of his neck.

"That's a dangerous area for a fracture. The complete severing of her spinal cord meant that the nerves from that point down, including those controlling breathing and circulation, were unable to function. I imagine her death was very quick. A fall down a long flight of stairs would do it, depending on how she landed and how her head and neck were bent."

"Were there any other findings, like tissue under her fingernails or defensive wounds?"

Craig shook his head. "It doesn't mention any defensive wounds, but it was the fifties, they didn't do the extensive forensic evaluations that we do now unless there was something that suggested foul play. It's unlikely they'd have checked for that, and many of the tests we use now for toxicology and DNA were just emerging back then. Remember too, this is a small town and the medical examiner wouldn't have had access to those types of tests if they were available. To do that, they would have had to take her body to Denver. It looked like an accident, and there was nothing to say differently. The autopsy was essentially to confirm what had killed her."

Kate sighed. "Okay. Was there anything else that seemed out of the ordinary?"

"She was pregnant at the time, according to the autopsy. It was early enough that she probably wasn't sure of it, although she probably suspected it. According to McClelland's chart, she'd had three living children and two stillborn babies. His notes indicate that the husband was pretty upset when the sheriff told him about the autopsy results. Sounds like he was sure it wasn't his."

"Cody," Kate said quietly. Unexpectedly Evan reached out, took her hand, and squeezed it. Then he dropped it quickly as if he'd touched something hot.

Craig paused, and shifted uncomfortably in his chair. "He also notes visits from her for injuries that, if she'd been my patient, I would have tagged as abuse related and tried to put a stop to it. It was a different time, though, and he didn't intervene."

"Can I have a copy of the chart?" Kate frowned and tried to discretely wipe at her eyes. *No wonder Daddy never wanted to talk about his life,* she thought.

"I guess it wouldn't hurt." He paused and gave her a slight smile laced with empathy. "Your grandmother's death happened a long time ago, Kate. I'm sorry about what happened to her and very sorry about your father. Suicide is so hard to deal with and leaves so many questions. Sometimes all you can do is figure that the person was in serious enough pain to want to die and accept that, unless he or she left a note, there's no way to know what the reason was. It's hard, but keeping the wound open just prolongs the pain."

Kate nodded her head and didn't respond. It was just so hopeless, and her heart broke for her father. What a horrible life he'd had.

"I'm gonna go start the truck, get the heater going," Evan said getting up.

Craig excused himself and returned with a manila envelope with all the papers in it. Kate tucked the copies of the police report from the sheriff in there as well and said goodbye.

CHAPTER THIRTY-ONE

IT WAS STILL snowing when she walked out to the truck. Evan opened the door for her and then spent several minutes clearing snow from the windshield before getting in. A frown had taken up residence on his face.

"It sounds as if it probably was an accident," he said, turning toward her. "Your theory about your father may be exactly what happened. He may have surprised her and that caused her to fall, which set off the dreams and the withdrawal, then he suppressed the memory. Maybe some event triggered his memory."

Evan took a huge breath and continued. "The package your dad sent me, the one I told you about, arrived before his death. You said you didn't want it, that I should keep it." He reached across her to get to the glove compartment where he retrieved the wrapped package. "Anyway, I opened the package last night, and it's a diary, it might have belonged to your grandmother. Do you want it? I didn't read it."

"No, I don't want it. She's not going to reveal how she died. She might confirm that Cody's the father of her baby but with an abusive husband that's not likely. They're all dead and so's the child so it's irrelevant now. You can keep the other stuff I left at the house as well."

Evan watched as she held the copies in the oversized envelope that Craig had given her, clutched to her chest.

"Your friend is right. I'm torturing myself. I'll never know why he killed himself and in the end what does it matter? He's gone, Cody's gone, and my aunts know nothing helpful. I only hope that he's found some peace now, and that he's with mom and happy."

She looked down at the envelope as if it was the first time she'd seen it. "In fact, just take these." She thrust the envelope at him. "I don't know what possessed me to ask for copies. He gave the diary to you, keep it, do what you want with it. It's like I said, it's just one more thing he shared with you that he didn't share with me."

"Kate…"

She shook her head abruptly. "No, it's true. You're the son he never had, I was just window dressing. He could share things with you that, for whatever reason, he felt he couldn't with me, and that can't be corrected. I just wish he'd burned the letters and his notes rather than hide them, and I wish he'd never left me the property. But this searching for answers is pointless and just too heartbreaking for me. I'd like to go back to the B & B and head home."

He put the truck in gear and headed to the B & B. "The snow's predicted to get worse. They're saying it'll probably turn into a blizzard before long. Wait until tomorrow, please, till the weather's better."

"I can't stand to be here any longer."

Evan shook his head and stopped in the street outside the B & B. "I'm going home, and I won't come back into town, so you don't have to be afraid you'll run into me or that I'll force myself on you."

Kate turned to him. "Evan that's not the problem. You don't frighten or threaten me in any way. In fact, there's a part of me that wishes desperately I had met you under different circumstances.

But I don't think you understand. He took you under his wing, he shared things with you that he never did with me. He never even *mentioned* you to me or that he helped you build your house. Clearly you were important to him and not something he wanted to share with me."

She stared out the windshield at the swirling snow. "I feel like…like the two of you *erased* me. I can't look at you without this anger toward him, and this jealousy toward you, welling up and taking over. It's not your fault…I just can't do this right now. I'm a mess. I'm sorry about coming to you when I was last up here. I felt so alone, but it wasn't right and it wasn't fair to you."

Kate clutched her hands together. She wore no gloves and her fingers were white with the cold. "I care about you Evan, I wish things were different, but I can't figure out how to get past my father and what you meant to him. I'm so sorry."

She turned to the truck's passenger door and opened it. Stepping out into the snow she said again, "I'm so sorry," and closed the door.

He watched the wind and snow buffet her. It whipped her hair in a cloud around her face as she walked to the door of the B & B, looking as if she were trapped in a snow globe, before she disappeared inside.

"I'm sorry too," he said, putting the truck in gear and driving toward home.

————◆————

EVAN PUT the truck in the garage and walked into the house, dropping the large envelope on the kitchen island along with the diary that he'd rewrapped in its original package. He fixed himself a drink, walked over to the fireplace and turned it on, settling on the couch and staring blankly at the gas flames, his stockinged feet propped on the coffee table. He'd left the house lights off and as afternoon moved toward evening, the house grew dark. The weather had gotten considerably worse, and he was worried about Kate trying to drive back.

He fished his phone out of his shirt pocket and called the B & B. "Hazel, it's Evan Hastings, I was calling to see whether Kate Earnshaw had decided to stay until the weather improved or if she left."

"Well, she came back and checked out. I suggested she stay, what with the weather and all, but she said she had to get back to Denver. Hope she made it before they closed the highway."

Evan frowned. "I hadn't heard that they closed it. Okay, I just wondered."

"They just closed it an hour ago. She had plenty of time to make it at least to Greeley or the interstate. Try not to worry." When Evan didn't respond she said, "She has a cell phone, if she gets into trouble, she'll call or text you."

Except she won't. "Thanks Hazel, stay inside and stay warm."

"Same to you."

He stood at the living room window and watched the snow blowing outside the house. It had turned into quite a storm. He wondered whether he ought to drive to the point where they'd closed the highway in case she'd gotten into a jam. He shook his head. He wasn't her knight in shining armor. She had a phone. She could call the highway patrol or AAA if she needed help. Just then his phone pinged, and he brought up the text.

<Safe in Greeley. Plan to stay the night.>

He shook his head, relieved but annoyed that she clearly knew he'd be worried, and returned the phone to his jeans pocket not intending to respond. Then he fished it out and texted back a 'thumbs up' emoji and let it go at that.

———◆———

IT HAD been a hellish drive in near whiteout conditions to get to Greeley where she stopped for the night, hoping the roads would be better in the morning. According to the news, CDOT had finally closed the highway between Greeley and Ardwell because of blowing and drifting snow. She'd made it out just in time.

It took some time before she'd found a hotel with a vacancy and settled in. The hotel had a restaurant, and the food didn't look bad, but she wasn't hungry. At least they had wine. Two glasses in, the exhaustion from driving in the snowstorm hit, and it was all she could do to make it back to her room and fall into bed.

She'd texted Evan to let him know she'd made it to Greeley and received his thumbs up. Drifting off to sleep, she thought about him. Here was a man she could have something good with, a man who wanted something good with her, and she'd put up walls. Not walls that could be breached, but impenetrable walls that she hid behind.

What she had told him was true though, her anger and jealousy and grief stood between them. And now, more than likely he'd reached his limit for being jerked around. Once she had her head on straight, she doubted he'd be interested. Her eyes drifted shut, blocking out the memory of Evan and her father and the raw emotions she carried with her.

CHAPTER THIRTY-TWO

*"**B**UT MOMMY, WHY'S Daddy like that?" Her mother knelt in front of her and took her hands.*

"Daddy's not feeling well, Kate."

"But he just sits there, he won't talk to me. Did I make him mad?"

"No sweetheart. Daddy gets sick sometimes, and it's hard for him to talk or do much of anything until it passes."

"Should he go to the doctor?"

Her mother smiled and hugged her. "Don't you worry, the doctor knows, and he says Daddy will be fine."

Daddy didn't look fine and neither did Mommy. "But Mommy…"

"How would you like Jessica to take you to a movie?"

Kate wondered why it felt like Mommy wanted her gone, she wanted to ask, but Mommy looked worried. Instead she went with Jessica. She was six years old, she didn't need a babysitter, but she was pretty sure Mommy didn't want her there or to leave Daddy alone.

Kate sat up in the dark and was grateful for her familiar bedroom. She'd been stuck in Greeley another night until the snow finally stopped and the highway crews had managed to clear the main roads to make the interstate more drivable. It had been a slow slog home, people either driving forty miles an hour or well above the sixty-five mile an hour speed limit. She'd white-knuck-led it all the way, afraid she wouldn't notice how slow someone was going until it was too late or that one of the lunatic speeders would spin out of control and collide with her.

The dream drifted back to her as she lay down and pulled the covers up over her shoulders. She remembered those periods when her father had gone into a depression that lasted sometimes for several weeks. Even when little, and had no name for it, she knew that his illness was different than just being sick. Visitors didn't come, her mother didn't leave the house except when Jessica could come over and give her a chance to grocery shop or run other errands. And her mother spent a fair bit of time on the phone with her father's employees to keep the construction jobs running.

Her mother would sit next to her father and read to him, talk to him, or take him out for walks. She would bring him to the table and insist he eat something. She helped him dress each day and brought him out to sit in his recliner where she would try to engage him in conversation. Occasionally Kate would wake up after hearing her father cry out or shout something before hearing her mother's soothing voice trying to calm him.

Eventually it would pass and when it did, no one mentioned what had transpired. At a young age Kate had understood, in the instinctive way kids seemed to, that talking about it outside of the house was not okay. It had always felt to her as if talking about it to her mother or to her father after his emergence from an epi-sode would somehow, possibly trigger another. So after a few brief conversations when she was very young, like the one she'd dreamt about, she never said anything.

As she lay in the dark, she remembered how in her teens her father seemed to go for a very long time without suffering the kind of depression she'd witnessed as a kid. Going through his bedroom and bathroom after his death, she'd found a prescription antide-pressant among his blood pressure meds. The last real depression he'd experienced was after her mother's death. He'd functioned then, he hadn't shut down completely, but he had drifted through his days in a fog of sadness. Perhaps the antidepressant had prevented it from worsening. Before his death maybe the drug had stopped working and that's why he killed himself. Maybe the cops were right, and it was suicide.

Aside from her mother's death, she'd often wondered what triggered the earlier episodes. It was never clear to her if there was a cause, but being a kid she might not have been able to connect the dots. She'd decided to stop pursuing these fruitless efforts to discover what had happened. She'd contemplated contacting the physician whose name was on the prescription when she found the meds, but at the time there were so many other more pressing issues to take care of she'd put that on the back burner. Maybe she should do that.

Maybe I should make up my damn mind, she thought in frustration.

"I'M SORRY Ms. Earnshaw, privilege extends to a client even after death. Without a court order, I can't discuss what your father and I talked about."

"But…I can't figure out why he killed himself. It might help if you could tell me what triggered the depressive episodes."

"I'm sorry, I can't."

"Can you at least tell me if he contacted you right before his death? Did he say anything to you about meeting with someone? Did he tell you what he was upset about?"

The man on the other end of the phone sighed. "I can't." Kate began to cry then. "Ms. Earnshaw, all I will say is that I wasn't aware that your father was contemplating suicide or I would have done my best to intervene. Contact your father's lawyer and ask that he get a court order so that I can discuss this with you."

"It's just one dead end after another. I can't find anyone who can help."

"Sometimes answers aren't possible. Sometimes it's just what it seems, a person reaches the end of his or her rope and decides to end it. If I can be of any help to you, other than discussing your father, please feel free to call me. I'm sorry I haven't been able to answer your questions. Get a court order, then I can."

Kate hung up and wiped the tears from her eyes. She didn't need psych help—at least she didn't think she did—she needed answers. Maybe it was worthwhile to contact her father's lawyer and see if she could get access to the information. She sighed. Continuing to pursue this was like picking at a scab, the wound never healed and, in the end—when you forced yourself to leave it alone and let it heal—the scar was much worse than it needed to be. But she couldn't stop picking at it.

———— ✦ ————

"KATE, WHY do you want to do this?" Her father's lawyer looked at her with the same pity she'd seen in Craig Williams' eyes.

"My father was not suicidal. I saw him two days before his death. He was fine. Something was bugging him, but he wasn't depressed. The psychologist won't tell me anything. He said I'd have to get a court order. I want one."

"He also told you that he had no idea your dad was suicidal. If he didn't know or had no idea that your dad was that depressed, I don't see how his notes will help."

"I won't know until I see his notes."

"I don't see how seeing them will help."

"It may not, nothing else has, but I want to know. I want to see his records, so do what you need to do to get them."

The lawyer shook his head and then nodded. "Okay, if that's what you want."

"It's what I want."

CHAPTER THIRTY-THREE

EVAN FORCED HIMSELF to work. He had several unfinished canvases and none of them required him to think of something new to paint. All they required was for him to finish them. The work enveloped him as it always did, pulling him into the paintings, requiring his full attention and skill. It had always been a refuge and, during the day, it took his mind off Kate and her father. Once he'd stopped for the day, however, it was another matter. To avoid the thoughts, he often worked late into the evening until exhaustion took over and he could sleep.

He'd stowed the envelope and the diary in his office and left them there. He'd been angry since she'd left and digging further into the diary would just prolong the agony, so he put it where he wouldn't see it and obsess about it. He tucked his portrait of her away in his storage rack turning it so he wouldn't see that either. He did the same with the portrait John had done of him.

A simmering heat of anger toward Kate and her father followed him like his shadow. Why the hell hadn't John told her about him and why the fuck was that *his fault*? Why hadn't John explained to her what he was doing or brought her with him so they could have met? And he was pissed at himself for allowing her to convince him he was more than a temporary source of comfort. She'd managed to make him stop listening to that little voice, so he could make love to her and get his fucking hopes up. Time to move on, he told himself every time he began to think about her. So far moving on had been impossible.

He stood at his bedroom window and looked out across the snowy fields toward the fence separating his land from Fred Johnson's and watched the cows bedded together in the snow. He knew they'd eventually end up on someone's table, but they had a pretty peaceful life until then. He often found himself caught up in absurd fantasies about keeping the current herd on his property and just letting them live out their lives.

He'd grown up in Ardwell and he knew what life in a farming and ranching community was like. Farm animals were food and profit, not pets. And pets were expendable too. Barn cats had shelter, and they were useful in keeping rodent populations under control, but they were on their own for food and at the mercy of predators. Dogs were useful and when they weren't, they were put down. When horses were no longer rideable, they were either put down or sold for meat or glue. It wasn't true for everyone, but it was a cold, practical way of life.

He'd never quite fit into that mentality. That infuriating need to rescue had gotten him into trouble more than once with neighbors and townspeople, and it had played a part in his attraction to Kate. He wished he could go back to the peaceful life he'd had before she had shown up on her father's property. Granted, his life had been a little isolated and lonely at times, but it had been peaceful and had a daily rhythm that wasn't constantly irritated and frustrated by her.

One step at a time. He'd heard his mother say it more than once. Actually, she'd said it enough times it pissed him off to hear it, but he supposed she was right. He realized he'd forgotten to get back to his parents after talking to his mother. It would be Thanksgiving in a week. *It might be a nice break to see them for a day or two*, he thought, picking up his phone and making the call.

———◆———

THE HOUSE smelled wonderful when he walked in. The smell of roasting turkey and stuffing competed with the scent of pumpkin pie and reminded him what a good cook his mother was. He put his coat away in the hall closet and made his way to the kitchen where he deposited the two bottles of wine he'd brought.

"Evan!" his mother cried, turning from the bowl of boiled potatoes she was mashing to smile at him. "You made it, I'm so glad. Your friend didn't come?" She'd extended an invitation to Kate, which he had not delivered.

"No, I didn't ask her." He really didn't want to talk about it, but he guessed she was going to pursue the subject.

"That's too bad. I was looking forward to meeting her."

He sighed. She was relentless. "Mom, I don't know how many times I have to say this, but nothing's happening there. Nothing. So, just let it go."

She put down her potato ricer and flung an arm around his neck, pulling him in for a kiss on the cheek. "Well, she doesn't know what she's missing."

"Yeah, the food smells delicious as always."

His mother rolled her eyes. Clearly the food was not what she'd meant. "Your father is watching the parade, go on in and say hi."

"Do you need help?"

"Heaven's no, go." So he went.

His father was ensconced in his recliner and nursing a drink. "Damn things, they blow all over the place," he muttered as one of the cartoon blimps on the screen wavered dangerously. "I never understood why people go to watch the parade in person. Can you imagine being in a crowd that big? All those people crowding in to watch the parade and freezing their asses off and probably getting their pockets picked while they freeze."

Evan laughed. "It's part of the fun, I guess."

His father snorted and took another drink. "Help yourself." He raised his glass and used it to indicate the wet bar on the back wall of the living room. Evan walked over and poured himself two fingers of scotch then sat on the couch. "Your mother said you wanted to talk to me about the Earnshaws. How come?"

"Curious I guess."

"She also said you'd taken up with John Earnshaw's daughter and it wasn't going well." Evan blew out a breath and shook his head. His father waved his hand in the air dismissively. "If you don't want to talk about it, that's fine with me. Can't really help with woman problems. I got enough on my hands with your mother."

Evan had to laugh. His parents had been married forty-three years and counting. Both seemed to love each other and be very well suited as far as he could tell.

"Nothing to talk about there anyway," Evan replied, sipping his scotch and settling into the couch. He could hear his mother banging around in the kitchen.

"Then why the curiosity about the Earnshaws, hoping to score some points with her?"

"What *is it* with you two? It has nothing to do with her. I knew her father, John, we were friends, and he committed suicide. He was always very private. I'd like to know him better, know what went on with his family." Evan sighed. "I miss him. I feel guilty that I didn't suspect he was having problems, and wasn't able to intervene. I didn't even know he was gone until she arrived on his property."

"Sorry to hear that. I knew him as a kid in school. He was a nice kid. None of them Earnshaws were very social though. The kids didn't, or weren't allowed, to stay in town and hang out with friends, if they had any. We weren't friends, I was older, but Clark Talcott and John were."

"Clark, the pharmacist in town?"

"Yep. They hung out all the time at school and Clark would walk with John nearly all the way home some days."

"What d'you remember about his mother's death? Anything?"

His father muted the TV and scratched his chin a few times. "Not much. I never heard John talk about it. He may have talked to Clark, but Clark was good at keeping confidences. Guess that's good since he knows everyone in town's medical problems, being the pharmacist and all."

"What do you remember?"

"She fell down the stairs and broke her neck. It was an accident is what I heard. All I know is that John and his next oldest sister, Ellen, were pretty shook up about it. He just sort of went through the day at school in a daze for quite a while. He looked wasted, tired. Maybe he wasn't sleeping well. Ellen cried a lot as I remember."

"What about Madelyn?"

"She was in high school then, so was I. I never had much contact with her. She never showed how she felt one way or another, but I heard guys talk. You know when you're that age, you want to make yourself out to be a lot savvier than you are."

"Yeah? In what way."

His father frowned and took another sip. "Well, you know teenage boys, they exaggerate, brag, and just plain lie about their exploits. I heard she played the field a lot, never stayed with any one guy for long. She never tried to start anything with me, but I was pretty occupied with school and had quite the crush on your mother then. Couple of the guys claimed to have had sex with her, but others said she was a tease. Said she'd lead you down the garden path but she never finished the walk, if you know what I mean."

They sat in companionable silence watching the muted TV, listening to his mother in the kitchen. "Hope that's not what this woman's done to you," his father said at last.

Evan pressed his lips together and frowned. "If you two don't let up on this, I'm going home."

"Now don't get all pissy with me. We just care about you. What happened with you two?"

"Nothing and everything and now she doesn't want any part of me. Her father never told her about me. She thinks somehow I cheated her out of time with him, I guess. Hell, who knows what she thinks."

"Hmm." His father ran his hand through what was a surprisingly thick, although predominantly gray, head of hair. "You know it took me a while to convince your mother that I was the one she was going to marry. She's a bullheaded woman. Sometimes you have to talk them into things."

"I'm done talking to her or anyone else about this." He heard his mother bustling in and out of the kitchen and dining room. He stood up and walked toward the kitchen. "Mom? Let me help you bring that stuff to the table."

CHAPTER THIRTY-FOUR

H E ENDED UP spending the night in their guest room and left early the next morning loaded up with Thanksgiving left-overs. He decided on the way home that he'd arrange to talk to Clark Talcott and see what he remembered. He wasn't sure why, other than it gave him something to do besides stare at canvases.

"We were best friends in school. In fact, when he was coming up here to help you, and staying in town, he'd drop by and we'd go get dinner or just sit and talk. Sometimes he stayed here. I'm very sad to hear about his suicide. I'd heard from Clyde Davies that he'd passed, but I had no idea how."

Evan sat in Clark Talcott's living room. It was a quiet Saturday afternoon, and Clark's black Lab was stretched out in front of the fire.

Evan shrugged. "There doesn't seem to be a clear reason why he'd commit suicide. I hoped perhaps someone who knew him could help fill in some of the blanks about his life here."

"Well, maybe he's at peace now." Clark crossed his ankle over the opposite knee. He sighed. "I liked John a lot, but he wasn't a happy person as a kid or an adult."

"Because of his father?"

"That was a large part of it. Jake Earnshaw was one of those men who was…I'm not sure mean really captures it. He was quiet, sullen, and carried a chip on his shoulder all the time. Truth be told, he scared the hell out of me."

Clark smoothed the leg of his jeans, tugging at the hem. "He never did anything to me or yelled at me, but a couple of times when I walked John home and we ran into his father, I could tell he wasn't happy that John had allowed anyone to come home with him. I never hung around. He had a way of looking at you that'd freeze the blood in your veins. John was scared of him too."

He sighed and the dog raised its head and looked over checking, Evan supposed, that all was well and then returned to sleep. "I wondered if the old man abused all of them. I got the impression no one in that family was happy. I know John wasn't. It just got worse after his mother died. I suspect his mother was the kids' only source of comfort."

"Did John ever talk about any of that?"

"Those kids never talked about what went on at their place except in very general terms—you know like, if they got a new horse, or one of the ranch hands had taught John a new trick. John was pretty withdrawn after her death. I saw his older sister berating him for something one day not long after their mother's death when she showed up to collect him from school. It wasn't the first time. She was on her younger sister a lot too. I guess Madelyn had to take over her mother's role, and she probably resented that. John didn't like Madelyn, maybe because of that. He avoided her if at all possible."

"Sounds like the kids were afraid to talk."

Clark stared off into space. "Probably. We had a blizzard about six months after John's mother died. It had started snowing the night before and never let up. All of us were at school when it really hit. The principle allowed the kids who lived in town to go home once their parents showed up for them. The rest of the kids who lived outside town ended up being bedded down in the gym for the night. The roads were pretty impassable, and the temperature had dropped well below zero. I spoke with my parents over the phone, and they let me spend the night at the school so I could keep John company." He laughed. "Seemed like a great adventure at the time."

"I'll bet."

"Was pretty frightening as it turned out. John woke everybody up in the middle of the night screaming, and I mean screaming, absolutely hysterical. I remember him hitting the air as if fighting off someone and screaming, 'I won't tell, I won't tell. I promise I won't tell.' One of the teachers managed to calm him down eventually, but it shook everybody up. I asked him about it later and he blew me off, said it was just a bad dream and not to ask him about it again."

"Any idea what it was about?"

"Hell, who knows? But my feeling was it had something to do with his mother's death. I wondered whether he'd seen what happened. Whatever he was promising not to tell was anybody's guess. His dad was even harder to live with after his mother's death. Maybe he'd told John not to talk about their life at home or his mother and threatened him if he did. Maybe that's what he was promising not to talk about."

Clark smiled when the dog, curled up in warm sleepy bliss by the fire, twitched under the spell of its doggy dreams. He glanced at Evan and said, "He'd always been a pretty chatty kid about school and books—things like that—at least he was with me. He used to talk in general about his home life, but after that dream in the gym, he was as good as his word. He never talked about how things were at home, and he never talked about his mother's death."

Nothing to really add to what he knew so far, Evan thought as he returned home. John's life growing up had been unhappy, probably abusive, and keeping secrets was a way of life. Some things you never outgrow.

————◦◦————

THE THERAPIST'S transcribed notes obtained by Kate's lawyer bore witness to her father's long struggle against depression. He began taking antidepressants when she was in high school. That matched what she remembered about his depression no longer being so debilitating. The therapist had tried a number of meds over time, some worked, some didn't, which as Kate understood it, was par for the course. During her mother's final illness, the therapist found one that worked well for her father, and he was still taking it at the time of his death.

In the early therapy sessions, her father talked about his life growing up and about his mother. She could see once again why he hadn't wanted to talk about his family. It didn't explain why he'd kept the property or continued to visit Ardwell. Unless Evan was the connection.

J describes an isolated, abusive childhood with a father who behaved unpredictably, making it difficult for his mother or J and his sisters to know what would "set him off," as J calls it. His father was undemonstrative and according to J "an angry, hateful son of a bitch."

J remembers seeing his mother with bruises on her arms and face and describes how cowed she was by his father. J's father isolated the entire family, and other than time spent at school, he was not allowed to have friends over or spend time outside of school with peers, nor were his sisters. He states that his father behaved similarly with his mother, preventing her from making friends and restricting her to the ranch. According to J, his oldest sister, Madelyn, was better at convincing her father she had school responsibilities that allowed her to remain after school was out and socialize.

Relations with his next older sister, Ellen, were what could be described as normal within that family system. They were close with the usual brother/sister interplay and annoyances. The relationship with his oldest sister, Madelyn, was distant, which he attributes to their difference in age.

J does not like to discuss Madelyn. He deflects and redirects the conversation repeatedly to avoid talking about her and only if confronted will he say much. Primarily, he describes her as aloof, and because of the age difference, they had little in common. I believe there is something that underlies that relationship that needs to be explored, but it will take time because of his resistance. It's clear he doesn't hold much affection for her and his contact with her is limited. This could simply be a personality conflict and a lack of desire for contact on both sides.

Kate had picked up on the mutual coolness between her father and his sister, but she knew others who, for one reason or another, were either estranged or just not close with a sibling. She paged forward, skimming more entries that were similar to the one she'd just read. In one, the therapist and her father had discussed his mother.

J describes his mother in an idealized way as is common in children who have lost parents, however, she was clearly the refuge in this family. He remembers her reading to him and comforting him after confrontations with his father and doing that with all of them.

From his current perspective, he describes his mother's relationship with his father as abusive. At the time, he knew only that she was sad much of the time and when he asked about her injuries would say she 'was clumsy' or give some other excuse for them. A few months before she died, he believes that something had changed for her. She seemed happier to him, but also dismisses this as being wishful thinking on his part.

Cody, Kate thought. The sadness that Cody and her grandmother hadn't been able to make something of their relationship hit her. She thought of the chances, opportunities, and moments in time when decisions, or the lack of them, altered the course of a person's life and not always for the better. She sighed, shook her head, and continued to skim the notes.

Kate had spent the evening paging through the notes, stopping when something jumped out at her and skimming the rest. The notes covered years of intermittent treatment. When the depression would resurface, her father would return for sessions until he felt better then discontinue them. The frustration of the therapist over the lack of progress to get at the heart of what caused the depression was clear. He called it resistance, an apt word to describe her father's approach to the subject of his family from Kate's perspective.

The therapist repeatedly expressed the belief that her father had repressed memories tied to the death of his mother. He tried, when her father would return, to get him to open up. It became clear over time her father either wasn't willing or wasn't able to fully explore the causes of his depression, he simply wanted it treated.

According to the notes, in the year before he died, he began having dreams. Initially the fragments he could remember, were simply puzzling and left him uneasy. As time went on, the fragments coalesced and the dreams turned into nightmares. Nightmares that he was unable to describe, just that they woke him in a cold sweat terrified of some unknown threat.

J states that he had dreams after his mother's death that affected him similarly. He cannot describe those dreams or his current ones. He admits that he saw his mother fall down the stairs and huddled in the corner, afraid. He believed he couldn't talk about what had happened without terrible consequences, which he cannot expand on. Even now, talking about the dreams elicits a panic attack response that leads me to believe that J was either somehow responsible for or witnessed something significant about his mother's death.

Little boys, Kate thought, exuberant, into games, and not fully aware of the consequences of their actions. Perhaps he *had* surprised his mother and that had resulted in her falling. Perhaps he had been afraid to say anything for fear of being punished. With a father like he had, retribution was a very real possibility. As an adult, surely he could see that he wouldn't be punished for what happened, that it had been an accident? But perhaps he had so successfully repressed whatever had happened to his mother that he truly didn't know what it was.

The dreams continued to occur, leaving him anxious and agitated. The therapist had been working to help him remember the dreams in the weeks before his death. The final note, the week before his death, was frustrating.

J has agreed to try hypnosis, although he is apprehensive about it. He says that some family archival material has come to light and that he is sorting through it to see if it pertains to the dreams. He plans to bring it in when we meet in a week.

The next note was to document being contacted by the police regarding her father's suicide. It was another dead end. What her father remembered was lost. Not even the therapist knew what it had been. Nor had he known whether her father was suicidal.

It was midnight. She tidied and stacked the notes on her coffee table and went to bed. She continued to ruminate on what she'd read as she undressed. Alone in the dark, the thoughts continued to circle, making her toss and turn. At last she got up and took one of the sleeping pills her physician had prescribed for her in the days after finding her father. Tomorrow was Saturday, she could sleep in if need be. She had been careful with the pills as they made her feel foggy and muddleheaded the next day. Tomorrow it wouldn't matter.

CHAPTER THIRTY-FIVE

KATE DEBATED ABOUT it for most of the day until, at last, she threw a few necessities into her overnight bag and got in the car. All the way to Ardwell she debated whether showing up at Evan's was a good idea or one of the worst she'd come up with. But he had the diary and the letters she'd left with him. He said he hadn't read the diary.

Perhaps the diary was worth reading after all. Maybe her grandmother's entries could shed some light on what had happened and maybe not. After all, she wasn't going to describe her death. Kate wasn't sure what she hoped for. She had argued with herself all day about whether to ask Evan to help.

Changing her mind seemingly every five seconds about whether to pursue her questions or not was making her crazy, and it was most likely making Evan just as crazy. A small, niggling voice chastised her for not contacting Evan first and for trying to involve him further in her futile and frustrating search for answers. But he had the diary, she had to read it, and she didn't want to wait for him to mail it.

And a part of you would like to see him again, wouldn't you? That small voice asked.

"Maybe so," she said, then shook her head. "You are so fucked up."

———◆———

AT THE sound of the knock on the back door, Evan looked up from his book, slipped his bookmark into place, and laid it on the end table. It was dark, nearly nine o'clock, and visitors this time of night, this far from town, were unusual. He reached for his shotgun that hung on a rack by the door and, looking through the door's window, was taken aback to see Kate standing under the porch light. He opened the door and waited for her to say something as he angrily fought back the hope that had risen when he saw her. He saw her surprise when she noticed the shotgun he held at his side.

"This is a surprise," he finally said. He didn't step aside for her to enter.

"I'm sorry to just show up like this, I should have called."

"Yeah, you should have."

He waited, forcing her to ask, "May I come in?"

He stepped aside allowing, but not welcoming, her in. He'd be damned if he was going to make things easy for her. "Why'd you come?" He asked as he closed the door and replaced the gun on its rack.

He saw color flood her face and could see her struggling with what to say. Finally, she put her satchel on the kitchen island and opened it, fishing in it until she brought out a packet of papers and laid them on the counter.

"I got the records of my father's sessions with his therapist… um…I thought…I thought maybe I could read through that diary he sent you…maybe you'd like to read through these records, maybe it'd help explain what led to his death."

He watched her impassively. "So you thought you'd just pop up here and we could play detective, invade your father's privacy, to satisfy your curiosity about it?"

"I…"

"Never mind." Evan abruptly turned and disappeared into his office returning a few moments later with the diary and the other papers and letters she'd left with him the last time she'd been in Ardwell. He slammed them down on the countertop, making her jump.

"Here. They're all yours." He stepped around her and plucked his coat off the hook by the door and shrugged into it. "Make yourself at home. I'm not sure if I'll be back."

He moved to the door and she grabbed his arm. "Where are you going?"

"Out."

"But why?"

"Because," he said, leaning in close, watching as she took a step back. "I don't want to play your games anymore."

He heard the barely controlled anger in his voice, and he saw her eyes go wide with…what? Fear? That pissed him off even more than her showing up uninvited. He'd be damned if he'd let her turn him into a monster. He could smell her scent, see her huge brown eyes, and could, if he took a step, touch her lips. All he wanted to do was kiss her. He moved closer, reaching out and taking hold of her shoulders. His heart rate jumped with the contact and his breath was short.

"I want *all* of you or nothing. I refuse to be a comfort fuck, and I refuse to let you use me when it's convenient."

He heard her breathing quicken. She'd backed into the door and closed her eyes, making a small whimpering sound. His voice was low and angry. "Since you're here, make yourself comfortable. As much fun as it might be to fuck your brains out again, I don't intend to stay. I'm tired of being jerked around by you, so there's what you wanted. Take it, read it, burn it, I don't care, just be gone in the morning."

With that he released her and stepped back abruptly. He snatched his keys off the hook by the door, jerked the door she'd been pressed up against open, sending her stumbling away from it, and left, slamming the door behind him.

———◆———

STUNNED, KATE stood in the entryway and listened to him drive away, hearing gravel spit from under his truck's tires. It had been stupid to come, stupid to think he'd welcome her, but she never imagined he'd be so angry or that he might not want to help her. She hesitantly walked to the island where the collection of papers and the diary lay and ran her hands over it. Kate closed her eyes and could smell the scent of him that lingered near her and sent a stab of longing for him through her. She had yearned for the comfort of his arms and his reassurance, his steadiness. And, like Evan, that was gone, leaving her feeling empty.

———◆———

"YOU LEFT her there?" Craig exclaimed. "Why the hell did you do that? I thought you liked her."

"I do, but I'm tired of being jerked around." Evan paced Craig's small living room. "She just showed up out of the blue—no phone call, no nothing—and expected me to drop everything and help her sort through all this crap she brought with her. I don't want to read John's therapist's notes. Christ what possessed her to think I would?"

"Maybe it was an excuse to see you."

"I doubt it." Evan flopped onto the couch, rested his elbows on his knees, and dropped his head into his hands. "Look, I'd appreciate you letting me sleep on the couch tonight. I can't be there, I'm too angry and I don't want to do something stupid."

"Like sleep with her again?"

Even raised his head and glared at Craig. "We didn't sleep much that night, but yeah, I don't want a repeat performance."

"Wanna get drunk instead?"

"No. Last time I did that I ended up getting laid in my truck by a working girl and drunk dialing Kate at one in the morning."

Craig laughed. "Oh, man, you are so messed up."

"Tell me about it."

Craig walked into the kitchen and returned with a bottle of bourbon. "I'm out of beer, I was going to go grocery shopping today and got waylaid by a couple of patients. Want some?"

Evan nodded and watched as Craig poured them both a drink. "Can I stay on the couch?"

"Of course, you dumb ass, anytime."

It was late when Craig retrieved a pillow and a couple of blankets and dropped them on the couch. Evan held out his phone and said, "Take my phone with you so I don't call her."

"Sleep well." He patted Evan's shoulder and walked a little unsteadily toward his bedroom.

———◆———

EVAN WOKE with a stiff neck. It had been a cramped and uncomfortable night for a lot of reasons—the couch had only been one of them. The smell of coffee had woken him, and he lay there for several minutes trying to decide what to do. Did he go home and potentially find Kate still there or did he find something else to do?

He stood and stretched, hoping to ease some of the kinks from the night on the sofa. Something in his back popped. He walked to the bathroom, used the facilities, and made his way to the kitchen.

Craig looked up from the coffeepot. "Want some?"

Evan nodded and fixed himself a cup. He sat at the table and massaged his temples to ease the headache that pounded there. "Your couch is a piece of shit to sleep on."

"Says the ungrateful, unexpected guest."

Evan sighed. "Sorry I'm in a really bad mood."

"You up for breakfast?"

"How about I treat you to it at Joe's? I owe you for the lunch the other day and last night."

Craig shrugged. "Suits me. I'll go get dressed. There's a comb in the medicine cabinet in the bath. I'd recommend using it. I don't have any extra toothbrushes—don't use mine."

"As if," Evan replied irritably.

He returned to the living room and pulled on his boots, running his hands roughly through his hair. He didn't feel like making the effort to comb it. The coffee had helped the headache, but he sat on the couch in a bit of a stupor. What if she was still there when he got back? He'd been rude and explicit about not wanting her there, but she was unpredictable and stubborn. He hoped she'd gone home.

Joe's was noisy when they got there and found a booth that was unoccupied. Evan was hungry and attacked the food when it arrived.

"So, what're you going to do about her?"

"Nothing. There's nothing I can do. I'm just hoping she's gone when I get home."

"And if she isn't?"

"Then I'll escort her out and lock the doors." Craig ate and watched Evan. "What? What're you looking at?"

"You really care about her, don't you?"

Evan stopped eating and glared at Craig. "I don't want to talk about it."

Craig shrugged and began to eat again. "Just saying, you're in pretty deep and you're making yourself miserable. Maybe let her stay if she's still there and see what happens."

Evan put his fork down and stared at Craig. "I'll tell you what'll happen. Either we'll fuck our brains out again, then she'll leave and tell me to go to hell, or I'll spend the rest of the weekend with an unrelieved hard-on and be even more pissed than I am now. Let it lie Craig, it's unfixable."

"Never seen you so rattled by a woman before. It's a shame it hasn't worked out."

"Yeah, well, that's how it goes sometimes." They finished the food and Evan signaled the waitress for the check. "Look, I'm going home. I'm in a terrible mood. I appreciate the couch and the company last night. You want me to drop you at home or your office?"

"Don't worry about it. I need to stop by the Cameron's and see how their kid is anyway. That's not far and I could use the walk. You might take one when you get home." He caught Evan's scowl and laughed. "Just a suggestion, Evan, just a suggestion."

————◆————

HER CAR wasn't there when he got to the house. Craig was right, she had him rattled and he needed to figure out how to get her out of his head.

He walked in and closed the door behind him before he saw the note on the kitchen island. He closed his eyes and let out a breath. He stalled, taking off and hanging up his coat, putting the keys on the hook by the door, before he walked over and picked it up. He saw the diary and the packet of information lying near the note. Christ, she hadn't taken any of it with her. He wished she had.

> *Evan,*
>
> *I'm sorry for showing up uninvited. I should have realized that you wouldn't appreciate it. I spent the night reading the diary. Thank you for allowing me access to it. I'm sorry I've made such a mess of things between us. I hope you can forgive me at some point.*
>
> *Kate.*

"Forgive you?" he said aloud. "Hell, I'd forgive you for anything except not wanting me."

CHAPTER THIRTY-SIX

THE CONFRONTATION WITH Evan had surprised her. She'd seen the anger in his eyes, but more importantly she'd seen the hurt, and had wanted badly to make it go away. And responding to it would have been so wrong. She'd begun to realize during the time that they'd been out of contact, that the anger toward him was misplaced. He was as innocent as she was. Her father had deliberately chosen to keep them apart, to not share things with either of them. But it had also occurred to her that perhaps leaving the property to her was her father's way of ensuring that she and Evan met. That angered her too.

You should have just told me about him, Daddy, instead of putting us both through the wringer.

The anger at him had spewed onto Evan. And now Evan was the angry one. It was anyone's guess whether that could be changed. She thought, hoped, maybe she could change it. She'd see whether there was any possibility of repairing the damage she'd caused with him when she had taken care of the issues raised by reading the diary. She picked up the phone and dialed. She might get some answers about her father's death at last.

———◆———

HE MADE himself work after coming home, but it hadn't been a good idea. His bad mood ended up forcing him to scrape the fresh paint off the new canvas he was working on after he'd made a number of mistakes. In frustration and because he felt claustrophobic, he took Craig's advice, geared up, and went for a long run.

Heading back home, he detoured to John's deserted house and stood in the living room. Most of the floor was covered in snow that had entered through the hole in the roof and the damaged floor on the upper level. He edged around it and sat on the landing at the base of the stairs. It was a long, steep staircase, and it didn't surprise him that John's mother had broken her neck. All it would take is a misstep and down you'd go.

Or a push, he thought. *Christ, she's infected my brain with her suspicions.*

He sat for several minutes head leaning back against the wall. "You really fucked both of us up, John," he said aloud. He got up and left, heading back home chilled from sitting motionless at the base of the stairs. He had a gallery event in LA on Monday and was scheduled to leave very early the next day.

He fixed himself dinner, packed, and settled on the couch with a book. The diary, still sitting on the kitchen island, kept dragging his attention back to it, seeming to reproach him for avoiding it. He continued to try to ignore it until around eleven he closed his book and sighed, getting up and walking to the island. *Not tonight,* he thought. He'd read it on the plane. Tonight, he was tired. Tired from the run and tired of this whole debacle over John.

"Jesus, John, you could have at least told her I existed or left a damn note and none of this would have happened. Better still you could have called me. I'd have done anything to help you," he said as he walked into his bedroom. He swiped at his eyes and cleared his throat roughly to try to rid himself of the painful constriction that had suddenly materialized.

His sleep was restless, and his phone alarm jarred him awake nearly as tired as when he'd gone to bed. He didn't mind traveling to LA, but these gallery events were a pain. He didn't like talking about his work but that seemed to be what people wanted to hear. He didn't like the effusive praise patrons gave him and how the gallery owners made him sound like some sort of western Rembrandt. It was embarrassing, but if he wanted to keep selling his work, it was required.

Evan had fully intended to read the diary on the plane. He'd packed it in his carry-on, but having to arrive at the airport for an eight a.m. flight meant he had to leave Ardwell at three-thirty. So despite the best intentions, he slept nearly the entire way. The gallery owners had sent a car to pick him up and deposit him at a hotel they routinely used. Around five, he showered and dressed in a clean shirt and jeans, adding a sports jacket as a concession to LA dress codes. The event was scheduled for eight that night, but he liked to get there early and make sure his canvases were up and that there were no surprises.

Erik and his partner, Gavin, the gallery owners were in their usual state of excitement and anxiety over the pending party. They were a mixed race quirky couple, their differences in coloring and personality seeming to complement each other well.

"Evan! Oh thank heavens you got here early." Erik said, looking his usual pre-party frazzled self. Nothing was ever as catastrophic as Erik imagined. "Let's take a look at the layout and make sure you're happy with the presentations."

"I'm sure it'll be fine, take a deep breath, Erik."

"How is it you're always so calm? Is it something they put in the water in Montana?"

"Colorado, Erik, it's Colorado, and no the water's fine."

Erik flapped a hand at him. "Colorado, Montana, same difference. Gavin! Evan's here."

Gavin materialized, a huge grin lighting up his ebony face. "Evan, good to see you, how was the flight?" He grasped Evan's hand and pulled him in for a clap on the back before releasing him.

"Fine. How've you two been?"

"Great, just great. I'm thrilled about tonight, there are several big names coming. *Mucho dinero* for all of us if things work out like I think they will."

"Fingers crossed," Evan said with a smile. Things pretty much always worked out like Gavin planned.

"How've you been, handsome?"

"Good, good."

Gavin squinted at him appraisingly. "You look tired. Let's look around, make sure you're happy with the layout and then let's go get some food and you can tell me all about life in the Wild West."

The party went like most of them did and several of the larger and smaller canvasses sold. Evan returned to the hotel at about one in the morning. His feet hurt from standing all evening and he was heartily sick of talking about himself and his work. He planned to stay tomorrow and leave Wednesday morning. A little break, a little sun, and some relaxation seemed like just what he needed.

Sitting at the pool bar the following day, he ate lunch then found a lounge to stretch out on and relax with his beer. He'd brought the diary with him to the pool. If he didn't end up falling asleep in the sun, now was as good a time as any to read it. The pages were yellowed and a musty smell drifted out of them. Evan settled into the lounge and sipped his beer as he read.

———— ◆ ————

IT HAD taken three calls before Kate connected with her aunt on Tuesday morning. She could hear her sigh in exasperation.

"Kate, I was fourteen. I had a crush on the stupid man and he spurned me, which of course makes perfect sense. What in God's name would a man in his thirties see in a fourteen-year-old? I was nothing but jailbait."

Kate could almost see her aunt's brows crease together and draw down into a frown. She could certainly hear the anger in her voice.

"Of course, I was mad at him, wouldn't you have been? I threatened him with the photos and told him I'd tell Pa if he didn't take me away from there, but that's *all* I did. He was in a no-win situation. If I told Pa, at best Cody would lose his job and at worst my father would have fired him and then taken it out on my mother. He did the only thing he could—he left. I had no leverage then and I finally realized that he wasn't worth bothering with."

"But you denied knowing him when I asked."

"Of course, I did. It's embarrassing and it's especially embarrassing now that you've read the diary. If you had one, how would you feel if someone read it?"

Kate persisted. "You said he was attracted to your mother and that you were upset with both of them about it."

Madelyn laughed, but she didn't sound very amused. "Kate, Mama was nice to all of them, she was a nice woman, but she failed to see how her niceness could be misconstrued by the ranch hands and my father. Pretty much all of the hands had a crush on her. He just happened to be someone I liked so it was hard to watch. This is absurd really. Do you honestly think I had something to do with her death?"

Kate felt foolish now and wished she hadn't called her aunt. "I wondered, you said they would have to pay for it. And they did, so I just…"

"You just wondered if I pushed her down the stairs?" She asked indignantly. "That's what's wrong with people today, you watch too damn much TV. And you young people, none of you ever face the fact that sometimes life just doesn't work out the way you think it should. I had to face up to that. I wasn't going anywhere until I was old enough to manage it myself."

Her aunt huffed out an exasperated breath. "I didn't push her down the stairs—she was my mother for God's sake! I was a typical teenager, I was mad at her *and* him. Her behavior toward the ranch hands was partly responsible for my father's treatment of her, and I wanted her to leave Cody alone. But I didn't kill her over it.

"Adolescents spew in their diaries about all the things that happen to them, all the people they hate or who've treated them badly, all their revenge fantasies, and all their crushes and ridiculous ideas. Adolescents are idiots, and I was one of them. I'm done talking about this, and I hope you'll move on. I'm sorry your father committed suicide, and I don't know why any more than you do. Neither of us ever will." With that, Madelyn hung up.

It was true adolescents did spew in their diaries, but some of them took guns to school and killed people as a result of real—or imagined—insults or threats. Kate shook her head. This was her aunt, how likely was it that she'd pushed her mother down the stairs? After talking with Madelyn she was beginning to believe that her father had surprised or scared his mother and she'd tripped. That was enough to push someone to suicide under the right circumstances. Perhaps he had finally remembered the dreams and had been unable to live with what he'd repressed.

CHAPTER THIRTY-SEVEN

EVAN GREW MORE concerned as he read. He'd been surprised that the diary didn't belong to Kate's grandmother; it
had been her aunt's. Initially the entries were pretty much
what you'd expect from a teenage girl, but over time they changed
in tone and topic.

*Yesterday Tom Jacobs told me he's in love with me. That
should relieve some of the boredom around here. I'm fourteen
and I can't wait till I'm older. Then I'm leaving and having a
life. I just can't stay here. I would die of boredom, and I want
to get as far away from Pa as possible.*

*I'm not sure Tom is all that interesting, but he's cute and like
most boys he's interested in kissing and other things. The kissing is fun, but I'm not sure about the other things. He says he
has a way to keep me from getting pregnant if I let him go all
the way, so maybe I will. Boys have always pressured me for
it and so far I've held all of them off, not saying yes but not
saying no. It's easy to keep them interested if you dangle the
possibility of that in front of them.*

I did it, mostly just to see what the big deal was. It was hot and sweaty and messy and nasty, and it hurt, so I guess the only reason women do it is to get what they want. I might try to tempt one of the ranch hands, maybe I could get one of them interested enough to take me away from here. Some of them are so gross though. Sex is disgusting, but I've found you can tolerate just about anything to get what you want.

A new ranch hand named Cody hired on six weeks ago. He's handsome and very polite and friendly. I've talked to him a few times. I think I make him uncomfortable because he finds reasons to end the conversations quickly. I saw him talking to Mama the other day. He looks at her differently than he looks at me. I don't like it. Pa caught me talking to Cody, and he told me to leave the hired hands alone or he'd make me wish I had. Maybe I'll tell Pa about Mama's conversations, that'd give Pa something to think about.

Pa is off to Greeley for the weekend to buy some horses. It's so nice when he's gone. I was surprised when Mama said that Cody asked to take pictures of all of us. I asked why and Mama said Cody'd bought a Brownie camera and wanted to try it out. So I dressed for the occasion and gave him some looks that would let him know I wasn't a little girl and am younger and prettier than Mama. I'm not sure if he's attracted to her, but I see them talking a lot.

I saw Ellen taking a picture of Cody and Mama out back of the barn. They looked very cozy. He's avoided me since he took pictures of all of us, and it makes me really mad. Seeing him standing there with an arm wrapped around Mama makes me mad at both of them. She's married and has no right to him. I ought to tell Pa, he'd fire Cody and put Mama in her place.

But maybe I can force him to leave and take me with him. I'm going to see if I can find the pictures. If I had them I could threaten to tell Pa unless Cody leaves and takes me with him. I found them and took them. He knows they're missing, I heard him asking another ranch hand whether he'd seen anyone going through his footlocker. He said some mementos had gone missing. No one saw me. I'm not stupid. Then I saw him talking to Mama when she was alone weeding the garden. He kissed her. They both need to pay. She's going to ruin my plans to get away from here.

I caught him in the barn saddling a horse today and showed him the photos. He grabbed me and tried to take them back, but I told him if he didn't let go I'd scream and say he attacked me, so he let go. I told him he had to leave and take me with him or I'd show Pa the pictures and he'd make sure Mama paid for her behavior. Cody was pretty mad and told me he'd never take me anywhere and if I wasn't careful he'd tell my Pa what I'd said. I told him he'd better leave and take me with him or I'd see Pa knew what he and Mama had been up to. He cleared out during the night. No one saw him leave. She's ruined everything for me.

Pa was pretty angry when he realized Cody was gone. And Mama looks at me differently now. I think she knows about what I told Cody. I don't want her to make up a story about me and tell Pa. Maybe I'll show her the photos and threaten to tell Pa if she doesn't mind her own business.

Mama fell down the stairs and broke her neck. Everybody's upset. John's acting like a lunatic, Ellen cries all the time, and now I get to shoulder all her work. I hate it here! I hate all of them! I wish they were all dead!

The last entry made Evan's lunch threaten to come back up. Madelyn had made no confession and maybe it was just a…a what? An adolescent's angry ranting? A hateful, manipulative, young girl trying to get her way? Evan shook his head. Her mother *had* fallen down the stairs a few days after the next to last entry, and after reading the diary he was pretty sure Madelyn was responsible for the fall. And he was equally sure that John Earnshaw had witnessed it.

Then his heart rate kicked up a couple notches as he abruptly sat up from the lounge chair. The California sun wasn't hot enough to prevent the chills that made him shudder. Kate had read the diary as well, dear God he hoped she hadn't called her aunt and confronted her. He stood up and gathered his belongings and nearly ran to his room.

"Evan?" Kate sounded surprised to hear him.

"I read the diary, Kate. Please tell me you haven't talked to your aunt."

"Don't worry about it, she explained it. She said she was just fourteen and pretty angry at Cody and her mother. She was embarrassed about my reading the diary, but that's all."

He sighed. "I don't think it was as innocent as she claims. When did you talk to her?" His heart was still pounding as he went into the bath and gathered up his Dopp kit and threw it into his carry-on. He had the phone clamped to his ear with his shoulder as he began dragging the few clothes he'd brought out of the closet and dresser drawers and shoving them into his bag.

"Yesterday. She had a reasonable explanation about it and was mostly irritated that I'd read the diary and invaded her privacy. I think what happened is just what everyone thinks, an accident. And I think when my father saw his mother fall it traumatized him. Nothing more. Her explanation made sense."

"I don't think so. I think she had a hand in your grandmother's death. She didn't confess on paper, but it's pretty coincidental that your grandmother fell down the stairs a few days after Madelyn threatened to tell her father about the photos. According to the sheriff's report, Madelyn was upstairs. She may have confronted your mother and pushing her was the end result. She was in a position to have done it. Maybe that's what your father saw."

"Oh for heaven's sake, Evan, I think she was angry with Cody and her mother, but why would she kill her? I'm more and more convinced that my father had some connection to the accident and when he remembered it he couldn't live with it."

"Where does she live?"

"In LA, why?"

"I don't like it. I think, now that she knows you read the diary, you're at risk."

"For what?"

"If she killed your grandmother, she may have had something to do with your father's death. If she did, she's not going to want anyone to know. You've read the diary, and you told her you read it. You're a threat to her. There's no statute of limitations on murder." There was silence on the line.

"And what?" Kate asked at last. "You think *she'll kill me?*"

"I…I don't know, but think about it, your father must have read the diary, too. Maybe he did just what you did and asked her about it." Hearing himself, Evan felt like he sounded insane, God only knew what Kate thought, but for him the pieces were finally coming together.

"Your dad said he intended to talk to someone about what he'd found. Maybe it was Madelyn, maybe your father saw her push your grandmother and reading the diary triggered his memories. Maybe Madelyn had something to do with his death."

"Or maybe it was his shrink he intended to talk to. I've known Madelyn all my life. She's an unfriendly, unpleasant, old woman, but if she did what you think she did and my father saw her, why wouldn't she have done something to him a long time ago? Why wait till now?"

"I don't know." He ran his hands roughly through his hair. "Two deaths so close together might have raised suspicions about both. Since your dad was so shut down after his mother's death, she may have thought he was no threat to her. You said he couldn't remember the dreams. I'm pretty sure they related to his mother's death. If your father talked to Madelyn and she knew he'd read the diary and now she knows you have, you could be in danger. What's her last name? I'm here in LA, I can go make sure she's still here."

"What're you doing in LA?"

"A gallery thing. Please just humor me."

"Don't go visit her. You'll make both of us look like fools. Take a deep breath. She's not insane. I'll be fine."

"For Christ's sake, just give me her last name. Tell me where she lives. I won't talk to her, but I'm going to make sure she's still here."

"Fine, it's Madelyn Clayton. She lives in Santa Monica. Hang on and I'll give you her address. I don't want you to talk to her. Check to see if she's there, if you feel you have to, but otherwise leave her alone."

CHAPTER THIRTY-EIGHT

H E HAD THE taxi driver pull to the curb a block away from the house and asked the guy to wait for him. Walking down the sidewalk toward the small, white stucco bungalow, its red roof tiles seemed overly bright in the California sunlight. The neighborhood was quiet. It was the middle of the day, and he guessed most residents were at work and kids were in school.

Taking a calming breath, he walked up to the front door and rang the bell. He had no idea what he would say to her and had been frantically trying to think of something as he stood and waited. Finally, he decided to pretend to have gotten the wrong address. He rang the bell again then knocked. No answer.

A woman exited the house next door, a small yapping dog clutched against her side. "She's not there. Ring all you like, but no one's going to answer. Sparky for fuck's sake shut up!"

"Do you know where Ms. Clayton is?"

"Who's asking?"

"I'm her sister's nephew." *Jesus,* he thought, *what was the other sister's name?* "Her...her sister Ellen hasn't been able to get ahold of her and asked me to stop by and check on her. Do you know where she is?"

"Well, she isn't there," she cackled. "She took off this morning. Called last night and said she was going to be gone and asked if I'd collect her mail. Sparky! Shut up!" She opened her door, leaned over and tossed the little dog in the house, pulling the door closed afterward.

Evan's heart began to race. "Did she say where she was going?"

"She never says where. Said she'd be back late tomorrow, didn't plan to stay long, just had something to take care of. Tell her sister not to worry, she's fine. She's too mean for anything to happen to her. You know what they say, the Devil don't want her and the Lord won't have her." She laughed again and went back in the house. The dog was still yapping.

Evan turned and ran back to the cab and had the driver take him to the hotel. Half an hour later he'd tried every airline with a flight to Denver and hadn't been able to get a seat at any price.

"Carlyle Gallery."

"Gavin? It's Evan Hastings."

"What's up? Are you still in town?"

"Gavin, I need your help. Do you know anyone who can get me to Denver as soon as possible? Maybe a private pilot? I have to get home, I can't get a regular flight and I…" His breath was coming in gasps, and he forced himself to stop and catch his breath. "Anyone, do you know anyone who can get me there?"

"Jesus, what's wrong?"

"Someone I care about is in trouble. You have all those connections with patrons. I hoped maybe one of them could help me." Evan heard the extension pick up.

"Evan, it's Erik, what's wrong?"

"Erik, talk to Evan while I go make a couple of calls." Gavin put down his extension.

"It's okay, whatever's the matter it'll be okay. Gavin will fix everything, he always does."

Evan pinched the bridge of his nose as he listened to Erik prattle on until Gavin returned.

"Okay, I've got you set up for two o'clock at Bob Hope Airport. A friend of ours has a private jet and he owes us favors."

Erik laughed. "Honey, if you were gay, he'd probably give you the plane, you're just his type."

"Oh my God, Erik, get a grip!" Gavin said. "Anyway, he's sending a car to pick you up and take you straight there so wait in the lobby, and the driver will text you when he pulls up."

"I don't know how to thank you guys. I…I just…"

"Stop. Take a deep breath, go down to the lobby, and wait. Then when you take care of whatever is going on call and let us know everything's okay. Promise?"

"I will, thank you so much."

He'd tried on the way to the airport to call Kate and gotten her voicemail. He'd left a message for her to call him back and not to meet with Madelyn. She hadn't called back. She hadn't answered his texts either. He could barely contain his worry as he sat belted into the private jet's cushy seat. Why the fuck wasn't she answering?

After several more attempts, he quit trying to contact her. He hoped that the reason for Madelyn's trip wasn't to see Kate. And if it was, he hoped he got to Kate first.

———◆———

KATE BLINKED several times and then her mouth went dry. She'd heard the doorbell and, without thinking to look out the peephole, opened the front door to find Madelyn on her doorstep.

"Madelyn, this is a surprise," she said, trying to smile.

Her aunt barked a laugh and raised her eyebrows. "It's not really, is it?" She pushed passed Kate and closed the door behind her. "I came for the diary. If you give it to me now, I'll leave and we'll forget it exists and go on with our lives. If you don't…well the outcome will be far less pleasant."

Kate stared in horrible fascination at the small gun Madelyn had taken from her purse and was aiming at her. "I…I don't have it."

"Oh don't start lying to me. Of course, you have it. Why would you know what was in it, if you didn't? Now get it."

"Madelyn, I don't have it. I swear I don't."

"Where is it?"

"A friend has it. I can get it. I just don't know how long it'll take."

Madelyn pursed her lips and frowned. "Call this friend and ask for it. Don't say why you want it and don't tell this friend I'm here."

Kate couldn't find her phone. "I think I left my phone in the car. I need to go check."

Madelyn nodded and followed her to the garage. "Don't try anything stupid."

"I won't." She found her phone in the car, saw all the texts and missed calls from Evan, and with shaking fingers, Kate called him.

"Kate, I'm almost to your place. She's not home…"

"Evan, hi. Hey I need you to bring that book I forgot at your house. I'm glad I caught you."

"She's there, isn't she?"

"Yes, if you could bring it now I'd appreciate it."

"I'm just a couple of minutes away. I'll…I'll think of something."

"Okay, see you shortly." Kate disconnected and turned to Madelyn. "He said he'd be here in a few minutes."

"Good, that's good." She held her hand out. "Give me the phone, then have a seat until he gets here." She took the phone and dropped it into her jacket pocket.

"You pushed your mother, didn't you? Pushed her down the stairs because she was in love with Cody."

Madelyn rolled her eyes. "I could not have cared less how she felt about him, but she interfered with my plan to leave. If it weren't for her I could have gotten him to take me away. And after he left, I was afraid she'd tell Pa. I had the photos, and I think she knew it, so she might not have said anything, but I couldn't take the chance. It hardly matters now, it's old news and everyone believes it was an accident. Of course, you found the diary. That might convince the police to take a closer look. Can't have that."

"My father saw you, didn't he?"

"Yes. I didn't realize he was there until I saw him in the corner. Stupid child, he was always sneaking around."

"How did you keep him from talking?"

"I threatened to tell the sheriff he surprised her and caused her fall down the stairs. I told him I'd say I had tried to catch her but missed. I told him that the sheriff would believe that and he'd go to prison for causing the accident. I convinced him that he was wrong about what he'd seen. It doesn't take much to talk a nine-year-old into doubting what he's seen. Then it only took a few threats to keep him from talking to anyone. I always wondered if Pa suspected it, but he never said anything."

She made a moue of disgust. "After you called, I realized he must have found the diary or something. He never mentioned the diary, but I suppose it was in with Pa's stuff. You don't think things through when you're fourteen unfortunately. I had hidden it away after Mama fell. I never wrote in it again and then I forgot about it. I didn't remember to take it with me when I took off. I took Pa's gun, but never thought about the diary."

She shrugged and the gun in her hand pointed away from Kate momentarily. "He said he'd begun having dreams like he'd experienced after her death. They'd triggered his memory, and he wanted to know what had happened. He insisted he remembered seeing me push her. I couldn't let him go to the police, he was a witness to what I'd done, so I had to figure out a way to shut him up. I didn't realize he had the diary or I'd have made him give it to me."

"Did you manage to convince him again that he was responsible for her death instead of owning up to it?"

Madelyn's smile never reached her eyes. "No. We talked for a while, and I explained that Mama tripped and what he saw was me trying to grab her, not push her. But he kept insisting that he'd seen me push her."

"It wasn't suicide, you killed him, didn't you?"

"Well he wasn't going to keep his mouth shut, was he? He was so worked up about it. The idiot said all he wanted was for me to admit what I'd done so he could have some peace. He said if I did, he wouldn't tell anyone."

She paused and looked at Kate with a funny expression on her face. "But men lie. They all lie, and I knew he wouldn't let it go. He'd go to the police eventually."

"What did you do to him?"

"I came prepared. I paid a kid in my neighborhood to buy some fentanyl pills on the street. It's very popular these days—did you know that? Anyway I ground up several before I got to his house. After we had talked and I finally admitted what I did, I suggested that we seal the deal—his not saying anything further—with a drink."

She smiled and waved the gun in the air. "I knew he wouldn't keep his promise, but if he was dead it wouldn't matter. I got two glasses out of your mother's china cabinet and poured the drinks and added the fentanyl powder to his. Then when he was pretty woozy I walked him to the den and put Pa's gun in his hand and held it to his head and pulled the trigger. Problem solved, until you started calling."

She stared at Kate and shook her head as if in regret. "You're a lot like your father. You should have taken my advice to leave well enough alone when you first called me. And you should never have told me you had the diary or let anyone else read it. But you did, and now look at the mess we're in."

The doorbell rang and Madelyn motioned with the gun for Kate to get up, took her arm, pressed the gun to her side, and guided her to the door. "Open it."

Kate opened the door, and Evan could see from her face that Madelyn must be standing behind the door. He closed his eyes, momentarily hoping something would occur to him to prevent Kate from getting hurt.

"Thanks Evan, I appreciate you bringing it over so quickly."

"Uh, sure. Hey how about I come in for a while? We could go get dinner or something?"

When Evan saw Kate hesitate, he pushed her into the room and behind him.

"Here's the diary, take it and go," he said, holding it out. "Neither of us will say or do anything."

"Let's not have this conversation in the doorway," Madelyn said closing the door and gesturing with the gun. It looked large in her hand, but Evan saw it was a relatively small caliber handgun. Just as lethal if it hit the right spots, but perhaps whatever she did with it was survivable. Evan moved into the living room, keeping Kate behind him. "Give it to me."

Evan handed her the diary and felt Kate shift to his side.

"You've read it too. No don't either of you deny it. That's just not going to fly." Madelyn stood with the gun pointed at him and contemplated the situation.

"I thought I could come here and convince Kate to give me the diary. Without it, she'd have no proof of anything, so there'd be no point in going to the police. We'd just call it square, but now she's got a witness to corroborate her story."

She sighed as if put upon. "This is so annoying and just complicates everything. I so wish you hadn't let him see the diary. This is your fault you know, Kate."

She pointed the gun at Evan. He shoved Kate out of the way and lunged at Madelyn as she fired the gun. The bullet hit his left arm but didn't stop his momentum as he pulled his fist back and punched her in the face. He watched her drop the gun and collapse onto the floor. He clapped a hand to his left shoulder and kicked the gun as far from Madelyn as he could.

"Oh lord, how badly are you hurt?"

"I'm fine, it's just a flesh wound. Isn't that what they say in Westerns?" He gave her a feeble smile.

"Not funny, dammit."

"It's not bad, Kate. Her shooting skills are pretty poor fortunately. Call the police." Evan sat abruptly on the floor and stared blankly at the blood running between his fingers and down his arm, which was beginning to burn and ache something fierce. He saw her pull a phone out of her aunt's pocket and could hear Kate on the phone with the operator. She returned shortly with several kitchen towels.

"Here let me take a look." She pulled his hand away and tore at his shirtsleeve until she could see the wound, then pressed a folded towel to it and held it in place. "The police and an ambulance should be here soon. Lean back against me until they get here, you look a little pale."

"Where the hell was your phone? I tried calling and texting you to warn you about her."

"I'd gone out this morning and I left it in the car. I never got the messages. I saw all the calls and texts when I retrieved it to call you."

"About gave me a fucking heart attack when I couldn't get hold of you."

"Hush, it's over now."

He let her pull him back against her and he closed his eyes. Her scent mixed with the metallic smell of blood. Her breasts were a soft pillow against his back. Maybe getting shot wasn't so bad if it allowed him to lean back against her and have her wrap her arms around him to steady him.

CHAPTER THIRTY-NINE

IKE ALL BUREAUCRACIES, hospital ERs had rules. He'd gotten an IV despite telling them he didn't need one. The nurse gave him a pain med through the IV, which made him re-think his objection to it. A doc had numbed and cleaned the wound, then cauterized the bleeders and stitched him up.

The bullet had apparently entered and exited the muscle of his upper arm, something the doc kept calling the deltoid muscle. Why they couldn't just speak English, he never understood. A nurse had bandaged his upper arm and helped him into an arm sling. And there he sat with a prescription for pain meds and antibiotics, discharge instructions, and extra dressing sponges lying on the gurney beside him.

They'd given him a patient gown in lieu of his bloody, torn shirt, which they'd bundled into a paper bag and labeled with his name. A police detective had shown up midway through the process to take his statement and the paper bag with his shirt—evidence he guessed—and then left. But the hospital staff wouldn't let him leave in a taxi, and other than Kate there wasn't anyone nearby to call to pick him up. To complicate matters, he didn't have his phone. It was probably lying on Kate's living room floor somewhere.

A nurse came into the treatment bay they had stationed him in, carrying a cordless phone. "You've got a call Mr. Hastings."

He hoped it wasn't his mother. She'd be beside herself with worry, although he wasn't sure how she would have heard about it. He wasn't thinking all that clearly, he guessed. "H'lo?"

"How are you?" Kate asked. "They wouldn't tell me, said they didn't have permission to talk to anyone about you."

"I'm fine."

"Sorry it's taken so long, I've been tied up with the police. They took Madelyn to the police department after the EMTs looked her over. The detective took my statement and took the diary into evidence along with the gun. I guess I'll have to go in and sign the statement at some point."

"Yeah, me too. The ER is done with me, but they won't let me leave in a taxi. I'd sure like to get out of here, if you wouldn't mind coming and getting me. Oh and bring a shirt, there's one in my bag in the truck."

"I'll be there shortly."

He settled back against the gurney. Despite a cotton blanket the nurse had laid over him, he was cold.

———◆———

HE DIDN'T look as fine as he claimed to be when Kate picked him up. He was pale and there were lines around his eyes and between his brows, which made her wonder if the pain meds they'd given him were wearing off. She stopped at a pharmacy and had the prescriptions filled, and when she returned to the car, he was asleep with his head leaning against the window.

He stayed the night, but refused to let her hover over him or take care of him. She had thanked him profusely for what he'd done, and told him what Madelyn had said about her grandmother and her father. His face, still pale, now looked weary and sad. The conversation seemed to make him uncomfortable.

When Kate finished telling him what Madelyn had said, Evan let his head drop onto the back of the couch and sighed. "Such a damn waste of so many lives. It tears me up me that she killed your dad. He would never have said anything to anyone about what he knew. I think he just wanted some resolution."

He raised his head and looked at Kate. "I guess now you know you were right."

She nodded numbly. "I guess I do." She was ashamed of all the anger she'd harbored for her father and for Evan.

They sat uncomfortably silent, neither knowing what to say. At last Evan steered the conversation elsewhere to more neutral topics. Each time she tried to tell him how grateful she was for his help and how wrong she'd been about him, he cut the conversation off, so she gave up. She heard him on the phone while she was fixing dinner.

"Things are fine, Gavin. Yeah everything's fine."

He was quiet and Kate strained to hear wondering who he'd called.

"Thank you so much for the help. Tell your fly guy I'll give him a painting."

Kate heard him laugh. "No, I'm not interested in switching teams to pay for the plane trip. Jeez, Erik. Gavin, do something with him, will you? I'll be in touch. Thanks again."

Kate carried a tray into the living room and set dinner out on the coffee table. "Everything okay?"

"Yeah, I just needed to touch base with some friends who were worried about me. Dinner looks good." He said, cutting off further conversation about the phone call. Kate felt lost and shut out, she felt him push her away.

He fell asleep on the couch after eating dinner and taking his pain meds. She sat in the living room watching him sleep while she tried to read a book. She debated about waking him up and helping him to the guest bedroom. He looked so peaceful on the couch. She put a blanket over him and decided to leave well enough alone.

At eleven, she walked over and sat on the coffee table resisting the urge to stroke his hair. He was a good man, a kind man, and she'd managed to ruin any chance for even a friendship with him. Maybe she should tell him how she felt, make him listen and somehow try to convince him to give her another chance. She sighed. It was probably useless to try. Without thinking she leaned over and gently kissed him on the forehead. His eyes opened and he stared at her.

"Kate, don't," he said wearily. "Just let this lie. I'm heading home in the morning and you and I both know nothing's changed between us. Let's don't complicate things any more than they are."

"But what if things have changed for me?"

"You don't know how badly I wish they had. What we went through today was frightening for both of us and as much as I want you, I don't want to be a temporary soother."

He reached up and tucked a lock of hair behind her ear, letting his fingers caress her face before he dropped his hand. "You've got a lot to work out and when you do, you may not want me at all. I can't get sucker punched again. So go to bed, and I'll be out of your life in the morning."

His words hit hard and a tear rolled down her cheek. "I don't want you out of my life."

"I know you think that, but staying in your life right now is a recipe for disaster."

"Sleep well," she managed to say despite the pain in her throat that made talking nearly impossible. She stood, turned, and disappeared up the stairs.

HE RUBBED his eyes with his good hand and stared at the ceiling. He'd meant what he said, but it had been the hardest thing he'd ever had to do. He sighed and tried to find a more comfortable position on the couch. He planned to leave before she woke to avoid any further discussions.

The drive home felt twice as long as usual and a rush of relief hit him as he pulled up at the back of the house. Once inside, he swallowed two pain pills and his antibiotic, walked toward the bedroom, and crawled into bed.

I T HAD BEEN nearly six months since she'd last seen him. Six months of sorting through her grief about her father and her feelings about Evan with a therapist, trying to decide what to do. Things looked different than the last time she'd been at his place she realized as she pulled into the drive leading to his house.

There was a small barn now that sat beyond the garage with a fenced area attached to it and a large corrugated metal stock tank inside the…corral? She wasn't sure if that was what you called it. She could see Evan there putting out hay for a couple of young cows. Cows. Was he keeping cows at his house now?

The sight of him in old jeans and a T-shirt, his summer weight Stetson on his head made her heart start tripping. Just then a woman poked her head out the back door and said something to him. Kate couldn't see her clearly because of the screen door and the slant of the sun. She watched as Evan turned and grinned before the woman disappeared into the house letting the screen door bang shut.

Kate's heart took a nosedive.

Evan had found someone. She'd waited too long. She nearly made a U-turn to head back to the road, but felt compelled to find out how he was, who the woman was. Maybe the woman was just a friend; maybe there was still a chance for her. She had to find out. When he'd turned to respond to the woman, he saw her car. He exited the corral and began to walk toward where she had stopped her car in the drive.

She watched him approach, pulling off his leather gloves and stuffing them into a back pocket of his jeans. His T-shirt was flecked with small bits of hay but hugged his chest. She flashed on the memory of the small tattoo over his left breast and watched as he got closer, the longing for him overwhelmed her. She lowered the window and waited, not knowing now what to say to him.

"It's good to see you," he said, standing next to the car door, giving her a smile that lit up his beautiful green eyes.

"It's good to see you, too. I'm sorry, I should have called."

"You have a habit of not doing that."

Kate couldn't tell if he was angry or kidding her. But he didn't look angry. "I wanted to see how you were."

"I'm good. You?"

"Good," she said, nodding like some idiotic bobblehead doll. It took all she had not to squirm in embarrassment. She felt heat rise up her neck. What could she possibly say to him?

"Pull up to the house and come in. You can tell me what you've been up to."

"No, I really should go." She didn't want to, she wanted him to hold her like he'd done before, before she'd ruined things. "I was just…just in the area and thought I'd stop by. I should have called."

He raised his eyebrows skeptically. "I'm glad you stopped by. Park your car and let's go for a walk."

The scent of him hit her through the window—warm and slightly sweaty from working in the sun. The smell of grass from the hay he'd been handling wafted in through the car window. Since she wasn't sure what else to do, and she desperately wanted to spend even a few minutes with him, she pulled in next to his truck, parked, and got out, waiting as he approached the car. He motioned for her to follow him.

"I guess you sold the place," Evan said. "They bulldozed the house last week. Any idea what the new owners are going to do with it?"

"I didn't sell it, I sold my dad's house in Lakewood. I wanted to get rid of the farmhouse. It was the source of so much pain. I thought at the very least it needed to be gone. But I thought I could do something good with the property."

"Yeah? Like what?"

"I thought maybe I could build a place where artists could come, a peaceful place where they could work or relax. Maybe have some visiting artists give classes. I don't know yet."

"It's a nice idea. Would you run it?"

She shrugged. She had intended to ask if he'd like to help, but now…she felt embarrassed for some reason. "I don't know yet."

"You should consider it. I think you'd be good at it." They fell silent again.

"So, have you decided to become a rancher?" she asked, not knowing what else to say, as they walked in the direction of the two cows.

He laughed as he opened the stock gate to the corral and she followed him into where the cows stood eating. "Nah, my need to rescue got me into trouble—yet again. I made friends with these guys after they were born. They were twins, and mom rejected them, and Fred couldn't get a foster cow to accept them, so I took care of them for him. He can't be up all hours feeding orphan calves when he has a ranch to run." Evan stroked their backs. Neither raised its head from the hay.

"People think I'm soft in the head for doing it. To most people around here, animals are just animals—food or money. These two, though, got to be like big dogs, they'd come looking for me, so I offered to buy them. They're basically pets." He laughed. "Big use-less pets, I guess. All they do is eat and leave cow pies everywhere."

She smiled. "You always did like cows."

They stood silently watching the cows swat at flies with their tails as they ate.

"What'd you really come up for, Kate?" He asked at last.

"To see how you were. To reassure you that I hadn't sold the property."

"You could have phoned and taken care of that."

"Yeah, I guess."

"So why the drive?"

"Like I said, I was in the area."

He watched her and finally raised an eyebrow at her. "Your nose is gonna grow, you keep telling tales like that. Why'd you come?"

"This was a huge mistake. I'm going home."

He grabbed her shoulders before she could storm off and held on. "No, you're not, not until you tell me why you came."

She pulled away. "Oh fine. I made the mistake of coming, no point in passing up the opportunity to make a fool of myself as well. It took me a while to work through everything about my dad. I'm still dealing with some of it, the grief mostly. I suppose that will always be there. And it took me a while to accept that he'd treated us both poorly by not telling us about each other, by keeping things from both of us."

She paced in front of him distractedly. "I don't know why he did that, I never will. I don't…I don't think it was malicious. Maybe keeping secrets was so ingrained that he didn't know how to share things. Who knows? At least I know he didn't commit suicide. Anyway, I had a lot to work through, and I'm still working on some of it."

He'd let her pull away but stayed close. "I…I missed you…a lot. I hoped, maybe, we could try again, but clearly your lady friend would probably object to that."

Kate looked at him and frowned. "That's how it always goes, isn't it? No one ever falls in love or even like at the same time. I can see I missed my chance, but I'm glad you're doing well. It was good to see you."

She turned and started to make her way to the corral gate when he caught up with her and pulled her into an embrace. "Kate, that's my mother. She's visiting for a couple of days. I guess you didn't get a good look at her." He pulled back and grinned at her. "She's a handsome woman, but she's married and neither of us go for incest."

She shoved away from him, her face bright red with embarrassment. "I've made a total fool of myself, but don't laugh at me. If you're not interested say so and I'll leave."

He stepped in, took her face in his hands, and kissed her, softly, tentatively at first then longingly, hungrily, and she returned the kiss in equal measure, wrapping her arms around his waist.

He broke away, his breath ragged, and smiled as he ran his hands through her hair and then held her face in his hands. "I've wanted you since the first time I saw you. That hasn't changed. If you want me, you've got me."

She relaxed into his arms, arms that felt so good, arms that she'd missed so much. "I want you."

"For now or forever?"

"Forever, if you want me."

"Forever it is then." He kissed her again. Taking hold of her hand, he opened the gate, and they walked toward the house. He stopped a few yards from the back door. "Mom's going to be beside herself when she meets you. She's been giving me hell about you for quite some time."

"*What?*"

"When she first found out about you she assumed we'd sort things out and when we didn't she was pissed that I walked away. So, I've heard an earful." He laughed. "She finally stopped ragging on me about it. And after I refused to cooperate, she stopped try-ing to set me up with other women."

He held her tightly, and she could feel his heartbeat, beating as it had when they'd made love. "God, I've missed you."

"I've missed you too," she sighed, wrapping her arms around his waist and laying her head on his shoulder.

"Welcome home, Kate."

ACKNOWLEDGMENTS

LEGACY OF SECRETS is set on the eastern plains of Colorado. I live near Denver and have never lived 'out east' as people here often call the area. The town of Ardwell is a complete fiction, as are the characters, but it's based on a couple small towns in Colorado and two in Montana with which I'm familiar. For readers who live, or who have lived, on the plains please forgive any errors or flights of fancy on my part.

Thanks to my sister Lorelei Starbuck, who's always there to bounce things off of, to Julie Cameron, Landon Literary Agency, for editing this book, for input along the way from the Nag Sisters critique group, and from my beta reader Natalie McDonald. Thanks to Jenn Brusco for her help with the blurb. Thanks to Mary O'Neale, Jan Hixon, Rae Mitchell, Dianna Marston, and Donna Lefferdo for volunteering to be on my street team. Also thank you to Jim Lefferdo for his suggestions about how guys handle certain issues.

Thanks to Kirsten Jensen at My Word Publishing for proofing, for help with the blurb, for getting it to publication, and for handholding. You're great at all of that and I'm so appreciative. Thanks to Gail Cross of Desert Isle Design for the beautiful cover.

Last but not least, thanks to Vince Gill for his touching song *Down to My Last Bad Habit* that calls Evan Hastings to mind every time I hear it. Take a listen, I think you'll see what I mean.

AUTHOR BIO

COLORADO NATIVE, OR nurse, and author of the award-winning Annie Collins Mystery Series, Helen Starbuck lives in Arvada, Colorado, and has written stories since junior high. She loves mysteries with a touch of romance, thrillers, and books involving strong women and interesting men.

Sign up for updates and follow the author at www.helenstarbuck.com, on Facebook facebook.com/helensstarbuck/, and on Instagram at @helenstarbuck. Reviews on Amazon or Goodreads are always appreciated.